Children of Tender Years

Ted Allbeury

NEW ENGLISH LIBRARY

First published in Great Britain in 1985 by
New English Library, Mill Road, Dunton Green, Sevenoaks, Kent.
Editorial office: 47 Bedford Square, London WC1B 3DP.

Typeset by
   Hewer Text Composition Services, Edinburgh.
Printed in Great Britain by
   The Thetford Press Limited, Thetford, Norfolk.

British Library Cataloguing in Publication Data
Allbeury Ted
   Children of tender years.
   I. Title
   823'.914[F]   PR6051.L52

ISBN: 0 450 06085 3

This is for Dr Barbara Ansell of Northwick Park Hospital
and Great Ormond Street Hospital for Sick Children –
with love.

The way we selected our victims was as follows: we had two SS doctors on duty at Auschwitz to examine the incoming transports of prisoners. These would be marched by one of the doctors, who would make spot decisions as they walked by. Those who were fit to work were sent into the camp. Others were sent immediately to the extermination plants. Children of tender years were invariably exterminated since by reason of their youth they were unable to work.

Part of a sworn deposition made at Nuremberg dated 5th April 1946, and signed by SS-Obersturmführer Rudolf Hoess, Commandant of Auschwitz

Chapter 1

THE SMALL bedroom window was wide open, the curtain lifting and falling slowly in the breeze. And in the distance the sound of tennis balls on taut-stringed rackets. The sounds of Hampstead on a summer's day. It seemed so senseless, but typical, that the old man had survived the bleak winter and the long drawn-out spring only to die in the first week of summer weather.

He knew it was going to happen. The doctor and the hospital had said that it was only a matter of days. And his father wanted to come home to die. There was no more that they, or he, could do, and he knew somehow that this was to be the day. It was no longer days but hours and minutes.

The old man lay with his head in the soft valley of the pillow, spots of bright red blood speckling his chest and his pyjama jacket. The washed-out blue eyes that dominated the shrunken face stared into the distance as if he were already walking slowly away from the world to some far-distant place. As he held the old man's hand its skin was as dry and fragile as an autumn leaf, and the hand itself was cold and flaccid.

Weeks ago he made out a list of the things he would have to do when his father died. At the time it had seemed just a routine. Notifying a few friends, the death certificate, the funeral arrangements and the sad bureaucratic paraphernalia of death. But now it was so near it seemed too cold, too little, to mark the end of a life that had been so distorted and yet so courageous.

The telephone rang in the hall below but he made no move to answer it. Affection and instinct made him stay, his eyes heavy with sleep as he sat on the edge of the bed.

It was ten minutes later when the racking, gurgling cough

1

made him hurriedly turn his head to stare transfixed at the flood of bright scarlet blood that gushed from the slack mouth to cover the thin arm, the chest and the sheets with its patina of vivid colour. The purpled eyelids were closed over the protruding eyes and when he laid his hand on the old man's chest there was no longer a heartbeat. For long moments he sat there, overcome with inertia, trying not to think of the years of willing sacrifice that had just ended. Sadness borne with few outward signs, with great faith that the best was yet to come. The violin-playing that had earned a living, and a man who shed tears too easily at Puccini love duets, Mendelssohn and Max Bruch. A man who laughed, embarrassed, as he brushed away the tears saying, 'For God's sake – that Bruch wasn't even a Jew. What was "Kol Nidrei" to him?'

They'd lived in Swietokrzyska Street and his father had said that they would be safe now that the wall had been built to mark off the Warsaw ghetto. But two months later they had come in the middle of the night. He was too young to understand who 'they' were, but he knew they were Germans and that they were called the SS.

The shouting and screaming had woken him, and the fear on his parents' faces had frightened him as they stood there trembling. And then the floodlights shining in through the window. His father kissing his mother, tears pouring down his face as he ran from the room. Then his mother had swept him up in her arms and they were going down the stairs. As they turned in the hallway to go to the back-yard he saw an axe-head splitting the wood of the front door.

She ran with him, panting and sobbing as she clutched him to her. Into another house, one that had already been searched. Up the stairs to an empty bedroom. Crouching behind the wreckage of a bed she had put her hand over his mouth as the noise of hob-nailed boots came up the stairs.

They had held their breaths as the two SS men shone torches round the room, and after a few minutes they heard the footsteps going down the stairs. The next morning another patrol had found them and an angry scharführer had shouted at his mother, calling her a Jewish sow. Then it had been a welter of screaming blows until they were with

2

all the others in the square. He had never seen so many people. There was no shouting, just silence and the stamping of the guards' boots. There were no other people in the Warsaw streets as they were herded like sheep to the train and the night.

For three days and four nights the waggons had rumbled south, the acrid, sickening stench of urine and excrement saturating the fetid air in the waggon with its freight of eighty or more men, women and children. And day and night he clung to his mother, frightened by the hysterical shouting and screaming of prayers in Polish, German and Yiddish.

Once a day the double doors were swung open, light streamed in and the cries and prayers stopped as they queued for the stale black bread and greasy water.

When the train finally ended its journey the men were separated from the women and children. The big banner across the arched entrance said, 'Arbeit macht frei.' 'Work brings freedom.' He asked his mother what it meant but she just shook her head.

As he sat there lost in his thoughts the doorbell rang downstairs. He shivered involuntarily as he stood up wearily and went down the stairs into the narrow hall and opened the door.

The man who was standing there was tall and thin. In his late thirties, but looking older because of his old-fashioned moustache. He was smiling.

'Hi, Jake. I've been trying to get you on the phone. They want to have a meeting. Something's coming up. They'd like you to come along.'

'You'd better come in. What time is it?'

'Just after three. You been asleep or something?'

Jacob Malik closed the front door when the man was inside and walked into the sitting room pointing to an armchair.

'Sit down, Arthur.'

As the man sat down he looked up at Malik's face.

'Are you all right?'

'What's it all about, Arthur?'

'Jenkins called a meeting after he'd been to the FO.'

'Go on.'

3

'There was a report from the West German desk.'

'What about?'

Then Arthur Palmer was staring at Malik's hand.

'Jesus, you've got blood all over your hand. What's happened?'

'My father died. He had a haemorrhage.'

'When? When did it happen?'

'About fifteen minutes ago.'

Palmer stared at him. 'You mean here? In this house?'

'Yes.'

'Oh my God, Jake. Why on earth didn't you say? I didn't even know you had a father. I'm terribly sorry. Is there anything I can do to help you?'

'No.'

'I'll go back at once and tell Jenkins. They can postpone the meeting.' He stood up. 'I'll be in touch in a couple of days . . . are you quite sure I can't help?'

'No, you can't help.'

'Well. You know where I am. I'll let myself out.'

Jake Malik made the phone calls, and all the rituals of bureaucracy and religion were observed. A few old men, friends of his father, came to pay their last respects. No relatives came because there were no relatives still alive. There had been only one small surprise. When he opened the cigar box there was a Will. Witnessed by Hyman Freytag, a friend of his father and a solicitor. Everything the old man had, the Will said, was for his son Jacob. It wasn't that that was the surprise. It was the tattered birth certificate. The name on the paper showed that his father was Jacob Malik, although he had always called himself Abraham Malik. It didn't take all that much working out. He had given his son his own real name and he'd taken Abraham as his own name because it was even more Jewish. It was a badge, a banner against the Germans, and maybe against the world. A small act of defiance? Or was it to mark the change in his life that came when the cattle trucks rattled their way to Auschwitz with his wife and son?

There were two other men at the graveside. Rabbi Rabinowitz said the last prayers and a man he didn't recognise stood there until it was over and then without a word or a glance had hurried away. Malik wanted to get it over but he exchanged a few words with the Rabbi and promised to keep in touch. The old man's days in the Warsaw ghetto with his father deserved whatever courtesies he could muster. Then he walked to Highgate station and bought a ticket to Waterloo. As he sat on the bench waiting for the train he looked across at a poster advertising Cadbury's Milk Chocolate. The blue paper and the silver foil were turned down to display a row of individual pieces. In Auschwitz, just one of those small cubes could have assuaged your terrible hunger, bought you sex if you were a man or saved you a beating from a Kapo. And as the train roared into the station he remembered why he kept thinking of his father's swollen eyelids as he lay dying. They were exactly like the eyes of the first person he had watched as he died. The old Jew in Hut 18, the second day they were in the camp. Sitting like a heap of rags against the wall he had cried out several times as he was dying but nobody had done anything. They just left him there to die. His eyelids had been swollen and red and protruding like his father's.

Jenkins had left a message for him at the security desk and he was escorted up to his office. Jenkins was a dark stocky Welshman. A tough but amiable man in his fifties who had been a department head in SIS for as long as anyone could remember. He was standing, waiting for his visitor after the call from downstairs. He held out his hand and then took Malik's hand in both of his.

'It was good of you to come in, Jake, and I warned the others if you're not up to it we shall postpone the meeting until you are.'

'I'll be all right.'

'I was so sorry to hear the news. I remember the few minutes I spent with your father. When was it? Must have been two, maybe three years ago. He was so proud of you,

5

you know. In his modest way. A grand man. You'll miss him, I'm sure.' He paused, head on one side. 'How about you take some of your leave to have a break?'

'No, sir. Maybe I'll take a break later on.'

'It's up to you, my boy. Well, let's go down to the others.'

There was Jenkins; Arthur Palmer, Jenkins' PA; and Truslove from the German (West) desk. A thin, brown file lay in front of Jenkins' place at the table, and it was he who started the meeting. He looked at Jake Malik as he talked, and it was obvious that the others already knew what it was all about.

'As you know, Jake, we've got an arrangement with the West Germans that if they get involved in certain kinds of problems with the KGB, we have the option of dealing with the problem ourselves instead of involving Bonn. They have a similar deal with the Americans. It looks like we've got one of those problems now.' He leaned back in his chair. 'Not a major problem, thank God, but a tricky one.

'There's been an outbreak of anti-Semitism in several West German cities. Anti-Jewish graffiti, daubings on synagogues, graves defiled. The usual sort of hooliganism. But the Germans think that it's KGB-inspired. That's why we're involved.'

Malik frowned. 'What would the KGB gain in supporting anti-Semitism?'

'To create anti-German feeling in the rest of the world. Evidence that the Nazis are still there, biding their time. The Russians are probably reckoning that the West Germans will be more amenable to reviving Soviet–German detente if they feel isolated. That's just speculation. We just don't know.'

'Maybe it was genuine anti-Jewish groups.'

'Could be. That's why you've been brought into it. We want you to check it out, one way or another.'

'What sort of team can I have?'

'None, I'm afraid. You can have all the facilities you need but no bodies. But the Germans have offered one of their men to work with you,'

'You mean just two of us to penetrate all these groups? How many groups are there?'

'We don't know. The estimate is eight or nine. You don't have to do anything about breaking them up, or getting in deep. That can be done later when we know what they're up to.'

'Why the obstacle course?'

Jenkins shrugged. 'It's pretty low-grade stuff, Jake. We're only obliging Bonn so that they don't make things worse by blowing it up into a full-scale diplomatic incident. We just want to know what's going on.'

'Why me, sir?'

'You've got the experience, Jake, and the qualifications. You speak German . . . you know your way around . . .'

'Nothing more than that?'

'No. What had you got in mind?' Jenkins looked mildly irritated.

Malik shrugged. 'Can I see what we've got on file?'

Jenkins pointed to the file on the table. 'It's all there, Jake, and Truslove can fill you in on our talks with Bonn.'

'When do you want me to start?'

'As soon as you're ready. The flap died down once we told the Germans we'd deal with it.'

'Who do I report to?'

'To me. If I'm not around you can contact Palmer and he'll pass it on. I don't need daily reports. Just keep me in the picture when there's anything worthwhile.'

'Who's in charge? Me or the German?'

'You. It's an SIS operation now.'

Jenkins stood up and so did Palmer, and after they had left Truslove leaned back in his chair smiling, and said, 'D'you want me to translate what the Welsh Wizard was saying?'

'I got the message, Tony. Don't make a nuisance of myself. Don't probe too deeply. Don't get exposed, but keep the Germans happy.'

Truslove smiled. 'That's about it. Let's go for a beer and I'll fill you in on the politics.'

It was eleven o'clock when he left the pub in Victoria. The night sky was clear and he decided to walk back to Hampstead. He needed to slow down his mind. He wondered whether Jenkins wasn't right and that it might be wiser

7

to take a few days' leave. He wasn't physically tired but his mind was out of gear and just sleeping might do him good. The black thoughts didn't really start until he got to Mornington Crescent, when he heard the goods waggons being shunted in the sidings outside Euston Station. For a moment he stood still, his eyes closed, his fists clenched and he cried out in the darkness before he shivered and walked on.

Those bloody waggons. The sound of them still made him cold with fear.

'I don't remember the date, Father. I really don't.'

'But the year.'

'I'm not sure; I think it must have been 1944.'

'Why do you think that, son?'

Jake Malik sighed again and shook his head. 'I wasn't old enough to know, Dad. I didn't know about dates.'

'Was it summer?'

'I think so.'

'What happened?'

'I don't know. She just didn't come for me in the hut.'

'Did you ask where she was?'

'Yes.'

'What did they say?'

'Nobody knew. Nobody answered. You know how it was.'

'Did they say she was dead?'

'No, nobody said anything. She just didn't come back.'

The old man's voice trembled. 'I need a date to remember, boy. Just something. Anything.'

'I know, Dad, I'm sorry I can't help you.'

The old man had put his arm round the boy's shoulders.

'I'm sorry, boy. Don't be upset. It's just one of my bad days. I'll be better tomorrow. Have you done your homework?'

'Yes, Dad.'

'You like some warm milk or chocolate drink in bed?'

'Just water, Dad. In a glass.'

And upstairs in the dark, tucked up in his bed, he lay there trying to remember. At first they'd let her take him in the other hut, the guardroom

8

alongside the Lager Kommandant's house. She'd warned him not to talk or move or do anything. And he'd watched her undress and get on the guardroom bed with the SS man. It was always three men. One after the other; and afterwards his mother and he would sit at the table by the telephone and the typewriter and eat the black bread and a bowl of soup. He hadn't known then what they were doing to his mother but he knew now. And he knew that he must never tell his father. And he knew that she had had no choice and that it was to try and keep them both from the gas chambers.

He had no idea what had happened to her. After a time she had started going alone to the hut and she would come back for him every morning. But that day she hadn't come back. And he had never seen her again. An old woman had told him that the guards had grown tired of her and she'd been sent to the ovens. But the old woman was a crazed skeleton, and anyway he hadn't understood what she meant. He understood now. It must have been 1945 when she didn't come back. January or February. Because it was only a few months later that the Russians had come.

He was asleep when his father came up to bed and the old man had switched on the light to look at his son. He stood there silently, his eyes on the boy's face. The long black eyelashes, the neat nose and the soft full lips were just like hers.

Chapter 2

IN SOME musical circles the world divides into devotees of Tchaikowsky or lovers of Mozart, or, on a lower level, between the protagonists of Sinatra and the fans of Bing Crosby. For the young man lying stretched out on the comfortable sofa the separation came from whether, out of the two Schubert Piano Trios, you preferred the one in E flat major to the one in B flat major. If, like him, you preferred the latter, you would admire the cello that was propped in the angle of the piano stool and the pre-war Steinway that took up one corner of the spacious room. The young man was listening to a cassette of the old Casals version of the Trio, smiling to himself from time to time at the maestro's energetic grunting in the second movement.

An accomplished cellist, with callouses on the balls of his spatulate fingers that bespoke long hours of practice, he listened with his eyes closed. His father, mother, and two sisters were all professional musicians. It was a tolerant, civilised family, interested in all the arts, and living in comfort in the fine house on the outskirts of Cologne. The young man, Heinz Fischer, was the odd man out. Not that he didn't play the cello with feeling, and not that any member of the family treated him as an odd man out, despite the fact that he was the only one of them who wasn't a professional musician. But he *was* a professional. Heinz Fischer was a member of an élite group that most Germans refer to as the 'Popos'. Despite the cosy, almost cuddly name, the Popos are, in fact, the *Politscher Polizei*.

Ostensibly the Popos were just a specialist group in the normal German police force. No different in status from the other specialist groups who concerned themselves with vice or fraud. They were frequently to be seen, young men with alert eyes, guarding cabinet ministers and visiting worthies. But the population never believed that these were the Popos' main duties. Their activities were so secret that there were people, mainly dissidents, who swore that the Popos were the modern-day version of the Gestapo. In Berlin they were known as *Abteilung I*, in Bonn as K14, and in Munich as KA III. When, on rare occasions, a spokesman had to respond to media questioning as to their role, they were always described as 'special protectors of order', which, even in German, was virtually meaningless. As it was intended to be. What they could correctly claim was that they were members of the normal West German uniformed police force. The same claim rightfully made about Special Branch officers in the United Kingdom.

Heinz Fischer was almost thirty-two, and because of his fair hair, blue eyes and good physique the Nazis would have claimed that he was typically German. He was wearing a light-green corduroy jacket, a check shirt and denim trousers, the universal garb of young men in most countries of the western world. At least of those who didn't work for banks, the big conglomerates and the international fiefdoms of IBM, Siemens and the like. He had joined the *Kriminalpolizei* straight from university, but his talents and languages had led to an early transfer to the Popos. He liked his job and had been promoted twice. And promotion meant that he was seldom part of a team, and spent no time guarding public figures as they hurried from their Mercs, Rolls Royces or Citroens into palaces and parliaments. Although all his family knew that he was a Popo officer they always referred to him as being a police officer, and none of them, not even his father, had much idea of what he did. Some things he did would have shocked them, but most of his work they would have seen as odd but possibly necessary in a wicked world.

When the cassette-player eventually switched itself off Fischer lay there for several minutes in silence before he looked at his watch. Sighing, he swung his long legs off the sofa and stood up. He had to be at Wahn in less than an hour.

Malik checked in his luggage and picked his seat on the Lufthansa flight to Cologne. He sat with a cup of coffee in the cafeteria, his canvas holdall between his feet. Truslove had brought him to Gatwick by car. A generous gesture that made him feel guilty at his lack of response to Truslove's chatter on the journey. When the car pulled up in front of the terminal he had turned to Truslove.

'There's something I'd like to know, Gordon.'

'What's that?'

'Why did they decide to send *me* on this job?'

'Like Jenkins said. You speak perfect German and you're experienced.'

'No other reason?'

'What other reason could there be?'

Malik had seen the embarrassment in Truslove's eyes as he asked the question. Embarrassed because he knew the answer.

'Because I'm a Jew?'

'Oh, for God's sake. What's that got to do with it?'

Malik had reached over onto the back seat for his hand-luggage and he said softly, 'Is the boot unlocked?'

'Yes. Let me help you with your kit.'

'Thanks for the lift, Gordon. I don't need any help.'

They must have known how much he hated dealing direct with Germans. He didn't just hate them. All of them. He was afraid of them. At the monthly conferences in Hamburg he never stayed overnight no matter how long the meeting went on. If there was no convenient direct flight back to London he would fly to Paris or Amsterdam rather than wait around at Fuhlsbüttel. In the early days he had even taken sandwiches and a flask so that there was no need to eat their food. There was nothing about his features or his appearance that indicated that he was a Jew but he was sure that the bastards knew. They had always been amiable and respectful, seldom arguing with his evaluations, accepting his decisions without apparent resentment. But there had been times when he wanted to shout it out loud. 'I am a Jew. You bastards murdered my mamma.' He knew there was no point in doing it, but was ashamed that he had never done it. And now he would be there for weeks, maybe months.

12

He fetched another coffee but as he got back to the table they were calling his flight. For a split second he closed his eyes and thought of catching the train back to Victoria. Then he reached under the table for his holdall and walked to the loading gate.

It was nearly an hour later when the plane took off. He looked out from his window seat and the houses became smaller as the plane shuddered its way up through the candy-floss clouds. When the warning lights went out he lit a cigarette and reached into his holdall for the paperback copy of Palgrave.

It was dark by the time they swept over the woods on the approach line to Wahn, and it was spitting with rain as he clattered down the metal steps to the tarmac. At the bottom of the steps a Lufthansa ground hostess stopped him. 'Herr Malik?'

He nodded and, smiling, she said, 'Will you follow me, please?'

Malik followed the girl to the main doors and then away from the main processing area, along a corridor to an office marked 'Private'. She opened the door and waved her clipboard to indicate that he should go in.

A young man in a tweed sports coat was sitting on a metal table, one leg swinging until he saw Malik. He stood up and held out his hand. 'Mr Malik. Heinz Fischer. Welcome to Cologne.'

'Good evening.'

'They're putting your bags in my car then I'll take you into town. Would you like a drink while we're waiting?'

'I'd be glad of a coffee.'

'Sugar and cream?'

'Please.'

Fischer picked up the phone, dialled twice and ordered two coffees. He laughed at something that was said and then hung up, turning back to Malik.

'I think you know Cologne quite well. You've been before, I think.'

'A couple of times only, and I didn't leave the hotel.'

'Ah well. We must put that right this time.'

13

A girl brought the coffees and Malik guessed that Fischer was known at the airport. The coffee was in china cups not plastic. Or maybe it was just that undoubtedly handsome face that did it.

'Do you live in Cologne?'

'I live with my parents in one of the suburbs. Lindenthal. It's very green out there. Woods and lakes and a nature sanctuary. My father sends you an invitation to dine with us tomorrow evening. Just the family.'

'Thank you. Have we got a base, an office or something?'

Fischer smiled. 'They don't want us in Police HQ, that's for sure. It's not that they're uncooperative but I think they want to be able to sweep us under the carpet if anything goes wrong. I've been given funds and I've rented a small apartment in town. There's room for the two of us to live there and two rooms spare for offices.' He smiled. 'I gather you don't want to waste time.'

'Have you got much information already?'

'Not really. A few leads here and there, but I didn't want to do anything much until you came.'

A man in Lufthansa uniform opened the door and nodded to Fischer. 'It's loaded and out front. I've put the parking lights on, so don't be too long.'

Fischer turned to Malik. 'Let's go.'

The apartment was in one of the small streets near the radio station. It had obviously been rebuilt after the war, but although the interior was modern its façade was much the same as it must have been when it was originally built before Germany was a state. The front windows looked down on to a cobbled pedestrians-only shopping precinct and the back windows on to a small public garden with two wooden benches and a few rose bushes just coming into leaf.

The apartment was comfortably furnished with good, solid, German furniture in walnut and mahogany. When Fischer had shown him the layout they both sat together in the main room, and it was Fischer who voiced the first doubts.

'I haven't much background to contribute to this job, you know. It got handed down to me from above as if it were all cut and dried, but as soon as I started looking for real facts – something that would stand up in court – there was very little.' He paused and looked amiably at Malik. 'We could be wasting our time.'

'Where did the information first come from?'

'That's hard to pin down. The first official document is a telephone conversation between a Member of Parliament and the Police Chief in Hamburg. The guy said he had received information that the East Germans were sending agents into the Federal Republic to organise subversion groups. He wouldn't say where he got the information. I don't think it was taken too seriously at first, but a couple of weeks later there was a similar report from Berlin. That was from a journalist who is normally reliable. He had picked it up at a students' meeting at Humboldt University.'

'What party was the Member of Parliament?'

'CDU – a right-winger, but not an extremist by any means. Neither is the journalist, and as his information came via a definitely left-wing source it was treated as a strong indication that there was something in it.'

'Have you been on it full-time?'

'I was for the first couple of weeks, but I was put onto another case and after that I've only put in a day or two here and there. For the last month Bonn have been negotiating with London about our agreement, and since SIS agreed to take it over there's been very little done. Everybody seemed to lose interest.'

'Do you think there's anything in it?'

Fischer smiled. 'Officially I've got no idea. Nothing concrete one way or another. Unofficially . . . yes, I do think there's something in it.'

'What makes you think that?'

'God knows. Just instinct. It sounds right somehow.'

'How long have you been in the racket?'

'Just over eight years, including a year in the *Kriminalpolizei*.'

15

'Maybe we should start by having a word with the politician in Hamburg and see if we can trace his source.'

'I went up to Hamburg to interview him. When I phoned his office for an interview he said he'd check with Bonn. His secretary phoned back and said he regretted that it wasn't possible.'

'Who did he check with in Bonn?'

'He implied that he was checking with the Ministry but I suspect he was actually checking with CDU head-quarters.'

'Why shouldn't they want him to cooperate?'

Fischer shrugged. 'Politics. They wouldn't shed any tears if it was discovered that the government had been warned of left-wing subversives and had done nothing about it. They can claim they did their bit by reporting it, and it was up to the government to do the rest. Willy Brandt went down the river because of weak security and KGB infiltration, Schmidt has only been Chancellor for a few weeks, and the CDU would be happy for him to be shown as yet another security risk right now.'

'So why don't the Government pursue this more actively?'

'The agreement with London that we don't act unilaterally against the KGB, for one thing. And the fact that KGB stooges in West Germany are more than we can cope with. At the last count the estimate was 15,000. Give or take a thousand or two I'd say that's about right. And we haven't got resources to cope with that. The CIA are only interested in information about Soviet Intelligence, and your people . . . well, we're never quite sure what they *are* interested in.'

'Are you married, Heinz?'

'No. Are you?'

'No.'

'Steady girlfriend?'

'Girlfriends, but not steady.'

Fischer laughed. 'I've got a steady but I can't see any girl putting up with my sort of life. Or me for that matter. She says she wouldn't mind, but I'm not so sure that she really knows what it would be like.'

'What does she do?'

'She's a musician. Teaches harmony at the School of Music. My whole background is music. All my family are musicians.'

'A large family?'

'Mother, father, two sisters and me. I guess that's large these days.'

'You don't look like a policeman.'

Fischer smiled. 'Why not?'

'You look too happy.'

'I am happy.' Fischer shrugged. 'I've got my family, music, my girl, a job I like, and reasonable pay and conditions. What more could a man want?'

'How old are you?'

'Thirty-one. Thirty-two next month. I guess you're a little older.'

'I'm thirty-eight.'

'Tell me about your family.'

Malik stood up and Fischer was momentarily shocked by the look on his face, but the young German was too sophisticated to linger with what was obviously a gaffe. He stood up too and said, 'There's food in the refrigerator. I'll move in with you tomorrow and we'll get down to it. If you don't mind I'll stay at home tonight.'

Malik's face was taut and grim as he shrugged. 'It's up to you, Fischer. Do whatever you want.'

After Fischer had gone Malik walked over to the window. He could see the lights of the main railway station and the massive silhouette of the cathedral and very faintly from below he heard men shouting. He looked down and saw a policeman struggling with a belligerent drunk as a crowd of youths stood watching. At the far end of the shopping precinct the blue light of a police car was flashing as a police driver opened the doors at the rear. Malik turned away and walked to the bedroom where Fischer had put his bags. All his life when he heard people shouting in anger they seemed to be shouting in German. German was the language for shouting.

17

He undressed slowly and lay with the bedside light on, looking up at the ceiling. It stayed on all night as he slept.

Day after day, Abraham Malik's group had fought back against the Germans. Both the Germans and the Polish Resistance had expected the Red Army to come to Warsaw's rescue, but day after day they just sat there on the other side of the river, waiting and watching. A few aircraft parachuted food and medical supplies to the beleaguered fighters but they were only token supplies.

As the days went by and the numbers of Polish dead mounted, the Nazis reinforced their troops. Berlin had realised before the Poles that the Resistance fighters were going to be sacrificed by Moscow. The Red Army had no doubts about its ability to crush the SS forces around Warsaw, but Stalin was looking ahead. Resistance fighters could harass occupying armies no matter whether they were Russian or German. Let the Nazis do the dirty work of wiping them out. Forty thousand Poles died in those last few days of fighting the Nazis.

Abraham Malik was thirty-two the day the Red Army tanks rolled into Warsaw. Rabbi Rabinowitz lay with him in the rubble that had been the basement of the telephone exchange. Malik had a long, pus-filled gash, that spread from his ribs to his thigh, from an SS grenade, but as Rabbi Rabinowitz tried to comfort him it seemed certain that he only had a few hours to live. And again and again Malik had wept for his wife and son. He was obsessed by the thought that they might think he had deserted them. She had known that he was one of the Jewish Underground leaders but maybe she would feel that his duty should have been to her and their child. And maybe she was right. They had failed. They had fought against the Nazi occupiers only to exchange them for the Red Army. The Rabbi had feared that Malik's depression would only hasten his death. But when a Red Army medical team took Malik to the tented field hospital the obsession became an advantage. It seemed to give the Jew the reason he needed for living. He would find them and explain. And they would understand.

He had not been discharged from the hospital for two months and it took fourteen soul-destroying, frustrating months of bribery and persuasion before he eventually found his son in a Displaced Persons Camp near the Polish–Russian border. He was just ten years old.

18

The Rabbi came round to the Maliks most Sunday evenings to play chess with Abraham Malik and it was on one of those nights that Jake Malik had first learned of his father's life in the ghetto.

The Rabbi had just won a long-drawn-out game and as he sat sipping his coffee he turned smiling to the boy.

'Your father had more courage against the SS than he has playing chess.' He turned to look at the older man. 'Remember what you used to say, my friend? He who has nothing to lose can try anything.'

Jake remembered the look on his father's face as he looked up from rearranging the chessboard.

'I was a fool, Leo. We all had things to lose if only we had realised it. And what did we gain? Nothing. Thousands dead who could still be alive. Poland exchanged one tyrant for another. We were all fools, Leo. Especially me. I had a wife and son to lose, and it haunts me that I was wrong.

'How were you wrong, my friend?'

'I sacrificed her for a cause. A cause that was doomed to failure. I curse myself every day. It doesn't bear thinking about.'

The Rabbi sighed. 'Remember the words in the Talmud, my friend. "When a young man's wife dies, the altar of God is draped in mourning."'

Abraham Malik shook his head. 'There's another line, Leo, that's more real for me — "There is a substitute for everything except the wife of your youth."'

Rabinowitz leaned forward to put his hand on Malik's knee as he turned to look at the boy.

'One of these days I will tell you about those times. He was a brave man, your father. There were many brave men and women in those terrible years.' He turned his head to look at Malik. 'Have you shown him your medal, Abraham?'

Malik's father shook his head. 'It's rubbish, Leo. Rubbish.'

Jake Malik said, 'Show me the medal, Father, please.'

His father stood up slowly and walked over to the small desk in the corner of the room. He came back with a case of dark red leather in the palm of his hand, offering it without looking at it to his son.

Jake Malik opened the case. On a bed of white silk was a red ribbon with narrow blue stripes at each edge, and a gold cross below. It looked pristine, as if the case had never been opened before. As he looked the Rabbi spoke.

19

'The Cross of Merit, Jacob. First class. In gold.'

The boy looked at his father, embarrassed, not knowing what to say and his father said softly, 'Keep it, boy. I meant to throw it away long ago.' Then he turned to look at the Rabbi. 'I hate them, Leo. I always will. It haunts me. For her to die would be bad enough but to die in that hell-hole . . .' He shook his head slowly. '. . . what can her last moments have been like . . .?' And tears flowed down his cheeks before he put his head in his hands and the Rabbi signalled for the boy to leave them.

Chapter 3

HEINZ FISCHER let himself into the apartment just before ten o'clock, carrying two small cases. He opened one of them, took out a dark red file cover and placed it carefully on the table.

'Pretty thin, but it's all we've got. Have you eaten yet?'

'I don't eat breakfast but I've had an orange juice.'

Fischer looked at him. 'What's your first name?'

'Jacob. People generally call me Jake.'

Fischer smiled. 'Was it Jacob in the Bible who worked all those years to marry Ruth?'

Malik half-smiled. 'It was Rachel and Leah. Seven years hard labour for each.'

'A pity. My girl's named Ruth, and I've always connected her with that story.'

'Ruth was the grandmother of David. That's even more romantic. Anyway, we'd better get down to work.'

'OK. Let me go over the file.'

They went through it item by item. No matter how routine or apparently insignificant the document, Malik read it carefully before going to the next, asking questions as he went along and making notes on a small pad from time to time. When they were through he looked back at his notes.

'I think the first thing is to interview the guy in Hamburg. Whatever he knows we need to know.'

'Then what?'

'We check whoever his source was.' He looked across the table at Fischer. 'Are your suspect records computerised?'

'Yes. But I haven't got authority to access them except with written permission.'

'So we get written permission or I get London to do it. No problem.'

21

'There might be, Jake.'

'Why.'

'Inter-party politics.'

'This is an SIS operation, Heinz. German politics don't come into it.'

'You know that's not true, my friend. If London wasn't going along with Bonn you and I wouldn't be sitting here.'

'What's that mean?'

'I think you know already,'

Malik smiled. 'Maybe I do, but you tell me.'

'These groups are all over the country. They must be. When they did the anti-Jewish stuff it was on the same night in ten or eleven different cities. All far apart from one another except for Cologne and Düsseldorf. The slogans in every town were in several places. That means a lot of groups and several people in each group. And there's just you and me on this operation. Whichever way you look at it it doesn't make sense. Not unless they either don't want us to succeed or they just don't give a damn one way or another.'

'How frankly do we talk to each other, Heinz?'

'For me, as frankly as you like. We're on the same side. Officially and any other way as far as I'm concerned.'

'You aren't going to wear a German hat to protect the national interest?'

'No. If I was told to hold back or my people started playing games I should tell you.'

'OK. How do we get to see the guy in Hamburg?'

Fischer shrugged. 'Let's play it the usual way. I'll phone him for an appointment.'

It was ten minutes before Fischer came back, looking pleased with himself.

'It was like getting through to the Pope. He said he was a very busy man but he can give us a few minutes tomorrow and we won't have to go up to Hamburg. He's going to be in Bonn for a few days.'

'Where are we meeting him?'

'He's got a suite at the Königshof and has granted us audience at eleven o'clock. He sounds a pompous bastard.'

'Can you contact the journalist in Berlin? Then we can book a flight for Friday.'

'I think we'd do better to go there and contact him on the spot. If I phone him he'll want to know why we want to talk with him, and they always have this thing about never revealing their sources. Face to face he'll probably do a deal.'

'Will you book the flight, then?'

'OK. Leave it to me. By the way, you're dining with us tonight, remember. They all want to meet you.'

'That's very kind of you.'

Fischer called for him at seven o'clock, and twenty minutes later they turned into the drive of a handsome house. The whole of the outside was white, and in the pale, evening sunshine of the spring day it looked peaceful and calm, with the wide lawns and tall yew trees. It looked like the kind of house that was advertised in *Country Life*.

There were lights on despite the sunshine, and a tall, thin man in a dark suit stood on the wide steps of the portico. As Heinz introduced him to his father the grey-haired man took his hand.

'My son tells me you're in Cologne for some time, Herr Malik. You must come and see us often while you're here. Despite your work you might be lonely.'

He took Malik's arm and led him into the house. He was introduced to Frau Fischer and Heinz's two pretty sisters, Heidi, aged twenty, and Lisa, who was a few years older. And then they went straight into the dining room to eat. The conversation was mainly about music. Even the news that the Chinese had launched their first satellite quickly strayed into a discussion on modern Chinese violin-playing techniques. They had almost finished the meal when Heidi said, 'Let's play favourites, Papa.'

Herr Fischer smiled. 'We mustn't bore our guest with nothing but talk of music, my dear.'

The girl turned her blue eyes on Malik. 'You start us off, Herr Malik. What's your favourite piece of music?'

Malik smiled. 'How about you guess?'

Heidi laughed and clapped her hands. 'A clue first. Just one.'

'It's cello music.'

'Ah, as you're English it's going to be the Elgar, yes?'

Heinz grinned across the table. 'The Brahms. I'm sure it's the Brahms.'

Malik shook his head. 'I didn't say it was a concerto – maybe it is, but maybe not.'

'The Bach Partitas?' Herr Fischer said, eyebrows raised.

'No. I'm afraid not.'

Frau Fischer laughed and shrugged. 'One of the Mendelssohn sonatas.'

Malik looked smiling at Lisa and she frowned. 'Can I have two guesses? I'm sure it's one of them.'

'Go on then.'

'It's either the Tchaikowsky Rococo Variations or it's the Max Bruch setting of "Kol Nidrei".'

Malik smiled. 'Yes. The Bruch setting. But I could easily have chosen the Variations if I'd remembered them.'

Frau Fischer leaned forward to look down the table at her daughter and then at Malik. 'You know, she worries me sometimes, that girl. If we lived in the Middle Ages I think she'd have been in danger of being burnt as a witch. She's got second sight. She knows things she couldn't possibly know.'

As if she were embarrassed, Lisa stood up. 'I'm going into town, Mama. I'll be back about eleven.' She turned to look at Malik. 'Goodnight, Herr Malik. Don't let them bore you with too much music.'

Malik stood up, knocking the table so that the china rattled. 'Goodnight, Fräulein Fischer.'

There were a few moments silence as the girl walked from the room, and then Herr Fischer said, 'Let's take our coffee in the other room. And you play to us, Heidi. Something gentle. Brahms, perhaps. Or something French.'

Heidi sat down at the piano and they listened in silence as she played a Ballade and the Rhapsody in G major. Then Heinz drove him back into the city. As they walked together up the shopping precinct and stood at the door of the apartment house, Heinz said, 'I hope we didn't bore you too much. We are bores with our music. We know it, but we can't help it. That's why we seldom invite anyone who isn't a musician.'

'I wasn't bored, Heinz. I enjoyed it all very much. It was very thoughtful of you all. I appreciate it.'

'Tomorrow I'll move in properly.'

'OK. Drive carefully.'

Malik stood in the shadow of the building watching Fischer walk away. He looked much younger than his age and he wondered if it was the music that made them such an attractive family. It was hard to believe that they were German. He wouldn't want too much of them. They *were* bores about music. They couldn't just enjoy it. All that talk of performances, and comparisons of one soloist with another. Arguments about tempi and treatment. Why was Toscanini always so fast? Was Karajan's Beethoven really definitive? He wondered if they ever just sat back and listened without analysing every bar. He wondered how the girl Lisa had guessed the Bruch. So few people had ever heard of it. And he'd been going to choose the Mendelssohn fiddle concerto but the lush setting of the Jewish hymn had come into his mind, because he had thought of how much his father would have enjoyed the talk of music and the enthusiasm.

For five days he had hidden between the bottom bunk and the floor. On the fifth day the Kapo had dragged him out by his feet and flung him against the wall. He tried to get back on his feet but there was no power in his skinny legs. He was surprised to see a woman with the Kapo. She had a lean Jewish face and piercing dark eyes as she looked down at him.

'What's your name, boy?' she said.

'Jacob Malik.'

'Your mother's name?'

'Rebecca Maria Malik.'

The woman turned to look at the Kapo. 'You bring him tonight, Ganiek, and you get the watch. Understand. If you try playing games there'll be no more Kanada or women's camp for you. I'll see to that.'

The Kapo shrugged, pretending indifference, but the boy could see

25

that he was scared of the woman despite the fact that there was a yellow Jewish triangle on her dress.

When the woman had gone, the Kapo made him get back under the tiered bunk. He had stayed there trembling for another two hours until the Kapo dragged him out again, shoving him past the rows of bunks to the door.

In the dusk they walked across the two sets of railway lines that divided Auschwitz camp from Birkenau, and by the first row of huts inside the wire the woman was waiting.

For just over two months he had never left the hut where the girls sat sewing at the long wooden tables. The woman who had come for him was in charge of them. At the far end of the room was a tailor's dummy. One of the girls had whispered to him that it was the dummy for Frau Hoess, the Camp Commandant's wife, for whom most of the sewing was done. The clothes were of high fashion and the woman in charge had been the owner of an haute-couture *house in Warsaw before the war.*

He was fed and given odd jobs to do, and at night he slept in the locked workroom. He had overheard two of the girls talking about him, discussing why the woman was taking the risk of protecting him. They were sure that his mother must have paid her.

Sometimes in the early morning before the workshop was open he would stand on a wooden box and look out of the windows. Beyond the barbed wire fence was a plantation of silver birches before the outer perimeter fence and the electrified wire. From the window he could see four of the guardtowers with searchlights on their roofs and machine guns mounted on three sides pointing inside the camp.

It was on one of those mornings that the woman had come into the room, so quietly that he had not even heard the key turn in the lock on the door. She was standing beside him before he realised she was there.

'Well, Master Jacob, and what can you see?'

When he jumped violently and she saw the fear on his face she put her hand on his shoulder. She said softly, 'Do you know my name?'

He nodded and she said, 'What is it?'

'You're Panna Felinska.'

For the first time since he had seen her he saw her smile.

'That's very formal, little boy. What else do you know about me?'

He shrugged. 'They say my mother gave you gold to save me, and you made ladies' dresses before the Germans came.'

26

For long minutes she looked at his face and he saw tears on the edges of her eyes. Then she slowly shook her head. 'They are just stupid . . . no, that's not fair . . . they are just victims. Victims of this hell-hole.' She nodded towards the window. 'Even the animals know what goes on. There are no birds, no squirrels, nothing, in those trees inside the camp.' She turned back to look at his face. 'Where is your father now?'

'I don't know, Panna Felinska.'

'Was he brought to the camp?'

'No. He went before they got us.'

She nodded and sighed. 'He always was a fool. He'll be fighting with the others. All men are fools. Especially if they're Polish Jews.' She sighed again. 'Why should they die for Poland? The Poles are just as bad. They hate us just as the Germans do.'

He stood silent and obviously embarrassed. Not knowing what to say. Not understanding what she said. She smiled at him.

'Will you do something for me one day?'

'Yes, Panna Felinska.'

'If ever you see your father again will you tell him that you met Grazyna Felinska?'

'Yes. I'll tell him when I see him.'

She shook her head slowly. 'Don't say it like that, little Jacob. Not when you see him. If you see him.'

Chapter 4

THE WHITE Merc had its hood down as Fischer drove them down the main road alongside the Rhine; they were out of the city just after nine o'clock, and in Bonn by ten. They parked the car in the hotel carpark and ordered coffee and toast in the breakfast room.

'Do you want me to introduce you as another Popo or as SIS?'

'He'll tell from my accent that I'm not German.'

'I doubt it. You've only got a very slight accent and it's not English. What is it, by the way?'

'Polish.'

'Were you born in Poland?'

'Yes.'

Fischer waited for Malik to say more but when he didn't he went back to his question.

'Popo or SIS?'

'I'd say at this stage, Popo. You be sweetheart.'

Fischer smiled. 'I don't understand.'

'You be the nice guy. Reasonable, and on his side if he argues. I'll be the nasty.'

Fischer shrugged, smiling, 'OK. If that's how you want it.'

'Don't go along with him too far. You gradually begin to see my point.'

'More coffee?'

'Yes. We've still got twenty minutes.'

Fischer waved to a waiter and he poured them more coffee. When he had gone Fischer said, 'My father was very impressed with you. Said we were all uncivilised hogging away about music all the time. Complained that we hadn't asked you about your family and your interests.'

'I enjoyed it, Heinz. It made me seem one of the family and not just a guest.'

'Tell me about your family. They wanted to know.'

'I don't have any family. My father died a month ago. He was the only relative still alive.'

'You must be rather lonely.'

'I don't think about it, Heinz. I just get on with being alive. Surviving.'

'You're obviously interested in music. Do you play anything?'

'A bit of piano. A bit of violin. I'm mainly a listener.'

'The family are performing next month. Would you care to go if we're here?'

'I'd like to very much. Did you do anything about booking a flight to Berlin?'

'Yes. Typical German efficiency. Provisional bookings for five o'clock today and ten tomorrow morning.'

'Does Lufthansa allow provisional bookings?'

Fischer laughed. 'They do if you're a Popo officer. We'd better pay the bill and go on up.'

Herr Doktor Fassbinder's secretary said that he would be only a few minutes and maybe they would like to take a seat. There was a copy of *Die Welt* and the *Frankfurter Allgemeine* if they wished.

The Herr Doktor kept them waiting for ten minutes which Malik guessed was about par for the course. He came through the big double doors from another room. A large stout man with a shiny, smooth, red face, rubbing his hands together as if they were cold. Bustling towards them with an electioneering smile on his face.

'Which one of you is Fischer?'

Heinz Fischer put out his hand 'I am, Herr Doktor.'

'And your colleague?'

'Herr Malik.'

Fassbinder turned his big body and looked at Malik like a general inspecting the guard, and then turned away dismissively. He didn't seem impressed. He pointed to two chairs and drew up a third for himself.

'What can I do for you, gentlemen?'

Fischer started them off. 'You spoke to the chief of the *Kriminalpolizei* in Hamburg some months ago about the possibility of the East Germans setting up subversion groups in the Federal Republic. We'd like to pursue that.'

'Pursue it? There's nothing to pursue. I assume that whatever needed to be done has been done.'

'Of course. But we are taking it very seriously, and we should appreciate your help.'

The Herr Doktor spread his fat hands like a Frenchman denying guilt. 'What possible help could I give?'

Malik said quietly, 'Who gave *you* the information, Herr Doktor?'

Fassbinder turned his head slowly to look at Malik, the folds of fat at his neck compressing as he turned. His eyes were half closed with overdone disdain.

'What I was told I was told in confidence, young man.'

Malik nodded. 'Of course. And we want you to tell us in confidence who gave you the information.'

Fassbinder shook his head. 'Impossible. Unthinkable.'

Malik sniffed. 'You realise that would mean you were obstructing the police in their enquiries.'

'Who, may I ask, is your superior officer?'

Malik smiled. 'Let's not play games, Herr Fassbinder.'

'D'you realise you are talking to a Member of Parliament? Perhaps you hadn't been told?'

'Yes, I have been told, Herr Doktor. And I checked your file. You were elected seven years ago with a big majority. Your Communist Party opponent withdrew at the last minute but you'd have probably won anyway.'

'This is preposterous.' And Fassbinder looked back at Heinz Fischer for support.

But Malik went on. 'Are you going to tell us who gave you the information?'

'Certainly not. And I shall raise this matter with your senior officers.'

'That's OK with me, Herr Fassbinder. By the way, I saw that on the British de-nazification report on your case that you claimed you joined the Nazi party in 1937. But they had the originals of the party documents and in fact you joined in 1933. Right at the start, when there was no pressure on anyone to join. And in your election address you claimed that you had never been a member of the party at any time. You're a capable politician, Fassbinder, and I could never understand why you had left yourself wide open in that way.'

Fassbinder heaved himself out of his chair and walked over to where a white telephone stood alongside a bowl of anemones on a small table. As he picked up the phone Malik said, 'You're being very unwise, Fassbinder. They don't know in Bonn what's on your file.'

Fassbinder's fat finger dialled once and then stopped, turning to look at Malik.

'What the hell do you mean?'

'I mean that you're giving yourself away. Nobody in Bonn has seen this file. But I imagine that the SDP would be delighted to use it if it came out.'

Fassbinder slowly replaced the receiver.

'Who the hell are you?'

'I'm a policeman.'

'You're a blackmailer, Herr Malik, and you could get yourself into deep trouble. I warn you.'

'Sit down, Herr Fassbinder. Just sit down.'

For a moment Fassbinder hesitated, and then compromised by sitting only on the arm of the chair. Malik looked at him amiably.

'I suggest you help me with my enquiry and that we forget the rest of our talk.'

Fassbinder looked towards the window for several moments and they could hear the typewriter clacking in the outer room. Without turning his head Fassbinder said, 'Where is this so-called file?'

'It's in the Central Archives at Century House in London. Or it was last night.'

Fassbinder turned his head quickly. 'What the hell is Century House?'

'It's the headquarters of MI6. I'm the MI6 officer in charge of this investigation. And I've no wish or intention to embarrass you. But I've every intention of finding out who told you about these groups.'

31

'You think they exist?' And the voice was suddenly con-
ciliatory.

'I'm sure they do. Don't you?'

'And they're a danger to the State?'

'Any clandestine organisation is a danger to the State.'

The fingers of Fassbinder's plump right hand played
clumsy arpeggios on the arm of the chair by his leg.

'That puts a different face on this matter. Let me think
about it. Call me tomorrow morning about this time.'

'I need to know now, Herr Doktor. We've got a lot of other
enquiries to pursue.'

Fassbinder smiled. An ingratiating smile. 'You must be a
very good investigator, Herr Malik. You're a very determined
man.'

Malik said nothing, and eventually, looking down at his
jacket and picking a non-existent speck from his lapel,
Fassbinder said, 'This will have to be in confidence, of course.'

'Of course,' Malik said.

Fassbinder smiled at him. 'We're men of the world you
and I, Herr Malik, so I know you'll appreciate my concern
for complete . . . er . . . confidence.' He paused and then went
on. 'I meet all kinds of people in my political life. I have to. I
need to know what all levels of society are thinking in my
constituency. Of course I have helpers – a trade unionist, a
church official, several leading businessmen and of course . . .
er . . . young people . . . Why don't we all have a drink?'

Fassbinder walked over to a cupboard, opened its doors to
reveal several shelves of bottles and turned towards his guests.

'Schnapps, whisky, vodka . . . what'll you have?'

'Have you got a dryish sherry?' Fischer asked.

'Of course. And you, Herr Malik?'

'Nothing for me, thank you. I've got an internal problem.'

'Nothing serious I hope,' Fassbinder said, with obvious
indifference, as he poured the sherry for Fischer and a large
whisky for himself before coming back to sit in the armchair.
He unbuttoned his jacket, loosened his tie and patted his fat
belly. He smiled.

'Too many official dinners. They ought to pay us danger
money . . . Cheers.' He took a generous swig of his whisky.

32

'Now, where was I . . . ah, yes . . . the young people. That's where all the trouble comes from these days . . . drugs . . . protest marches . . . demonstrations against authority and all that bloody nonsense.' He waved his hand dismissively. It was a standard litany and a standard gesture, like the unbuttoned jacket and the loosened tie. It showed that his audience were specially favoured. Intimates of the great man in his moments of relaxation from the cares of State. 'There was one of them . . . one of the young people . . . I took a special interest in . . . insecure, bad home background, wrong set of friends, but intelligent in her own way . . . and talented. A lovely voice.' He sighed. 'She was a singer in one of the clubs . . . I was able to help here and there . . . a word in the right ear. I suppose she saw it as more than it was . . . mind you, I was very fond of her, very fond . . . I helped her get the lease of a small flat . . . saw her from time to time . . . there was a fellow in the background . . . there always is with a pretty girl . . . played in a group at another club . . . a bad influence, drugs and all that . . . she told me he got money from some political source. And he boasted that he was more important than she thought he was. One day she'd see how important he was. Said that 'detente' was just a cover-up and when the time came he and his group would be on the winning side. She hadn't told him about her knowing me and it seems one day he looked in her handbag and found a watch I'd given her for her birthday . . . raised hell about it and she told him . . . no reason why she shouldn't, of course . . . anyway the long and short of it was that he forbade her to see me again. Threatened her, said he'd have her beaten up, disfigured. I told her it was a lot of poppycock but there was no convincing her. She was shit-scared and didn't want to see me any more. That's more or less it. I told my friend at the *Kriminalpolizei* but I heard no more of it.'

'What was the girl's name?' Malik's voice was barely audible.

Fassbinder closed his eyes as if he were trying hard to remember, but Malik knew that he didn't need to.

'Maria something or other. Yes. Maria Hauser.'

'Is she still at the flat?'

'Yes. He'll be there too.'

'Can I have the address?'

'You won't mention my name?'

'Herr Fassbinder, as far as I am concerned, when I leave this room I shall forget the whole of our conversation except that man's name and address. Our conversation this morning was concerned with getting your views on Federal police budgets.'

Fassbinder nodded. 'The apartment is at 17 Monkedamm. The name on the door is Hauser.'

Malik stood up. 'Thanks for your help, Herr Fassbinder.'

Fassbinder was relieved and jovial as he walked with them through the outer room and opened the door to the corridor to let them out. 'Good hunting,' he said, and Malik nodded and smiled.

Heinz Fischer reached forward to switch on the ignition and then stopped, leaning back in his seat, turning to look at Malik.

'How the hell did you get that stuff about Fassbinder?'

'I phoned London last night. They phoned me back about one o'clock this morning.'

'But what made you think there might be something compromising in his record?'

'I didn't, I just wanted to check.'

'It was virtually blackmail.'

'Nonsense. Just a bit of pressure to make the bastard tell the truth. He was withholding information about internal security.'

'What would you have done if he had phoned headquarters?'

Malik laughed. 'I knew he wouldn't. There was a lot more on the file than I said.'

'D'you think there's anything in what the girl told him?'

'God knows. He may have been lying, using his position to get his own back on the man who'd taken over the girl.' Malik looked at his watch. 'We could catch the evening flight.'

Chapter 5

IT TOOK them two days to trace the girl. She had moved out of the apartment the day before they arrived and had left no forwarding address, but a cleaning woman was able to tell them the name of the club where the girl worked.

The club was in St Pauli in the basement of a warehouse in Erichstrasse. Its unoriginal name, Klub Eros, was in red neon above the door and a man just inside the door asked for five marks each as a membership fee. The decor inside paid its tribute to the river a hundred yards away. Teak steps down from the street door and ships' barometers and compasses on the mock walnut walls. There were twenty or so tables and the soft pink lighting made both patrons and girls look healthy and glamorous.

A topless waitress led them to a table and they looked carefully at the price list and ordered two beers. Along the furthest wall was a long bench where half a dozen girls sat chatting. A pianist on a slightly raised dais was playing old-fashioned rock and boogie. About half the tables were occupied and the men looked prosperous. The two girls who came over to join them were quite pretty and they settled themselves at the table and started their traditional patter. Names, where do you two boys come from, how long are you staying and a desperate thirst that only champagne could quench. After about twenty minutes Malik asked where Maria was.

'Which one, honey? We've got two Marias.'

'Maria Hauser or is it Haufer?'

'She's gone to change. She sings as well.'

'As well as what?'

The girl giggled. 'There's a room at the back if you want to find out. We could have a foursome.'

Malik smiled back at her. 'Somebody recommended that I should have a look at Maria.'

'Well here she comes, mister.'

The dim lights were dimmed even further, and a spotlight came on to one side of the piano as a girl came on the stage. She was young, pretty and blonde, and she was wearing a white bikini so skimpy that she might just as well have been naked. She was obviously popular because there was some desultory clapping as soon as she appeared. She smiled and nodded to the pianist and after a few chords she started singing. It wasn't a good voice but it was distinctive. Girlish and clear with an attractive catch of the breath as she sang 'Falling in love again'. She was pretty, and her body was attractive, but not enough to explain the obvious sexuality of her performance. Malik guessed that it was her youth, her appeal to masculine protectiveness. The thing that made some men pay for whores to dress up as schoolgirls. A mixture of innocence and complaisance.

She sang again; this time it was 'Where have all the flowers gone?' The two Marlene Dietrich hits were both incongruous yet appealing when sung so differently from the original sultry versions. None of Dietrich's worldly knowingness and yet more sexual.

There was considerable applause and then the spotlight went out and seconds later the lights on the dais went up as the pianist started playing his version of Scott Joplin.

The hostess sitting beside Malik said, 'D'you want to meet her?'

'Is she a hostess as well?'

'Of course she is. But she'll cost you more than I would, honey.'

'Like how much?'

The girl shrugged. 'At least a hundred marks. I'll give you an hour for eighty.'

Malik opened his wallet under the table and passed the girl a ten-mark note. 'You fix it for me, pussy-cat. And maybe you and I can get together tomorrow night.'

The girl shrugged, looked across at her companion and they pushed back their chairs and walked away.

Fischer said, smiling. 'All this on taxpayers' money, Jake. "To surveillance of possible informant -- a hundred marks."'

'It's going to cost more than that, Heinz. I want her to take me to her place. How about you leave if she comes out, and check where we go?'

'OK. Here's your one coming back again.'

The girl bent down and said softly, 'She's waiting for you. Go through the curtains where I went. The room's got a red door, it's just past the toilets.'

As Malik stood up Heinz Fischer said, 'I'll settle the bill. See you later.'

Malik nodded and then turned to thread his way past the tables. Dust rose in clouds from the red velvet curtains as he pushed them aside and he found himself in a long corridor that stank of urine and disinfectant. The urine was a clear winner. He knocked on the red door and a girl's voice said, 'Come in.'

She was smiling as he closed the door and she was prettier than he had expected.

'Gerda said you wanted to spend some time with me. Did she tell you how much it is?'

'No.'

'It's one hundred for half an hour.'

'Can I pay for a longer time than that?'

She shook her head, still smiling. 'I can't. I sing every hour after ten until we close.'

He took out his wallet and slowly picked out a hundred-mark note. When he looked up at her he said, 'If I pay you now can I see you tomorrow afternoon?'

She laughed softly, 'You're a funny man.'

'Why?'

She shrugged. 'Most men can't even wait till I get my pants off.'

'You're too pretty to rush it.'

'OK. That's a hundred now and we'll see how long you want tomorrow.'

'What time can I see you?'

She pursed her lips. 'How about two o'clock?'

37

'Where?'

'D'you know Venusberg?'

'Where that garden is?'

'That's it. There's a paper shop on the corner. My door is next to their door. There's a card over my bell with my name on. Maria Hauser. Ring one long and one short and I'll know it's you.'

'I'll look forward to that.'

She laughed. 'So shall I.'

They had taken adjoining rooms at a *pension* in Grossneumarkt and ordered a meal in their shared lounge.

'How are you going to get the fellow's name out of her?'

'I don't know. I'll just have to keep fishing around. And now we know where she lives we can watch it until we spot him. He's sure to be shacked up with her.'

'Then what?'

Malik seemed intent on cutting his steak and then he looked up. 'What do you suggest?'

'I could maybe persuade the Kripo to arrest him on some charge or other and you and I could interrogate him.'

Malik shook his head. 'If he's what we think he is, he wouldn't talk. Why should he? He'd know the charge was phoney. He'd just wait us out.'

'What else is there?'

'We could keep him on ice until we've talked with the fellow in Berlin.'

'That's a possibility.'

'Or we could do a private job on him.'

'What's that mean?' Fischer looked genuinely surprised.

'Pick him up. Stash him away some place and put him through the mincer.'

'And afterwards, what do we do with him?'

'Get rid of him.'

'You mean kill him?' Fischer's whisper emphasised his disbelief.

'Yes. If it's necessary.'

'You're joking.'

38

Malik sat back in his chair, chewing slowly as he looked across at Fischer.

'You needn't get involved.'

'But I am involved.'

'I'll send you down to Bonn. That'd give you an alibi.'

'You'd really do this, Jake?'

Malik nodded. 'Sure I would. Why not?'

'You'd get a life sentence if they caught you.'

'They wouldn't get me, and if they did they'd just do a deal with SIS and bundle me back to London.'

'I can't believe you mean it.'

'Why not?'

'You aren't that sort of man.'

'Don't kid yourself, Heinz. I am.' But Malik could see how much the conversation had disturbed the German and he said, 'Let's forget about it until we've had a look at him. Then we can decide whether he looks like a real suspect or not.'

Fischer seemed relieved, but then, looking slightly embarrassed, he said, 'Have you done that kind of thing before?'

Malik pushed aside his plate and grinned. 'Forget it. Leave it to me.'

'But I want to know.'

'Why?'

Fischer shrugged. 'If I'm working with you I want to know what I'm in for,'

'You aren't just working with me, Heinz. You're working *for* me. I give the orders.' Malik smiled but it wasn't a friendly smile. 'I'm sure your people get tough at times.'

'Sure they do. But the guys who do that sort of thing are different. They're thugs, not intelligence men.'

Malik shrugged. 'Maybe you've got a bigger budget than we have. We do our own dirty work.'

'Do you actually get training for this . . .'

'Not everybody. We all get training in self-defence. Even those who are going to end up behind desks. But field agents get further training.'

'To kill innocent people?'

39

'No. To kill people who might kill us, or want to destroy the State.'

'But this man may know nothing. Or what he knows may be unimportant.'

'If he knows nothing then I'll let him go.' Malik paused then went on. 'You know the problem with people like you, Heinz? You don't like what's done in abattoirs, but you like juicy steaks.'

Fischer said softly, 'Or maybe we learned some lessons from the war.'

'What lessons?'

'That a senior officer's order doesn't have to be obeyed if it's a criminal order.'

Malik shrugged. 'Maybe you should just go back to Cologne right now, and wait until I get back.'

'I'll hang around for now. Let's see what happens.'

Malik nodded and stood up. 'OK,' he said.

As they lay naked on the bed she looked at his face, smiling up at him. 'D'you want to do it again?'

'Can I come back tonight and stay the night?'

She shook her head, still smiling. 'I can't do that.'

'Why not?'

'I've got a boyfriend.'

'Where is he now?'

'God knows. But he'll be back here just before one and I don't leave the club until half past one.'

'What does he do?'

'Plays guitar in a group at another club.'

'You could come to my place.'

'He'd raise hell if I didn't come straight back here. He's very jealous.'

'What's his name?'

'Karl. Anyway, why bother about him now? We've got half an hour left yet.'

'What club does he play at?'

She smiled. 'You wouldn't be interested. They're all queers. Not the group. They're straight.'

'Is he any good?'

She laughed softly and pulled him to her. 'Not as good as you, honey. Do it to me again.'

'Does he know you sleep with other men?'

She kissed him. 'Of course he does. Do it to me now. Come on, honey.'

Ten minutes later, as she was dressing and he was sitting on the edge of the bed, he said, 'You didn't tell me where he plays.'

'It's a dump called The Caliph but you won't like it.'

'Can I have your phone number?'

'Sure. It's on the phone, there. But don't call before eleven in the morning or you'll wake me.'

He took a taxi back to the *pension*. Fischer was out and he'd checked for the address of The Caliph in the telephone directory and with telephone enquiries. Neither was any help. He was coming out of the old-fashioned lift into the hall when Fischer came in, and they went back to their rooms upstairs, as Malik told Fischer what had happened.

'With a name like that it'll be in St Pauli somewhere. I'll get on the phone and check with the police.'

Five minutes later he walked into Malik's room. 'It's down by the Fishmarket. There's no proper address but I know how to find it.' He looked at Malik. 'The inspector said it's a dangerous place if you're not a genuine queer.'

'We'll have to risk that.'

'There is another way.'

'Tell me.'

'I could get the St Pauli police to find out who he is. They could find out more in a couple of hours than we could in days.'

'We couldn't do that.'

'Why not?'

'If I had to pick him up they'd connect it with us straight away.'

'I thought you might say that. There's an alternative but it's not so easy.'

41

'What's that?'

'I could go with one of the vice officers who cover the clubs. I could say I was doing a general security check-up on homosexuals. And I could ask him to identify various people. Including our friend Karl.'

'Why you?'

Fischer grinned. 'I could try and look at least neutral. Nobody's ever going to take you for anything but a raving hetero.'

Malik closed his eyes for a moment as he sat in the chair. When he opened them he looked at Fischer. 'It's a good idea. Go ahead and fix it.'

'Let me phone St Pauli and then we'll eat.'

It was four o'clock in the morning when Fischer came back. Malik was fast asleep, still sitting in the armchair, the dot on the TV screen still flickering. But as Fischer closed the door gently behind him Malik's eyes opened.

'It worked, Jake. It really worked. Are you too tired to hear it now?'

'I'm not tired, friend. Just cat-napping. What time is it?'

'Ten past four.'

'Jesus. I must have really slept.' He stood up and walked over to the TV set to switch it off. He turned, smiling, to look at the German.

'You look like Miss World just before they stick the tiara on her head. Shall I ring for some coffee?'

'There's nobody about. It's like a morgue downstairs.'

'OK. Tell me how you were belle of the ball.'

Fischer sat down facing him in the other armchair.

'I went with the sergeant who covers male prostitutes and homosexual brothels and clubs. I learnt more about queers tonight than I did at police school. It's a fantastic world and you don't know whether to be sad or disgusted. That club's like a volcano waiting to erupt.'

Malik smiled. 'What about our Karl?'

'I asked the sergeant who various people were. He knew the life-stories of most of them. Some of them were household

42

names, looking quite at home in that sleazy dump. Wearing
lipstick and rouge and eyeshadow. The lot. I got round to the
group and he told me that the singer was a queer and told me
a bit about him. He was a local. He didn't know anything
about the others, but they introduced the group one by one
over the microphone when they did solo pieces. Karl Loeb
was one of them,'

'What's he look like?'

'About twenty-seven or twenty-eight. Tall, skinny and
foxy-looking. Plays guitar well. It was all hard rock. Old stuff
and loud.'

'What time did he leave?'

'The group played on right until they closed at about 3.45.'

'Did he leave alone?'

'Yes.'

'Car or walking?'

'Walking. It's only about fifteen minutes to the girl's place.'

'Sounds easy. Well done. Let's get some sleep.'

Fischer grinned. 'It's better than that. They've got files on
all the members, including the group.'

'Have you got access to them without showing any interest
in them?'

'I've already arranged to look through them tomorrow.'

'What excuse did you use?'

Fischer shrugged. 'Just general interest. Background for
experience.'

Malik nodded. 'That's a good start, Heinz. Maybe it won't
take as long as we thought.'

Fischer smiled. 'You sound eager to get back to London.'

'No. Just eager to get the job done.'

Malik lay back on top of the bed, his arms behind his head, as
Fischer arranged the papers.

'You ready, Jake?'

'Yep.'

'Right. Here goes. Name . . . Karl Loeb, born 1945 in
Kottbus . . . father was officer in Waffen SS, rank unknown.
Notified killed outskirts of Berlin February 1945 . . . mother

43

fled to relative in Brunswick with child . . . poor scholastic record . . . didn't make High School. National service in signals unit. Then worked as electronics repair man for radio and TV dealer for two years in Wolfenbüttel. Sacked for indiscipline. Loeb claims employer was slave-driver . . . got employment with electronics company working on computer servicing in Rhine area . . . Düsseldorf and Essen . . . self-taught guitar, played in clubs after work . . . now full-time . . . has played with groups in Brunswick, Berlin and other towns. Moved to Hamburg thirteen months ago . . . earns one thousand marks a month with group . . . admits making no tax returns on earnings for approximately three years . . . denies poncing for girl. Flat in her name and she pays all rent but he buys all food etcetera . . . away large part of the day and has no control over what she does when he is away. Told he could still be charged with living beneficially off immoral earnings . . . became violent then verbally aggressive . . . made threats that influential friends would get charges dropped. Full face and profile photographs in green envelope addresses missing . . . police file numbers quoted where applicable.'

Malik lay with his eyes closed.

'That's it, Jake. That's all I got.'

'Sounds beautiful to me, Heinz. Better even than Brahms.'

Malik sat up, his eyes focused far away.

'It doesn't sound all that good to me,' Fischer said.

Malik turned to look at him and smiled.

'Kottbus . . . East Germany . . . relatives still there maybe . . . electronics . . . communications . . . radio network. He obviously isn't the mastermind, but he's one of them. And that's a good start.'

'What now?'

'Can you get the local Kripo to give you details on all the people on that known associates list? Names and addresses.'

'Yes. Some will be on the computer, but it'll probably take a week to cover the lot.'

'That's OK. You fix that. We'll go back to Cologne. Get it all down on paper. Then we'll go to Berlin and fish around there.'

*

44

They spent three weeks checking out all the names in the German police file, particularly where the addresses were in Cologne and Düsseldorf. They were mostly drifters, unemployed youths and so-called dropouts. Some of them had been prosecuted for petty theft and two or three had been involved in minor assaults. But there seemed to be no connection between them. They didn't appear to contact one another and some were untraceable.

Chapter 6

DURING THE weeks in Cologne Malik was a frequent visitor to the Fischer house. There were few days when he and Heinz did not drop in for a coffee or a meal and it was obvious that Malik had become Lisa's protegé. They sometimes went out as a foursome, Heinz and his girl, and Lisa and Malik, and Malik took Lisa to the cinema and on picnics in the nearby countryside when the other two wanted to be on their own.

There was no emotional involvement on Malik's side but he came to look forward to their meetings and was conscious of being lonely when she wasn't available. He made no special efforts to please her but it didn't seem necessary. She obviously cared about him, but he counted it as the affection of a favourite sister, even when it became obvious that it was possibly more than just friendliness. And she was understanding. She didn't probe about his background or why he was working with her brother. The talk was always of music and life in general but there were other things that he noticed. When he ate with the family it was Lisa who saw that he was well looked after and when she was asked her opinion about something her reply was often prefaced by 'Jake and I think . . .'

Because she didn't probe he put up no defences against her. He felt relaxed in her company and even her family vaguely treated them as a pair. He was relieved that her family seemed to accept their relationship without comment.

The phone was ringing as they got back to the flat and Fischer moved over to answer it. When he walked into Malik's room he said, 'That was Heidi. It's their concert tonight. They want us to have an early dinner with them and go on to the concert afterwards. What do you think?'

'Are you going anyway?'

'Yes. I'll take my girlfriend. She's invited too, of course.'

'So you go on your own. I'll be in the way. I'll have an early night.'

'They'll be very disappointed if you don't come.'

Malik smiled. 'You're a kind man, Heinz Fischer. And a very polite one. I don't mean anything to your family, and why the hell should I? I'm a foreigner who happens to be working with their son. They're kind, hospitable people so I'm invited along too,'

Fischer stood looking at Malik. 'You're a strange man, Jake.'

'In what way?'

'I'm not sure. I can't really make you out. You choose a piece of cello music as your favourite. A piece that is lush and sad, almost a rhapsody. That's one part of you. Another part contemplates beating up a man, maybe killing him, as if we were discussing the pros and cons of a bottle of wine. And then . . .' He shrugged and let his arms fall to his sides.

'Go on, Heinz. You'd got to "and then . . .".'

'I don't know how to say it.'

'Try.'

'You're obviously a senior SIS man. You're obviously very capable and experienced. But away from the work you seem kind of lost. Right now you can't believe that my family actually like you. That they enjoy having you around. That they'd like you to come tonight. They talk about you after you've been over. Saying how refreshing it is to have someone to talk to about music who is a listener not a professional. You don't seem to believe that anybody can actually like you.' He paused and sighed. 'You don't even seem to like yourself, and that's terrible.' He looked at Malik's drawn face and said, 'And now I've offended you.'

Malik exhaled a cloud of smoke then stubbed out his cigarette on an ashtray on the bedside table before he looked back at him.

'What time do we have to leave for dinner, Heinz?'

'About five.'

'What are they playing?' Malik's voice was very flat.

'It's a varied programme. I can't remember all of it. The family are playing one of the Mozart string quartets. I think it's K387.'

'I'd better have a bath and get ready.'

'Mother wanted to know if you'd drive their car. My father drives terribly badly and he's worse when they're going to play themselves.'

'What is it?'

'A Merc automatic.'

'OK. That's no problem.'

The hall was full and the audience enthusiastic. And the playing had deserved their applause. Heinz Fischer took Malik to the Green Room under the stage where the players and their friends were celebrating with champagne and Rheinwein. Malik was introduced to friends and friends of friends. But eventually he was standing alone, his hands defensively in his pockets. It was then that a slim hand gently touched his arm. It was Ruth, Heinz's girlfriend.

'Will you do me a favour, Jake?'

'Sure. What is it?'

'Heinz was taking me to dinner, but the family have been invited to a friend's house and Lisa doesn't want to go. So we've got a transport problem. Heinz has got his car and the friends will drive the family back. Would it be asking you too much to drive Lisa home and then keep the car yourself until tomorrow at your place?'

Malik smiled. 'What's the matter with Lisa?'

Ruth frowned. 'It's a bit complicated. The friend's daughter is engaged to a boy that Lisa used to go out with. It wasn't ever going to work out and it was all pretty cool. But she's embarrassed about going in case he's there. I think they'd be a bit relieved, too, if she stayed away.'

'OK. Where is she?'

'I don't know. I'll find her and bring her over. She's not in a rush to go or anything.'

Ruth brought Lisa over five minutes later and he said his thanks to the family before they left. It was still light as they walked out of the hall towards the carpark.

'Can you remember where we parked, Jake?'

'Yes. It's in the far corner by the trees. Would you like to wait here, and I'll bring it over?'

She laughed. 'Good heavens no. A bit of fresh air will do me good.'

'You'll have to tell me the way back to your house. I've no idea how to get there from this place. I just followed your father's directions on the way here.'

'It's not difficult. I'll tell you where to go.'

Twenty minutes later they pulled up in front of the house. She turned to look at him. 'Come in for a drink or a coffee. It's early yet.'

'Are you sure?'

'Of course I'm sure. Put the car in the garage and I'll make the drinks. Or would you prefer coffee?'

'Yes. I'd like coffee. With everything.'

She smiled. 'Don't be long.'

The front door was left open for him and as he closed it behind him she called out, 'Come in, Jake. I'm in the music room.'

She was pouring coffee for them both and she patted the seat beside her on the big tapestried sofa.

'Come and sit down. Help yourself to sugar.'

As he stirred his coffee she said, 'How do you think it went?'

'They loved every minute of it. And your quartet was fine.'

'Did you know it already?'

'Yes. I've got it on cassette.'

'Who's playing it?'

'The Melos.'

'Oh, lovely. How often do *you* play?'

'Not often. I can't read music. I play by ear and that drives the other players crazy. I can't count the stops accurately so I tend to come in too early or too late.'

She laughed. 'Why don't you learn to read?'

'Partly laziness, I suppose. But if I had to learn I'd have to

49

go back to exercises and pieces like "The fairies in the glen". I couldn't stick that.'

'Play something for me.'

'I haven't brought my fiddle.'

'For heaven's sake. This house is full of fiddles, cellos, violas, mandolins – everything. Let me get one.'

Without waiting she jumped up and went over to a tall cupboard and a few seconds later she came back with a violin, a bow and a block of resin. She handed them to him and he put them on the seat beside him.

'You play for me first. A nice piano piece.'

'And then you'll play for me?'

'Yes.'

She walked slowly to the piano, smoothing her skirt as she sat down. She opened the lid and put her hands on the keys. Then she played. Soft, major chords, transposing the key as the simple melody developed. It was like a wind blowing over a mountain meadow, and heavy rolling clouds. She was wearing a black silk dress and her blonde hair was done up in a chignon so that her slender neck was emphasised. They looked very much alike, the two sisters. Very pretty, but their personalities somehow made their good looks less obvious. Heidi was the cooler one. Or perhaps more sophisticated, and Lisa, despite being a few years older, was livelier, more extrovert and more impetuous.

'What are you thinking about, Jake?'

She sat on the piano stool, smiling at him, the music ended.

'I was thinking about you and Heidi.'

'And what were you thinking?'

He smiled. 'Nice thoughts.'

'And what did you think of my music?'

'It was beautiful. What was it?'

'Guess.'

'Could have been Brahms . . . or Schubert, even . . . but I think it was more modern.'

'You're right, my boy. It's by Lisa Gertrud Fischer. Now come and play for me. You'd better check the tuning. I'll give you an A.'

50

He stood beside her at the piano and tightened the nut on the bow before he wiped it slowly with the resin. She gave him an A and he tuned the two strings that were out. Then he tucked the violin under his chin and played. And the girl looked up at him, watching his face. It was an odd face she thought. Strong and dark-skinned like an Italian. High, prominent cheek-bones, and muscles at the corners of his mouth. But the long black lashes that lay curved on his cheek made him seem vulnerable. Younger than his years, though it wasn't a young face. It was too lived-in for that. He was playing the Beethoven Romance. Lingering too long on the bits he liked but playing with feeling. More feeling than she would have expected.

She watched his fingers on the strings. They moved surely and accurately but the vibrato was slightly overdone. His fingers on the bow were out of balance, too close together and his wrist was too stiff. And then she was staring at his wrist where it disappeared into his sleeve. She closed her eyes for a moment but it was still there when she looked again.

And then he stopped playing, smiling at her. 'I can't remember any more.' Then he saw her face and was shocked. 'What's the matter, Lisa?'

She reached out her hand and took his arm and turned it over. The numbers were strangely distorted. Elongated, but still readable. She could make out the first three numbers in the faded bluish-purple. They were 493. And she knew that she'd never forget them.

She looked up at his face, but he looked puzzled. He was looking at her face, not at where her eyes had been.

'What is it, Lisa? Tell me.'

'When did it happen, Jake?'

'What?'

'The numbers on your wrist.'

For a moment he didn't understand, then his eyes went to her hand on his wrist and he pulled it angrily away. Throwing the bow roughly onto the polished top of the grand piano. Pushing the violin towards her.

'Take it, Lisa. I've got to go now.'

'Don't be angry, Jake. Tell me. Tell me what happened.'

51

He saw the tears brimming at the edge of her eyes and taking a deep breath to get himself under control he said quietly, 'You know how it happened, Lisa. Everybody knows. I don't want to talk about it.'

'But you weren't old enough, Jake.'

And then she saw him trembling, his whole body shaking; and she stood up, putting her arms round him, and like a child he put his head on her shoulder. Slowly and gently she stroked his hair and his neck. For long minutes they stood there until he raised his head, averting his face as he wiped the tears from his face with his hands. When he turned his face to look at her she bitterly regretted that she had spoken at all. It was gaunt, like a corpse, the brown skin grey, the eyes protruding and the mouth helplessly agape.

She said softly, 'I'm so sorry, Jake. I was stupid. I shouldn't have said anything. But don't go. Sit with me until you've recovered. I couldn't bear to be alone until they come back. Please forgive me.'

He went with her, unresisting, to the big sofa, and as they sat there he turned his face to look at her. He opened his mouth to speak but then closed it tight so that the muscles showed at the side of his mouth.

'Don't talk, Jake. Just rest. Shall I get you a whisky?'

He nodded, and she left to pour the drink. When she came back he looked more composed and the colour was coming back into his face.

'I brought you a brandy. Brandy will be better.'

He took a sip and made a face, leaning forward to put the glass on the low table in front of them. He sat looking at the girl.

'You knew I'm a Jew didn't you? That's why you guessed the Max Bruch.'

'No, Jake. I didn't know. I never thought about it. You were just Jake Malik, a nice man who knows my brother and who likes music.'

'You knew when you saw the tattoo on my wrist.' His voice was harsh.

'Jake, my love. Calm down. No. Even then I didn't think about it. All I thought of was how the hell it got there. How you could have been in one of those camps. That you must have been a child.'

'I was a child. But there were hundreds of children in the camps. They killed the children first. Some adults were Germans but all the children were Jews. They only gassed Jew children.'

She sat there in silence. Not knowing what to say. She wanted to say that at least half the musicians they played with were Jews but it sounded too much like that terrible joke.

'I'd better go, Lisa. Will you be OK?'

'No. Don't go. And I won't be OK. I don't think I'll ever be OK again.'

He reached out his hand for hers and she held it tightly as she looked at him.

'Will you forgive me, Jake?'

'There's nothing to forgive. It's not you. It's not even me.' He sighed. 'It was other people. Animals.'

'I was so happy playing to you, Jake. And so pleased when you played for me. It all seemed so right. And then in one thoughtless second I brought it all crashing down. And it won't ever be the same again.'

'Not the same maybe. But better in other ways.'

'What other ways?'

He sighed. 'You know me better. I know you better. For a moment you cared about me.' He shrugged. 'And that means something to me.'

'Will you walk me in the garden, Jake? I hate this room.'

'A good idea. Do you need a jacket or anything?'

She shook her head and they walked to the french windows, opened them wide and walked into the garden.

In the moonlight they could see the blossom on the apple tree, and Malik looked up at the moon. And as he looked she put her arm round his waist, her hand resting on his hip. He turned to look at her. She was looking up at his face and she said softly, 'Don't be unhappy, Jake. And don't be lonely. I care about you.'

He smiled back at her and said, 'I sometimes have nightmares. And those few minutes in there were like one

53

of those nightmares. Or they would have been except for one thing.'

'What was that?' she said softly.

'You called me "my love".' He shrugged, embarrassed.

For a moment she looked away and then she turned her head and put her mouth up to his. He kissed her gently. Lovingly, but without passion. And his arm went round her waist as they walked slowly across the lawn back to the house.

As she closed the door behind them she turned to look at him.

'I do care about you, Jake. I really care.'

'And I care about you too, Lisa Gertrud Fischer. Very much.'

She smiled. 'You must make a very good policeman.'

'Why?'

'You notice everything and you remember everything.'

'Shall I take you out to dinner or the cinema tomorrow night?'

'I've got rehearsals until six-thirty. I could be back here ready by say seven-thirty. So yes, Jacob Malik, the answer is yes.'

And Malik smiled as she laughed up at him. He said, 'Will you be all right now?'

She nodded. 'Yes. They'll be back soon. Drive carefully. Do you know the way?'

'I think so. No problem.'

She laughed. 'You're always saying "no problem".'

'And you're always saying "good heavens".'

'On your way, policeman. Sleep well.'

'And you.'

She was still standing at the door when he drove past and he flashed the headlights as she waved to him.

It was a door closing that woke him and he turned his head to look at the luminous fingers of his travelling alarm clock. It was just past three. And then his bedroom door opened and the light went on. Heinz Fischer stood there staring at him, his fair hair ruffled, a woollen scarf looped round his neck.

'What is it, Heinz?'

'Lisa told me about what happened. She's terribly upset about it.'

'She seemed all right when I left.'

'Oh, *she's* OK. She's worried about you being on your own. Are you OK?'

Malik nodded. 'Yes. I'm OK.'

Fischer sat down on the edge of the bed. 'I'm terribly sorry about what happened, Jake. I really am.'

'We're both OK now. Forget it.'

'I don't mean that. I mean what must have happened in that bloody camp.'

Malik closed his eyes and shook his head. 'Forget it. I don't want to talk about it.'

'I understand. Will you do me a favour?'

'The car's parked in the usual place.'

Fischer smiled. 'It's not that. But I was going to use you as an alibi tonight. I was going to Ruth's place but telling the family I was here. Lisa made me promise I'd come back here. Word of honour and all that. The lovely Ruth is sitting down below in a taxi with its meter running. Would you mind if she stayed here tonight?'

Malik grinned. 'Not at all. She can have my bed and you and I can sleep in your room.'

Fischer stood up smiling. 'Thanks, Sir Galahad.'

Chapter 7

THE PLANE came in low over Berlin, sweeping over the forest and lakes, banking and levelling onto the flight path for Tegel. When it had landed and taxied to the terminal stand, there was the usual Gadarene rush to the exit doors, but Malik and Fischer stayed in their seats. It was ten minutes before the steps were latched in place and the door opened, and five minutes later they reached for their hand luggage and left the plane.

Fischer showed his ID card at Immigration and vouched for Malik, and the Customs man recognised Fischer and waved them through. The flight had come through from Madrid but there was only a handful of passengers.

They took a taxi to Fasanenstrasse and booked into the hotel. Fifteen minutes later, they were walking down the Kurfürstendamm towards the number shown on Paul Radtke's union card as his permanent address.

It was over a travel agency and there was a grilled loud-speaker alongside the doorbell. When Fischer pressed the bell a garbled voice said something that they couldn't under-stand. Fischer gave his name and police rank and the door buzzed and opened to a push.

A man of about thirty was standing at the top of the stairs watching them as they went up towards him. He was dressed in a red shirt and blue denims and his feet were bare.

Fischer went up first and held out his hand. 'Herr Radtke?'

'That's me. I didn't get your name.'

'Fischer, and this is my colleague Herr Malik.'

'Did you say something about the police down there? This goddamn speaker's hopeless.'

'Yes. We're both police officers. We wanted to have a word with you.'

56

'OK. Come in.'

It was a small office with a door leading into another room that looked like a bed-sitter. The walls were lined with shelves, and the shelves were packed with box files. A cheap office desk was against the window with a typewriter, a phone and a pile of telephone directories.

There were only two office chairs and Radtke waved towards them and perched himself on the edge of his desk.

'What can I do for the *Bundespolizei* today?'

'A couple of months back we had a report through from Berlin that you'd picked up a rumour about the East Germans sending people over to organise subversion groups in the Federal Republic.'

'Christ. Which one was this? I'm always picking up rumours about infiltration and terrorist groups.'

'This was from Humboldt University.'

'Ah yes. I remember that.'

'Can you tell us what was said?'

'Not unless I kept my notes.'

'But you do remember it?'

Radtke laughed. 'All I remember is that the chick who told me had got real big tits.' He stood up and walked to one of the shelves, touching the labels on files as he went along the row. He pulled one out and carried it to his desk.

'If it's anywhere, it's in here.'

He leafed through a pile of papers and newspaper cuttings then pulled out a shorthand notebook, flipping the cover open and slowly turning the pages.

'Yeah. Here we are. It's not much. I went over because there was a debate between students from the Free University and students from Humboldt. Subject was . . . I can't read it . . . yes – "The dangers of the proliferation of nuclear weapons to world peace".' He looked up and shrugged, smiling. 'All the usual crap. Both sides doing their standard pieces. Their lot better informed. Our lot better debaters. There were about sixty people there, and coffee and sandwiches afterwards, courtesy of the Faculty of Political History.' He laughed. 'They used to serve Beluga caviar at these things until some stupid bastard got up and asked where they got caviar from in East Germany. A lot of laughter but some quiet grinding of teeth.

'Anyway, this bird latched on to me. Very pretty, tight sweater and all that. Bent my ear about how many countries were developing or trying to develop nuclear weapons. Egypt, India, Pakistan, Israel, our old friend China, and the usual list.

'She seemed to know quite a lot about what was going on. Things that journalists hear about that don't get printed in the papers. I asked her why it was necessary for the KGB to ruin Willy Brandt's career by planting a spy on his personal staff. He'd been working hard for detente between Moscow and Bonn, and with the East Germans. I asked her if they would prefer dealing with Franz-Josef instead. She huffed and puffed a bit and then came out with this comment. I couldn't make notes at the time but I did when I came back. As near as I can remember, she said ... quote ... true detente isn't possible and never was . . . and that one of these days Bonn would realise that playing double games didn't pay off. But Moscow was well aware of what the revanchists in West Germany were trying to do and they had people there who would rise up and expose them when the time was ripe . . . unquote. I genuinely didn't understand what she was getting at so I asked her what she meant and she went on . . . quote . . . there'll be a day of reckoning and we've got the people there who would bring down the war-mongers of Bonn . . . unquote. It didn't seem all that startling, but she seemed to want to take back what she'd said. Said it was off the record, unofficial. Only her own thoughts. She went on so much I thought I should report it and I did.

'I told the police I was going to try and date her and see if there was anything more. They said it was a good idea.' He grinned. 'I was looking forward to it but they phoned me in the afternoon and said maybe it wasn't such a good idea as she was being screwed by a KGB officer based at Karlshorst. I agreed it wasn't a good idea.'

'Did you get her name?'

'I never record informants' names in my notes. I've put an

58

A in a circle and I think her first name was Anna. She was a student, so you should be able to check her out.'

Fischer stood up. 'Thanks for your help, Herr Radtke.'

'Are you people taking this seriously?'

'Not particularly. We do what we can to check these things, but they generally end up in a cloud of smoke.'

Radtke laughed. 'Too true. Anyway, remember me if there is anything. First call so that I can earn an honest buck.'

'We will. Thanks again. We'll let ourselves out.'

'OK. All the best.'

They stood in the sunshine looking in the travel agent's window. Malik said, 'More than I expected, but nothing of any use except the girl's name.'

'Let's walk along to Kempinski's and have a coffee.'

'OK. Let's do that.'

They sat at one of the outside tables and when the waiter had brought the coffee Malik said, 'Is it likely the West Berlin police could trace this girl?'

'I'd say it was certain. They wouldn't have been able to tell Radtke that she was being screwed by a KGB man if they hadn't identified her.'

'Of course.' Malik nodded, thinking. 'You're absolutely right. Can you contact them?'

'I'm not allowed to contact them direct. I have to go through *Abteilung I*.'

'How long will it take?'

'I don't know. There's friction between them and the Kripo.'

'There always is. I think governments like it that way.'

'I'll go along and see them.'

'Where are they?'

Fischer looked embarrassed. 'I'm not allowed to tell you.'

'Ah well. It doesn't matter unless they take too long. If they do, I'll put London onto Bonn.'

'Have another coffee and I'll get on my way and we'll meet back at the hotel.'

'When?'

'God knows. I'll have to do some bowing and scraping first.'

Malik phoned the Fischers' number in Cologne but Lisa was out and he was embarrassed at her father's friendliness and having to hedge about giving his phone number so that she could call him back. He left a message that he would call her again.

Ten minutes later the phone rang and it was Lisa.

'How did you know the number?'

'Heinz scribbled it on the pad by the telephone. Said he'd give the room number when he called.'

He laughed. 'So much for security.'

'Hang security. Are you OK, Jake?'

'I'm OK. How're you?'

'Fine. I played tennis this morning as it's Saturday.'

'Is it Saturday? I'd lost track of the days.'

'When will you be back?'

'I don't really know. Soon, I hope.'

'Try and get back for the Sunday concert.'

'I'll do my best.'

'We must . . . aren't telephone conversations terrible? I'd hoped you'd phone me and now I've got nothing to say . . . Mama has just gone past. Says she sends you her love and say the same to Heinzl. OK. I'd better go.'

'I'll call you again tomorrow.'

'Bye.'

'Bye.'

He waited until she had hung up before he put down the receiver.

For several minutes he sat there thinking about the Fischers. The old man reminded him of his father, with his sudden enthusiasms and the loving way he tucked his violin under his cheek. And his insistence on not using a chin-rest. Tuning by ear and that last minute swish of his bow which they both claimed settled the horsehair into its proper place.

Heidi, despite being the younger sister, was more serious

and reserved than Lisa, and their mother tended to keep to the background until there were decisions to be made. Almost like any Jewish matriarch. Lisa was the emotional one. Pretty, impetuous, enthusiastic like her father and easy to get on with. He wondered what they all thought of him now that they knew that he was a Jew.

Fischer looked pleased with himself when he came in, a brown envelope in his hand. He was smiling.

'I got photocopies of the whole file.'

'Is it useful?'

'In a way.' Fischer sat down at the small table. 'Plenty of names, but no common thread that I can see. Maybe you can see something.' He shoved the envelope across to Malik.

'Lisa phoned. Your mother sends you her love.'

'Thanks. I'll give them a ring later. I'm going to get a haircut. I'm beginning to look like a policeman trying not to look like a policeman.'

Malik nodded without looking up as he opened the file. The pretence that they were policemen was beginning to irritate him. Fischer was more of a policeman than he was, but to keep up the public pretence between themselves was pointless. And he had a suspicion that Fischer was emphasising it so that he could play it by the rules. There was a strong element of the Boy Scout in Fischer. Or was it just the German instinct for bureaucracy? *Befehl ist Befehl.* He turned to the first sheet in the file.

There was half an hour's reading and then he went through it again. Despite his dislike of the policeman attitude the file showed one of the advantages of playing it that way. It was typical police work and typically thorough. It must have taken a lot of man-hours to put it together.

Anna Bauer was twenty years old and a student at Humboldt University, the crown jewel in East Berlin's educational system. She was in her second year and unlike most students she had a room of her own not far from the University buildings. There were a dozen or so photographs. Grainy and contrasty because they were taken undercover and with long lenses. They still showed a girl who looked more like a beauty queen than a political agitator. Some of them were taken in the street as she left her flat, but most of them were in cafés or clubs and the captions on the back of the prints gave details of the place and sometimes the names of the people she was with. There were two photographs of the KGB man, Anatoli Simenov. Malik knew more about him than was on the report. He was in his early fifties and one of the more sophisticated KGB operators. He had started in the 9th Directorate as one of the special guards protecting top Party leaders and their families, but nowadays he was used on special assignments. He'd worked in the United States, had a short stint in F ris and a year in London.

The girl's recorded contacts were on both sides of the Wall, and there were two or three lines of background description when the contact was apparently more than social. The East Berlin contacts were mainly Party officials. Two of them, apart from Simenov, were Russians. One was a Red Army major who was unidentified apart from his artillery insignia and the other was a town-planning expert on loan to the East German government.

In West Berlin her contacts were almost all non-political. Several businessmen. A photographer. A radio announcer from RIAS Berlin and a magazine features writer. And the contacts were evaluated as being social and sexual, typical of the contacts a pretty girl would have. But not if she was from East Berlin. That made all her West Berlin contacts suspect. The mere fact that she could come through the Wall so easily and so often made her suspect. What was more significant was that several of her businessmen contacts were from outside Berlin. One was from Hamburg, another from Munich, one from Cologne and one from Frankfurt. And according to the surveillance she saw them every time they came to Berlin and they were always there at the same time, staying at the same hotel.

The surveillance had been for five months and had been intensified since the journalist's report to the police. The evaluation was non-committal and went no further than the suggestion that the KGB man was using her for gathering bits and pieces of industrial and economic information that would help pad out his reports to Moscow. It was a traditional method for agents of most Intelligence services to finance a mistress, but the evaluation classified the girl and her contacts as of only average security interest. Which was fair enough. They would have thousands of similar files in their Registry.

'What about the Cologne guy, have you ever heard of him?'

Fischer looked embarrassed. 'Yes I have. As a matter of fact I've met him several times. He's a friend of my father. Well, perhaps not a friend, but a close acquaintance.'

'What's he like?'

'Nothing like what we are looking for. Right-wing and ultra-conservative. Sponsors concerts. Happily married so far as I know. He's got a piano factory. Turns out pianos for schools and clubs. They're not Steinways but they're pretty good.'

'Doesn't sound a likely target for us, but nevertheless he does come up to Berlin to see our little Anna.'

'He may come up for business and she's secondary.'

'Is he the kind who screws on the side?'

'Who knows? I suppose nobody's past doing that if they get the chance, and she's very attractive.'

'But why should she let him?'

'I don't know. Money, maybe.'

'If she was doing it for money she'd move into West Berlin and make a fortune.'

'So what next?'

'I think we go back to base and then maybe we have a good look at our friend in Hamburg. We've got a lot of data but no clues. It needs digesting.'

For a few moments Malik looked at Fischer as if he were trying to make up his mind about something.

'Sit down, Heinz.' Malik said it quietly and pointed to the chair at the other side of the table. Fischer sat down and waited for Malik to speak.

'Has anything struck you as odd about this operation, Heinz?'

'Apart from the fact that we don't seem to be making much progress – no.'

Malik smiled. 'Just do the sums, Heinz. There are at least six cities that may have these groups. A group is going to be eight or ten people. So we're talking about fifty to sixty people who are involved. SIS have put me on to checking it out. And Bonn have given me you as an assistant and as a means of liaison. That's what's odd.'

'I don't understand.'

'Let's go back to square one. Bonn hears from two sources, the Member of Parliament from Hamburg, and the journalist here in Berlin, about possible subversive groups. But they must get that sort of information week after week. Then there are the anti-Jewish activities and Bonn suddenly get agitated. They assume that the people being planted in the Federal Republic are East Germans controlled by the KGB. It's a possibility, of course, but there could be lots of other solutions. They may be neo-Fascists, or old Nazis, or just anti-Semitic Germans. A dozen scenarios. But if it was any of those then Bonn would just deal with it. That's what the Popos are for. But they stick to the KGB angle and that means referring to London and Washington. So SIS take it over to avoid diplomatic problems with the Soviet Union. But after all this nail-biting and discussion all that happens is that two people are put on to it. You and me. Nobody's pressing us. Nobody's phoning every hour asking what we've got or done. Why?'

'Because they don't really care what happens.'

'That's one possibility, but I don't think it's the real one. Maybe London and Bonn do know what these people are up to and see it as harmless or even useful.'

'And we're being used just to keep the record straight. Someone to blame if something happens they don't like.'

'There's one other possibility.'

'Tell me.'

'That they think they know what's going on but they're wrong.'

'So what do we do?'

'The first thing we do is to check how serious they are about the operation. Both of us contact our seniors and say that we think it's a waste of time. If they agree then that's that. If they disagree and order us to carry on, we ask for additional man-power.' Malik smiled. 'We'll talk about it again when we've had their answers. Meantime we'll have another look at our friend in Hamburg.'

Chapter 8

'WHERE ARE you speaking from, Jake?'

'Police HQ in Cologne.'

'Have you got a scrambler?'

'Yes.'

'Let's go over to scrambler then.'

Malik pressed the red button on the black box and Jenkins was already speaking. '. . . getting on?'

'Slowly, I'm afraid. There are only vague leads to follow. That's why I called you. I think there's something going on but I'm not sure what. I need more bodies but I wanted to check that you thought it was worthwhile.'

There was a long silence at the other end and Malik said, 'Are you there?'

'Yes, I'm here, Jake. We can't spare any more bodies but we do want you to carry on.'

'But if you . . .'

'Jake. We've had a tip-off from Berlin that seems to link up with your operation. It gives weight to your feeling that something's going on. But we want to keep it low-key in case we're being conned.'

'What was the tip-off?'

'One of our chaps there is playing footsie with an East German KGB man. He's been hinting to us that the KGB are interested in a group of Germans who he thinks are up to something. He talked vaguely of some sort of high technology device.'

'What's the KGB man's name?'

'Hold on . . . I'll have to check the file . . . here we are . . . Simenov. Anatoli Simenov. He's based at Karlshorst.'

'What kind of device is he on about?'

66

'We don't know. Our chap couldn't look too interested. The implication was that a group of Germans were involved in the development of some piece of high technology. They might be official for all we know. Or a figment of the Russian's imagination. Or some little game the KGB have worked out. The impression was that he genuinely didn't know much and was fishing to see if we knew anything.'

'What makes you think that?'

'He offered a trade, Jake. A name we would very much like, if we could put his mind at rest as he phrased it. Which probably means no more than that he can close the file on some rumour they've made him check up on.'

'What makes you think his little gang are anything to do with my lot?'

'Instinct. Experience. A feeling in my water. How about you?'

'Yes. It fits the timing. Anyway, you want me to keep plugging away?'

'Yes.'

'Can I use SIS facilities at our embassy and the consulates?'

'Yes. But not Berlin.'

'Why not?

'Just not Berlin, Jake.'

'One last point. I haven't had any mail since I got here.'

'I'll check with Gordon Truslove and liven him up. I know we've been paying the standing orders, I saw the paper-work go through the other day. The mortgage, an insurance or two and I think it was HP on the car, so don't worry about those. I'll see about the mail, though. Anything else?'

'No thanks.'

Fischer looked gloomy as he let himself into the flat.

'How'd you get on, Heinz?'

'You know it's crazy, Jake, but I don't know. The best of German bureaucracy at work. Agreed that we haven't made much progress. Yes, they want the operation to continue. And no, I can't have any help. Facilities yes. Bodies no. Keep

at it but don't bother them with too many written reports.'
Fischer spread his hands. 'They're not interested, Jake.' He
sighed. 'How did your people react?'

Malik told him briefly of his telephone conversation with
Jenkins but he didn't mention the information from Berlin.
He wasn't sure why he kept that back but he rationalised on
the basis that he could always mention it later if it seemed
relevant.

'So what do we do next, Jake?'

'We go up to Hamburg again and fish around. If we draw a
blank we'll take Loeb for a long weekend.'

They watched the girl's flat for two days. Her name was still
on the card over the bell. Different men were there during the
day when Loeb was out. Fischer followed Loeb several times
but he spent most of his time with other members of the club
group in bars and cafés. Both nights he had left the flat
carrying his guitar in its case and both nights he had returned
in the early hours of the morning.

Back at the hotel Malik sat at the table looking through his
notes. Eventually he closed the notebook and looked across
at Fischer.

'Any suggestions?'

Fischer sighed. 'None that are worthwhile making.'

'Let's hear them all the same.'

'We can check on all those contacts of the girl in Berlin.
We can keep a watch on all Loeb's contacts here. And
maybe you could contact the girl again and see her a few
times. Gain her confidence and see what you could get from
her.'

'And by the time we'd finished we'd be ready for our
pensions.'

'I know.'

'How do we go about renting a house?'

'We could do it through an agent.'

'Do they have lists of places to rent?'

'Of course. And photographs.'

'That's our first job tomorrow.'

Fischer didn't reply but Malik was aware that he hadn't said no. And he would have realised what it meant.

They sat at the table looking at the details of the houses.

'Where's Harvestehude?'

'It's the other side of the Alster. The radio station's there.'

'Heavily populated?'

'Yes. It's a major suburb.'

'Which of these houses is likely to be isolated?'

'You'd have to go east towards the East Zone. This one at Gross Hansdorf is a possible and this one at Rausdorf's another.'

'How long do we have to take it for?'

'They wouldn't be interested in less than a month.'

'Let's hire a car and go and look at them.'

'If we want to go inside they'll want to send someone with us.'

Malik smiled. 'We don't need any company, Heinz. You go off and hire us a car.'

'I'll be about an hour.'

'OK.'

As Malik waited he wondered what to do about Fischer. The German knew, all right, what he was intending to do, even though he didn't acknowledge it. For the first time he was going to have to give the German an order. An order to go back to Cologne, or an order to join him in what he intended doing. He hoped there would be some sign, some indication of what would be best.

He had no doubt about doing it. They would sit around for months doing fruitless surveillance of a dozen or more people and at the end of it they would have to make one of them reveal what the groups were doing. It would take a team of eight or nine to penetrate even one or two groups, and even that would take several months. And his orders had been clear. He was to discover what they were doing and who they were. He was not required to penetrate them or round them up.

As soon as the Volkswagen pulled up at the house in

69

Rausdorf he knew it was the one. With high brick walls, it stood back from the road, its garden a jungle of weeds, its wrought-iron gates leaning half open because the bottom hinges had rusted away. They wrenched the gates further apart and drove the car up to the house. The gravel drive itself was thick with cow parsley and plantain but the house itself looked solid and substantial.

They walked round the house, clearing the ivy and bind-weed from the windows and peering inside, and Fischer stood looking slightly disapproving as Malik took out the soft chamois wallet and tried the skeleton keys. Water ran freely when Malik turned on the taps and when he pulled down the meter switch the lights functioned in most of the rooms, and the big refrigerator in the kitchen hummed satisfactorily as he opened its door.

As they stood again in the garden he said softly, 'Well, Heinz. This is the one. Let's go back. Pay them two months in advance, book yourself a flight to Cologne and bring the keys back to me in the hotel. Give a false name to the estate agent.'

'I'll stick around, Jake. You're going to need some help.'

'It's an order, Heinz. You don't need to be involved.'

'I'm already involved, Jake. Nobody will believe I didn't know what was going on.'

'They will if I say so.'

Fisher put his hand on Malik's shoulder. 'Forget it, Jake. There's more chance of success if there's two of us.'

Malik knew that was true. And Malik was a professional. 'We'll talk about it when you've got the keys.'

Fischer was already at the hotel waiting for him when Malik got back from the shops with a cardboard box full of food and a cheap canvas holdall that he didn't open. The keys to the house lay on the table, tied together with a shoe-lace that was knotted to a wooden tag. Malik picked up the tag and looked at the letters that had been crudely burned onto the wood. It spelt out *Das Waldhaus*.

They went out for a meal and then rested on their beds until ten o'clock, when Malik made coffee and they sat at the table.

'Can I ask you something, Jake? Something personal.'

70

'Try me.'

'Do you hate all Germans?'

It was a long time before Malik answered and then he said quietly, 'If you'd asked me that a month ago the answer would have been yes. Even now, when I think of Germans *en masse* the answer would be yes. But I don't hate the Fischer family. I like you all. I seldom think of you as Germans, though. I think maybe hate is the wrong word. Germans scare me. Really scare me.'

'But you're so tough, Jake. I can't imagine you being afraid of anybody.'

'It's not that kind of afraid, Heinz. I'm not afraid of men, just Germans. Sometimes on a TV documentary I see an old newsreel of a Nazi rally, or hear the bastards singing the Horst Wessel Lied and I almost pass out. They put men, women and children in chambers and gassed them. Millions of them. Some bastard supplied the pipes and built the ovens and put up the barbed wire. And everybody for miles around could smell the smoke. It's a smell of burning pork, Heinz. Except that it wasn't pork, it was people. And one of them was my mother.'

'Lisa thinks about it all the time. She told me she didn't know what to say. She asked me what we could say or do.'

'And what did you tell her?'

'I told her that there was nothing we could say, beyond how ashamed or angry we feel. But what we could do is remember. And see that others remembered. She said that at least we could try and help you.'

'Only a frontal lobotomy could do that, my friend.'

Fischer nodded. 'All I really want to say is that we do care, and we do understand. All the family. Not just Lisa and me.'

Malik nodded. 'We'll leave here at one. Is it too late to change the car for a four-door model?'

'We can change it tomorrow. They'll be closed by now.'

'We'll leave it. Let's put our stuff in the car.'

Malik stood in the shadows of the derelict warehouse waiting for Loeb to come out. He could see the lights of a freighter tied up at the dockside and there were lights at the head of a gantry. Far down the river he heard the wistful moan of a ship's siren. And it was beginning to rain.

In the next hour men left the club in twos and threes and then he saw Loeb standing in the doorway looking up at the night sky, turning up his jacket collar against the rain.

Malik let him go under the archway onto the cobbles and then he was alongside him.

'Loeb.'

Loeb turned to glance at him and walked on. Malik realised that the German thought he was a homosexual looking for a partner. Malik's hand went to the back of Loeb's collar, pulling it back until the buttons were at his throat. Loeb jerked his head as he heard the click, and opened his mouth to shout as he saw the long thin blade of the knife. And then Malik's hard fingers were over his mouth.

'Don't make a noise, little boy. Just keep walking. That's it. Keep going. Get in the car. Now.'

Malik bundled the German roughly into the back of the car, clambering over the angled front seat to follow him. As Malik leaned over to swing the door to, Fischer started the car and headed back towards the town centre. Ten minutes later they were on Federal Highway 435, Loeb crouching in the corner of the back seat, still clutching his guitar case, the glint of Malik's knife blade reflected in the rear mirror. As they got to the bridge over the E4 Loeb tried to stand up and Fischer heard him scream, 'For Christ's sake you've cut my hand.'

He heard Malik say, 'I'll cut your face next time, sweetheart.'

As they made their bumpy way up the drive to the house Fischer glanced at his watch. It was less than an hour since Malik had shoved Loeb into the car.

They took Loeb round the house to the back door. He put up no resistance, and Fischer prayed silently that he would stay that way.

Malik had led the way upstairs to the main bedroom and stood aside as Fischer followed Loeb inside. Malik pointed to a worn armchair.

72

'Sit down, Loeb.'

Loeb turned to put his guitar case on the foot of the bed and for an instant the blade of the knife flickered before Malik realised what Loeb was doing. As Loeb sat down Fischer saw how pale and gaunt the man's face was. His pale blue eyes were red-rimmed, his fair hair spiky and unwashed. His mouth was small and girlish, and his unshaven chin was covered with a fuzz of downy hair.

Malik sat on the edge of the bed looking at Loeb, and Loeb turned his head cautiously to look back at him.

'I don't have money, if that's what you want.' Loeb's voice quavered as he spoke.

'Tell me about the group.' Malik's voice was soft.

Loeb shrugged. 'It's just a group. Drums, vibes and two guitars.'

'I mean the other group. The political group who pay you. You told your girlfriend that you were more important than she thought. Tell me all about it.'

'I was just kidding her.'

'Tell me, Loeb.'

'There's nothing to . . .'

The sound of Malik's fist on Loeb's face echoed round the room. Dull, fleshy and sickening. The German had both hands up to his face and bright red blood trickled through his fingers to run down his arm. He was shaking his head in pain, gasping for breath, rocking backwards and forwards in agony. He screamed as Malik reached out, grabbed his hair and wrenched back his head.

'Tell me about the group.'

'Don't hurt me any more. Please . . . don't . . . I'll tell you.'

'Who's your contact?'

'The Herr Baron, and the boss.'

'Where do you meet?'

'At the Herr Baron's estate.'

'Where's that?'

'At Lauenburg.'

Fischer was frowning as he listened. 'Are you talking about von Busch?'

Loeb nodded, and Malik saw the doubt on Fischer's face.

'Is von Busch the man you called the boss?'

'No. That's Herr Meyer. Amos Meyer.'

Malik looked at Fischer to see if he recognised the name but Fischer shook his head.

'Where does Meyer live?'

'I don't know.'

'Where do you meet him?'

'At the Herr Baron's estate or at a hotel. Wherever they tell me to go.'

'How many are in the group?'

'I don't know. I've only met the two of them.'

'Why do you call it a group, then?'

'That's what they said. A group of patriots.'

'How much do they pay you?'

'Two hundred DM a month and then for the work.'

'Tell me about the work,' Malik said softly.

'It's just electronics, printed-circuit boards, decoders, pulse modulators . . .' Loeb shrugged. 'All kinds of stuff. Whatever they want.'

'What do you do for them?'

'Test the sample and then make repeats.'

'Where do you do this?'

'I've got a lab and workshop at the Herr Baron's place.'

'What are these things used for?'

'God knows. All sorts of things.'

'Like what?'

'Computers, measuring systems. It's impossible to tell from the bits and pieces.'

'What did they tell you they were for?'

'They didn't tell me anything.'

'And what do you pay you for the work?'

'Depends on how long. They pay well. Maybe four times the going rate. I've made ten thousand DM in three weeks sometimes.'

'Why is it all so secret?'

'I don't know, but they told me if I breathed a word to anyone about it they'd finish me off.'

'Why did you go on playing at the club?'

'I like it. And they told me to.'

74

'How long has this been going on?'

'About six or seven months.'

'How did he first contact you?'

'There was a note for me one night at the club. It said ring the telephone number it gave. And it gave a time and a day when I should do it. When I rang it was a woman's voice and she just gave me another number to phone, and said I would be paid for meeting someone.

'I rang the other number and I was told to go to the Botanical Gardens, by the cafeteria, and someone would contact me. That was for the next day. It was von Busch and he asked me about where I was born and my parents and my background. And then he said there were groups of people in Germany who were concerned that German politicians were leading the country astray. He wanted my help and he'd pay me two hundred DM every month.'

'Did he say what you had to do?'

'No. But he asked me a lot of questions about when I did my army service.'

'What were you in the army?'

'I was on electronics, radar equipment and computers and control systems.'

'But he never said that was how you would help him?'

'No. Whenever I asked what I had to do he just said that it wasn't dangerous and I would be told when it was necessary.'

'Where did he say the other groups were?'

'He said they were all over Germany.'

'How many?'

'He didn't say.'

'Did he mention any places or names?'

'Cologne was one and he mentioned somewhere in the Harz area. I think it was Goslar. He said the leader in Cologne was a business man named Reichardt, or maybe the name was Rechmann, and the man in Goslar was a retired judge. And I think he said the boss of the Hanover group was a retired general named Lomke, or maybe that was the judge's name. I can't remember. It didn't interest me.'

'Any other names?'

'I think there was a Weiss, but I don't really remember.'

'Why did he give you their names?'

'I think it was to impress me. I guess I looked doubtful and he mentioned them to convince me that it was serious.'

'What did you think about it all?'

'I didn't really believe it. You get to meet a lot of odd people in my sort of life. Important men, but real kinky in all sorts of ways.'

'Have you told anybody else about any of this?'

'God, no. He said I would be watched all the time and if I talked I'd get it.' And Loeb pulled a bloody finger across his throat. 'And they meant it, all right.'

Malik looked at Fischer and then reached for the canvas holdall and took out several lengths of rope. Loeb flinched as Malik stood over him, tying him to the chair and his ankles to the chair legs. When he stood up Malik looked at the German and said, 'Don't try any games or you'll be in trouble again.'

Malik nodded to Fischer who followed him out of the room. Malik went down the stairs, along the hall and into the kitchen, switching on the light. Inside the room he turned to look at Fischer.

'What do you think? Does he know any more?'

'I doubt it. But he's obviously met or seen Meyer. You could ask him about that.'

'Good point. Anything else?'

'I don't think so. He's obviously not part of the real group.'

'Is the guy in Cologne he mentioned the piano maker?'

'It's possible. It could be any businessman. It's not an uncommon name. And it depends on what you call a businessman.'

'What's the earliest flight we can get to Cologne?'

'We won't make the first flight. I guess we could make the nine-thirty one. What are you going to do with Loeb?'

'Leave him here. Don't worry about that. I'll deal with him.'

'But he'll talk.'

'He won't,' Malik said brusquely. 'Get the car ready. When we get to Hamburg, check it in and pay, and we'll take a taxi to the airport. Do you need any cash?'

'No. I've got plenty. What about the food you brought?'

'I'll bring that out when I've finished upstairs.'

Fischer nodded and walked out of the kitchen. Malik switched off the light and walked back up the stairs to the bedroom. Loeb was sitting just as they had left him but with his head back and his eyes closed.

Malik stood in front of him. 'Loeb.'

The German opened his eyes, shivering as he looked at Malik.

'Tell me about Meyer. What does he look like? What is he?'

'He's some kind of businessman. He's getting on. In his sixties. Biggish, dark hair, he's got a deep tan. Could be an Arab, or even a Jew. He was the one who told me what to do. He understood electronics, von Busch didn't.'

'What makes you think he could be a Jew?'

Loeb shrugged. 'He looks like one, and sometimes he used Yiddish slang words.'

Malik hesitated and then said, 'Were any of the groups responsible for the anti-Semitic things that have been going on recently? The synagogue daubings, and the slogans?'

'I don't know. I shouldn't think so.'

'Why not?'

'Well, a Jew wouldn't be doing that, and von Busch wouldn't get mixed up with that sort of thing. He's an aristocrat.'

Malik walked over to the window and stood there silently for several minutes. Then he put his thumb over the back of the blade of the knife to soften the sound as he pressed the button and the long thin blade flicked up.

The plane back to Cologne was full of business people and Fischer felt disturbed that he was almost glad that he and Malik hadn't been able to sit together. He hadn't asked Malik what had happened to Loeb but he was certain that he was dead. As he sat in the car he had watched Malik shove the keys through the letterbox after closing the door. There was no reason why anyone should visit the house for days or weeks. The rent had been paid for two months and he

77

realised now why Malik had insisted on two months instead of one.

Fischer was well aware that killings and brutality were weapons in the armoury of all intelligence services but he had never met a man who actually did such things. It seemed strange, uncomfortable, almost eerie, to realise that a man you knew well, a man who liked music, had eaten with you and joked with you, could kill, not in passion but coldly and efficiently because it was expedient. From the moment he decided to pick up Loeb, Malik must have known that it was almost certain that he would kill him. Even the blow with Malik's fist was so professional. Malik knew exactly how to hurt people. Not in anger. Coldly and precisely Malik's fist had smashed the man's nose. No build-up of persuasion to answer the questions. A few uncooperative replies and then that crunch of bone and gristle. Even when he started the questions again there was no anger in his voice. It was almost as if the blow hadn't happened. He had heard no scream, no cry, as he waited in the car and Malik had closed the door behind him, walking to the car carrying the holdall as casually as a housewife going shopping. He hadn't looked back at the house and he had sat with his eyes closed as they drove back into Hamburg. For a few fleeting moments he wondered if there was any element of revenge in killing a German in Malik's mind. He tried not to dwell on it. It didn't bear thinking about.

He could see the back of Malik's head as he sat in an aisle seat a few rows forward. The thick, curly black hair, the tanned skin on the cheek bone and the slightly misshapen ear. He wondered what it was that so attracted his sister to this man. Despite the closed-in face and the cautious eyes, there was an awareness in Malik's face. He listened, and seemed to take in everything that was said to him. He seldom indicated agreement or disagreement but you knew that what you said was weighed and considered. There was a safeness about Malik that would appeal to women. An obvious strength and self-assuredness that had nothing to do with "machismo". But

78

for all the understanding, the man inside Malik never came out. Whatever it was it stayed inside, looking out at people and the world through those soft brown eyes. Was it likely that that carapace of solitariness would crack or melt for a twenty-three-year-old girl? A German? He had grave doubts that it would.

There was no doubt that Malik had freed the log-jam in the operation. They now had definite leads to follow instead of casting around aimlessly in all directions. And when he thought it through he knew that if Loeb had been freed he would certainly have alerted von Busch. Maybe there really had been no choice. If they were to find out anything, somebody in one of the groups would have had to talk, and it was highly unlikely that they would have talked without being threatened. And after they had talked you couldn't put them back in circulation. His own instinct would have been to suborn the talker with money or whatever and turn him back to inform on the group. But that had sometimes proved risky. When it had been done in other operations four out of five had reneged. Maybe it was he who was the hypocrite and Malik merely rational.

Rain was beating against the windows as they banked over Wahn, the raindrops creeping like glass beads across the plexiglass from the wind against the fuselage. The plane was bumping and lurching as it circled the airport and the warning lights were on. Malik turned in his seat to look at Fischer, giving him a brief smile before looking away.

Malik sat on his bed looking at the envelopes of the mail that the consulate had delivered for him. There was nothing that looked interesting, at least half of them were obviously bills and he threw them all carelessly onto the bedside table.

He stretched and stood up, walking over to the window to look down at the small gardens. The rain had stopped and the old lady with the two little girls was there again. She was there most days, sitting on the wooden bench as the children played on the grass. She was always doing something, never just sitting there; today she was knitting, and from time to

79

time she called the taller of the two girls over to measure her work against the plump little body. Both little girls had straw-blonde hair, plaited and tied with ribbon, and despite the fact that it was the start of summer they wore typical German boots rather than shoes. They were both very pretty, but what moved Malik most were their slender necks that looked like the stalks of flowers. Malik had always felt great sympathy for small children.

The phone ringing interrupted his thoughts. It was Lisa wanting to know how he was and inviting him to dinner that night. Ruth and Heinz would be there, she said.

Chapter 9

THE LAWNS had been cut and the smell of mown grass hung in the air as they sat on the bench under the weeping willow, her head resting on his shoulder.

'How much longer will you be staying in Germany, Jake?'

'At least a month, probably longer.'

'You said something nice today when I phoned you.'

'What was that?'

'You said "We got home about two o'clock."'

He turned to look at her. 'We did. What's nice about that?'

She smiled up at him. 'You said "home" not Cologne.'

Malik looked away from her, across towards the house. She was right. He *had* said "home". And that was what it had felt like.

'Tell me about your house in London, Jake.'

'It's nothing special. Victorian. Solidly built. A distant view across Hampstead Heath. That's about it.'

'Are you fond of it?'

'I never think about it. I guess that means I'm not all that fond of it.'

'Heinz seemed very . . . I don't know what . . . edgy when he came home. A bit short-tempered with everybody.'

'He seemed all right at dinner.'

'Ruth always puts him in a good mood. Do you ever go to church . . . to synagogue?'

'No.'

'Don't Jews *have* to go?'

Malik turned to look at her, smiling, 'No more than Catholics or Protestants have to. I was born a Jew and nothing's going to alter that. But it doesn't mean that I do anything about it.'

'Aren't you proud of being a Jew? I would be if I was a Jew.'

81

Malik shook his head. 'I'm not proud of being a Jew. Nor of being born a Pole and naturalised as British. No more than I would be proud of being French or Italian or American. Whatever nationality you are it's an accident. Where your mother was when you were born, who she was married to and where some politicians drew lines on a map. There are people I admire who happen to be Jews. But there are Frenchmen and Italians I admire too. The individuals, not their nationality.'

'But you must feel proud of the Jews in the camps.'

'Why, for God's sake? They didn't go there voluntarily. They didn't go into the gas chambers singing hymns or chanting prayers. They thought they were going to be deloused. They were victims, not heroes. Being proud of race or nationality is what Hitler wanted. The master race.'

'But the whole world except the Arabs admire the Israelis.'

'Don't kid yourself, Lisa. The whole world just shouts for winners. Wait until the Israelis lose some war and see what the world says then. The people who praise the Israelis see them like their favourite football or baseball team. The boys who bring home the trophies and give the Arabs a bloody nose. Some day the Arabs won't just use the price of their oil as a weapon – they'll stop all supplies and the Israelis won't be the heroes then. Arabs are perfectly capable of cutting off their noses to spite their faces.' Malik turned to look at the girl. 'Are you proud of being a German?'

'How could I be, Jake, after what they did to you and your people?'

'You have to remember that there are Jews who are proud of being Jews because of what happened to us in the camps. They are stupid, too. What did we do? We died or we survived. Those who died didn't all die bravely. Some died without knowing what was happening and some screamed their way to heaven. I wasn't brave. I was scared all the time, and I didn't even know what was going on.'

'But you hate Germans.'

'Yes. I do. It's not logical but it's a fact. I can't help it. Germans scare me. I think they could do it again if they got the chance.'

'I pray for you, Jake.'

Malik smiled. 'Tell me.'

'I pray that some day you can forget. God must think I'm crazy. I pray that you can forget, but not forget your mother and your father. I pray that good things will happen to you.'

Malik put his arm round her shoulders and pulled her gently to him. 'You're a good thing that has happened to me.'

'I wish that was true.'

'It is, sweetie. You may not know it, but it's true all right.'

She sighed, and as she looked up at his face he kissed her.

'These are the newspaper cuttings. That's him presenting a cup to the headmistress. And this one is the panel judging a schools music competition. He's the one in the middle.'

'How can I get a look at him?'

'We could invite him home and you could meet him there.'

Malik shook his head. 'No. We won't do that.'

'Why not?'

'I don't want your family dragged into all this. It would be abusing their kindness. And it's not necessary. I can get to look at him some other way.'

'Why do you want to look at him?'

'It can tell you a lot, actually seeing a man's face and how he talks and looks. Have you got any background notes on him?'

'Yes. There's not much, though.'

'Let's have a look at it.'

Fischer pulled a file out of his brief case and passed a single sheet to Malik.

Franz Rechmann had been born on November 11th, 1918. And that was almost the only item of interest in the details of his life. His father had been the founder of the piano-making business. Well off, but not wealthy, he had never held any official post. He hadn't joined the Nazi Party until 1938 which meant he had held out as long as possible. During the war the factory had been turned over to making artificial limbs. The father had been killed in an RAF raid in January 1945.

83

There was no mention of what Rechmann himself had done during the war. He had two daughters. One was married to a Frenchman and lived in Paris. The other still lived at home. Malik shoved the sheet to one side.

'Nothing much there, Heinz. Has he got any enemies?'

'Not that I know of. He's quite a nice guy.'

'How about you run me out to look at the works.'

'OK. Let's go now.'

They drove up the main river road and turned off to cross the Mülheimer bridge. The plant was far bigger and more modern than Malik had expected. It was on the edge of an industrial estate, and the buildings were well-designed and efficient looking. From where they sat on the service road he could see a brightly painted crane loading huge wooden crates into a container lorry. There were thirty or forty well-made crates waiting to be loaded.

'He must be making a lot of bread, Heinz. Is he very rich?'

'A millionaire.'

'In what? D-marks?'

'Anything you care to name. Dollars, yen, sterling, D-marks. Don't forget that it's not only the pianos with his own name that he makes. There's dozens of well-known names in pianos all round the world that are in fact made here. He's considering making electronic organs in a deal with one of the Japanese manufacturers. Another two hundred jobs.'

'Where does he live?'

'He's got a big estate on the edge of the Königsforst.'

'Let's have a look at it.'

It took them half an hour to get to the edge of the estate and another fifteen minutes to find a vantage point so that they could see the house.

But it wasn't a house. It was a mansion, a *château*, a *schloss*. It was too far away to see any detail without binoculars, but visible enough to see that it was both imposing and vaguely menacing.

'Can we go round the whole perimeter of the estate?'

'Yes. But it's over five hundred acres and this is the only place you can see the house from.'

'Let's just take in the main entrance and then we'll get some large-scale maps.'

The main entrance looked normal enough. Two big wrought-iron gates and a pretty lodge-house with a small herbaceous border along the drive. The gates stood open and there were no obvious guards or security precautions. As they drove slowly past nobody came out of the lodge.

The concert ended early and the family had come back home for drinks and a sandwich. Heinz's father and mother were with a neighbour in the music room and Heinz and Malik were playing Scrabble with Lisa and Ruth in the sitting room. Heidi had gone up to bed with the portable TV to watch a play.

Ruth was checking a spelling in the *Langenscheidt*.

'He's right, Lisa.' She looked at Malik. 'Heinz is always right, Jake. It's a waste of time challenging him.'

Malik smiled and Heinz said, 'There ought to be a penalty for wrong challenges.'

Lisa laughed . 'And there ought to be a penalty for anyone who cramps up all the corners with two-letter words. It's your turn, Jake.'

As Malik looked from his tiles to the board Heinz walked over to the TV. The picture was on but the sound was turned down. As he turned the sound up there was a shot of a house on the screen and the newsreader said, '. . . on the outskirts of Hamburg. The body was discovered early today. The Hamburg police authorities are not prepared to comment until further enquiries have been made but a police spokesman said that they were treating it as a case of murder . . . In Paris today there were . . .'

Fischer turned off the set and turned slowly to look at Malik. Malik was arranging his tiles on the board and counting out his score.

'Eleven to us, Lisa.'

'Heinz says you've bought a car. What is it?'

'A five-year-old BMW.'

'Did you bring it tonight?'

'Yes. It's by the garage.'

'Can I see it before you go?'

'Sure you can. It's your go.'

They had played for another half hour and then Lisa had gone with Ruth to get her coat.

Fischer said tensely, 'Did you hear the TV news item?'

'Yes. Interesting.'

'It's going to mean trouble.'

'No, it isn't. Forget it.'

And then the girls were back. The four of them went into the music room to say goodnight and then walked in the warm summer night to where the cars were parked. Malik stood with Lisa, his arm round her waist watching the others get into Heinz's car and they waved as they turned and drove away down the drive.

Malik held the door open for her and then slid into the driving seat.

'What do you want to know about the car?'

She smiled, turning her face to look at him. 'Nothing. I just wanted an excuse to be alone with you.' She reached out and took his hand in hers. 'Tell me about your father.'

Malik leaned back and thought before he spoke. Then he said, 'He was tall and thin, perhaps fragile is more the word. When we first came to England he worked as a clerk in a dress factory in the East End. After a couple of years he became the manager because the old man who owned the place fell ill and the only person he trusted was my father.

'A Pole he knew from Warsaw got him a part-time job playing his fiddle in dance-bands for recording sessions in the evenings and the weekends. He saved the deposit for the house and we moved in about 1952 or '53 and we've been there ever since.'

'What was he like – himself, and with you?'

'He was a very gentle man, but scared. Afraid of people, afraid of losing his job, afraid that something might happen to me. He was delighted when I got a university place, and in a way I think he was relieved when I was away. I know he was lonely without me there, but I think he felt that all those smart professors would make sure that I was safe. When I

86

joined the service he was very agitated at first, but he got used to it. And I think about that time we changed roles. I seemed older and more capable of dealing with the world than he was. In a way I became the father and he was the child.'

'Was *he* proud of being a Jew?'

Malik smiled. 'Yes. He kept up the rituals, but because I wouldn't go along with it he treated it like it was some hidden vice. Not to be flaunted. You've got to realise that he never really belonged there. He admired the English but he belonged back in Warsaw. In a way he didn't live there, he just existed. Looking after me. Caring about me. And then when it wasn't necessary any more he was relieved, but he seemed to lose interest in all outside things. He had a pension, and he still played in orchestras and bands, but he was exhausted. He'd had enough of being alive. He never got over my mother's death. He didn't really believe she was dead. He imagined that one of these days she'd appear at the door and the clock would go back and we'd all start all over again where we left off.'

For a long time they sat there without speaking and then he said, 'You'd better go in, sweetie. They'll wonder where you are. Wave to me when I go by.'

He kissed her gently and watched her walk back to the house. She waved as he drove slowly past.

Malik hadn't realised how the time had gone by. It was past twelve o'clock when he parked the car and walked along the cobbled deserted passage to the door.

Heinz Fischer was waiting for him in a bathrobe.

'The Hamburg police have been on the phone. Said they'd been ringing all evening.'

'Was it the Kripo or the Popo man?'

'Aren't you worried, Jake?'

'No. Why should I be?'

'The piece on the TV news.'

'That doesn't worry me.'

'Not even when the local police phone a few hours later?'

'No. What did they say, anyway?'

Fischer shook his head in slow amazement. 'You really are a cool bastard, Jake. I was shit-scared.'

Malik smiled. 'What did they want?'

'It was Lauterbacher, the Popo man. I phoned him this morning and asked what they knew about a man named Amos Meyer. He was phoning to say that they know where he is.'

'Don't tease, Heinz. Where is he?'

'He's in hospital in Hamburg. In a private room. He was hit by a car.'

'Sounds interesting. Was it an accident or deliberate?'

'An accident.'

'How can they be so sure?'

'It was a police car that hit him. They were chasing a hit-and-run driver.'

'How seriously is he hurt?'

'They don't think it's more than superficial scrapes and shock.'

'Can we see him?'

'I didn't ask. There was no need to. He's just a guy in hospital. It's nothing to do with the police who sees him.'

'We'll fly up tomorrow.'

'I've already booked us on the ten o'clock but we'll have to drive up to Düsseldorf. The morning flights from Wahn are all booked.'

'Well done.'

'I've put in an alarm call for seven o'clock, so we'd better get some sleep.'

The other children were watching him. Standing silently. One of the little girls was crying as he threw the last of the dolls into the hole in the ground. The eldest boy had gone, leaving him to do the digging alone.

He hadn't heard the woman as she hurried down the garden path and her voice made him jump.

'What on earth are you doing, Jake?'

The boy looked up at her from the pile of loamy earth.

'It's for the bodies, Mrs Manson,' and he pointed tentatively at the

pile of dolls and soft toy animals heaped in the shallow pit. He saw the
look of incomprehension on the woman's face turn to fear and revulsion.

'How dare you frighten the girls like this? Give me that spade at
once.'

They boy handed over the toy spade with its bright red-painted blade.
'They weren't frightened, Mrs Manson.'

'For heaven's sake look at Debbie, she's crying her eyes out. You
wicked boy. Just you go right back home. Go on.' Her voice was shrill.
'I shall speak to your father when I see him . . . and don't you come
round here again . . . whatever next?'

Jake Malik looked at the woman's face. She was shaking with anger
as he stepped out of the mock grave, and he couldn't understand what
the fuss was all about. But it would be a lonely holiday without the
children to play with. They said they wanted a new game and they had
joined in enthusiastically at first. It was when he'd taken the clothes off
Debbie's doll and tossed it onto the heap with the others that the tears
had started. But they were interested, he could tell that. His father
would be cross. He had told him never to talk about it to anyone. It
would turn them against him, he said.

In Hamburg they booked into a small hotel near the Binnen-
Alster and Fischer phoned Lauterbacher to see if he had
any further information. A lawyer had contacted the police
lawyers regarding compensation and to the police lawyer's
surprise and satisfaction it seemed that Meyer was not
intending to make allegations of careless driving or to claim
damages beyond his medical and hospital expenses plus an
amount to cover day-to-day expenses. Fischer guessed that
Meyer didn't want to draw attention to himself. Von Busch
had been his only visitor apart from an unidentified business
friend from Cologne. Meyer was expected to be discharged
from the hospital in the next two days.

When Fischer told him this, Malik asked him to see if he
could sit in on the discussions between Meyer's lawyer and
the police legal department. Fischer was able to arrange this
for what was hoped to be the final meeting the following day,
and Malik made out a short list of questions that he hoped
the police lawyer could get answered.

Malik decided that they would go to the hospital after they had eaten, just for the opportunity of looking at Meyer. The police driver was in the general ward with a broken arm and they would use seeing him as their excuse for visiting the hospital.

They took a taxi to the hospital and the reception desk gave them directions to get to the police driver's ward. They had already checked and found that Meyer's private room was on the same floor.

Malik stayed chatting with the police driver for ten minutes, checking on the details of the accident. It seemed that it had just started to rain and Meyer had been struggling into a plastic mac as he stepped off the pavement without looking; the front wing of the car had caught his thigh, turning him so that he lost his balance and rolled into the gutter. As was normal, the police driver had been suspended until the legalities were concluded.

Malik left Fischer with the driver and walked down the long corridor to Room 734. He knocked, and without waiting for an answer he walked inside the room.

The man in the bed was balding and dark-skinned with heavy-lidded brown eyes, and he put down the magazine he was reading as he looked at Malik.

'Is there anything you want, Herr Meyer? Reading matter or toilet stuff? I'm just going out to get some things for the police driver.'

'You're a policeman?'

Malik nodded. 'Yes.'

'How's the driver?'

'Waiting for his arm to set. The X-rays indicate that it's healing OK.'

'Thanks for the offer, but I've got everything I need. And I'm expecting friends – they will be bringing me today's papers and a few magazines.'

There was a knock on the door and man put his head in.

'Amos, I didn't know you had a visitor. We'll wait outside.'

'No. Come in. This gentleman is a police officer who offered to get me anything I needed. He's just leaving. I didn't get your name, officer.'

'Malik, Herr Meyer.'

The man at the door nodded. 'Von Busch. Glad to meet you.' He opened the door and another man came in, ignoring Malik and walking over to the bed.

'Amos, it's good to see you. I was worried.'

'I'm fine, Franz. I'll be out in a couple of days they tell me.'

Von Busch moved to one side as Malik bowed slightly to the three of them and headed for the door.

Two things puzzled him. The first was the Israeli passport lying beside the watch and the coins on the bedside table, and the second was the man called Franz. He had seen him somewhere before, but he couldn't think where.

When he went back to the police driver, Fischer had gone. He had left a message that he was going straight back to the hotel and would wait there for Malik.

Fischer had left a note at the hotel reception desk that he was in the hotel's coffee bar, and Malik joined him there.

As he sat down at the table, Malik said, 'Why did you disappear?'

'I had to. I recognised somebody and I was scared he would see me.'

'Who?'

'I saw these two guys walking down the ward and I recognised von Busch. He's well known. I recognised him from newspaper pictures when he used to ride for our Olympic equestrian team. And then the other guy turned to speak to him, and it was Rechmann. Franz Rechmann.'

'The guy with the piano factory we looked at?'

'Yes.'

'Did he see you?'

'No. He was too intent on whatever he was saying to von Busch.'

'The two of them came into Meyer's room while I was there. I thought I'd seen him somewhere before. When could it have been?'

'He was in the Green Room that night when the family

played at the concert. You might have seen him there. And you saw the press pictures too.'

'Of course.'

'What excuse did you give when you went in?'

'I told him I was a cop visiting the driver. Just being helpful.'

'So von Busch and Rechmann will know you're a cop.'

'Sure. But that's fine. No need to pretend I'm anything else. They'll connect me with the accident rather than the groups. It won't matter if I meet him with you.'

'What was Meyer like?'

'Polite enough. He uses an Israeli passport.'

Fischer frowned. 'That doesn't fit in, Jake. You wouldn't have an Israeli connected with anti-Jewish groups.'

'So we think again about what the groups are up to. Apart from daubing swastikas on synagogue doors.'

'It rules out the KGB.'

'Not necessarily.'

'What's that mean?'

'A cover for a cover for whatever the real thing is. The KGB like playing these very convoluted games. Let's not cross anything out until we've got some hard facts. Can you find out when Rechmann will be back?'

'I should think so. I'll phone when we get back.'

The police lawyer's meeting with Meyer's lawyer had been brief and amiable. And all Malik had learned, despite his list of questions, was that Meyer was an Israeli citizen and the wealthy and influential owner of a group of companies based in Israel with its headquarters in Tel Aviv. The companies included insurance, engineering, a cotton mill, a freight company, a small shipping line and minority holdings in a variety of small local enterprises. He was sixty-one, he had no family, and he travelled a lot. The German Embassy in Tel Aviv had confirmed that he was well respected and had influence in all the places that mattered. He was much respected, both as a man and as a businessman.

Chapter 10

'THERE MUST be somebody who hates his guts. You don't get to be a millionaire without making enemies on the way.'

'I'll phone my father and see if he's got any ideas.'

'What about journalists? They always know the skeletons in the cupboards.'

'There's a freelance guy named Otto Prahl. He'd be worth talking to.'

'How old is he? How far back can he go?'

'He's in his early sixties and he's worked for US magazines, South American newspapers, and most of the European press services take bits and pieces from him. He knows what the dirt is if there is any.'

'What's he go for, money or booze?'

'Both, I should think.'

'Have you got anything you can trade him?'

'I can find something, I guess.'

'Where can we meet him without being noticed too much?'

'Let's take a private room at the *Dom* and give him a good dinner.'

'Fine. You can introduce me as British police and that will get him interested.'

Fischer looked up Prahl's telephone number in the directory and rang the number. Prahl accepted the invitation for that evening but couldn't meet them until nine o'clock.

Otto Prahl was nothing like the traditional newsman. He was tall and elegant with a bush of wiry grey hair and a lean ascetic face. He wore a tweed suit that was well cut, and an old-fashioned cravat with an opal pin. He carried an ebony

93

walking-stick with an ivory handle. He was obviously used to meeting people and used to assessing them quickly, and after they had discussed European politics over their meal he sat in the armchair with his glass of neat whisky, looking across at Malik.

'Am I allowed to ask what you're doing in our fair city, Herr Malik, or is that going too far?'

'Are we on or off the record, Herr Prahl?'

'It's up to you, my friend.'

'How about we talk off the record first, and then maybe we can go on the record later.'

'Why not?'

'I'm seconded to the Federal police for a few months to compare notes on various matters of mutual interest.'

Prahl smiled. 'You sound like Helmut Schmidt on his first day as Chancellor.' He waved his hand. 'I mean that as a compliment of course.'

Malik didn't smile. 'One of the things that concerns us is this latest rash of anti-Jewish outrages. Paris, Nice, London, and now it's happening in the Federal Republic. Why?'

Prahl shrugged. 'The wicked Germans at it again, I suppose.'

'So why doesn't it happen in East Germany too?'

'There's no need to daub synagogues over there. You've got an anti-Semitic government to do it for you.'

'So you think it's genuine, anti-Jewish Nazis?'

Prahl shook his head. 'No. I shouldn't think so. Things are never as simple as that. It could be people organising a few louts to do these things to make those governments that find the new Germany an acceptable partner think again. Once a Nazi always a Nazi, or better still, once a German always a German. The Soviet Union would benefit from that. They would like to see us isolated from NATO and the Common Market. We might turn to them. They have prizes to dangle. Even a vague hint of a unified Germany would keep any Federal Chancellor in power for decades. Even discussions about discussions would be a prize.'

'What about the Israelis?'

'I don't understand, my friend.'

'How does it affect Bonn's relationship with the Israelis?'

'For public consumption Tel Aviv will raise hell, and Bonn will make soothing noises. Underneath it will make no difference. We have paid every pfennig of the agreed reparations. We cooperate with them economically, politically and militarily. A few swastikas or even a bomb or two aren't going to shake that for a moment.'

'You don't see any benefit to the Israelis in these attacks?'

'None. Absolutely none. What benefit could there be?'

'Maybe Israeli domestic politics. The opposition blaming the government for what goes on. Or die-hard anti-Germans trying to break the link.'

Prahl shook his head. 'The Israeli politicians, government and opposition, have got more problems than they can handle, sitting all round their borders. Nobody's going to get any mileage out of finding a new one. Of course there are plenty of Jews who still hate the Nazis, maybe all Germans, but they aren't going to rock the boat for Israel. There's nothing in it for anybody.'

'So who does benefit?'

Prahl pursed his lips. 'The Soviet Union, marginally the East Germans. Nobody else.'

'So you think they could be behind these attacks?'

'Quite frankly I haven't given it much thought. It isn't really important.' He shrugged. 'Violence is an everyday symptom of the whole world today. Maybe it always was, and we are merely better informed now.'

Malik nodded. 'It's your turn now, Herr Prahl. What can I answer that would help you?'

Prahl raised his eyebrows and smiled. 'Two questions, if I might be greedy.'

'Carry on.'

'Are you a Jew, Herr Malik?'

'Yes.'

'How many Germans have noticed the tattoo on your wrist?'

'I don't know. Only one other person has commented on it. It's quite faint by now.'

'You must have been very young at that time.'

'I was seven when they tattooed me.'

'You seem a rather special sort of man, Herr Malik. Very analytical, very observant, but underlying all that I sense something else. You're not just a policeman are you?'

'Technically I am.'

Prahl smiled. 'Of course. I'll say no more, except to ask if I may put one more question?'

'Go ahead.'

'Do you think Englishmen could have behaved like the Nazis?'

Malik smiled, looked at Fischer, then away towards the picture hanging over the fireplace. He looked at it for a long time and shifted uneasily in his seat as he turned his head to look at Prahl as he started to talk.

'I know Englishmen who could behave like the Nazis. I can think of at least half a dozen who could murder innocent women and children because somebody ordered them to. But on the whole, no, they wouldn't behave like the Nazis. There wouldn't be enough thugs to go round to do it on a big enough scale.'

'Why not?'

'For an odd sort of reason, Herr Prahl. The English don't really respect the law. They are all half-anarchists but would be shocked if you told them that. They don't respect politicians or governments or bureaucrats, they despise them. Even if they voted for them. I think there's a difference, too, that Germans admire winners and the English have a soft spot for the underdog. And the English hate obeying orders. Even sensible ones.'

Prahl raised his eyebrows. 'What about the innocent women and children who died in their thousands when the RAF wiped out Dresden in one night?'

'I'm not defending that, Otto, but there is a difference. First of all it was the Germans who started that game. It was the *Luftwaffe* that started bombing cities rather than military targets. Coventry, Liverpool, Birmingham, London. And secondly, the concentration camps were nothing to do with the war. They existed long before the war, so did the campaign against the Jews. No other nation on earth has built gas ovens to kill millions of civilians because they were Jews, or anything else. It wasn't done in the heat of war, it was done in cold blood by barbarians.'

Prahl had noticed Malik's use of his first name and reached for his glass when Malik stopped talking. He lifted it towards Malik.

'*Shalom*, Herr Malik.'

'*Shalom*.'

Malik put down his glass and leaned forward. 'I met a man in Hamburg. He comes from Cologne. I'm told he's a millionaire. How do you get to be a millionaire in post-war Germany, Otto?'

'Who is he?'

'He was introduced to me as Rechmann. Franz Rechmann. He's got a factory or something.

Prahl leaned back in his chair. 'Well I guess it helps if you start off with a few hundred thousand from your father, and a business that's a going concern. When the old man died there were no other shareholders. Franz inherited the whole of the stock. He turned out the old plant, put in the latest equipment, took on bright people and spent money on promotion. And now he exports to over thirty countries.'

'He must have some skeleton in his cupboard. All millionaires have.'

Prahl smiled. 'Of course. Our dear Franz is no exception. Mind you, it's a comparatively small skeleton compared with some of them.'

'What is it?'

Prahl looked at Fischer. 'Do we tell him, Heinz? Or do we keep it in the family?'

'I don't know of any skeleton, Otto. I really don't.'

'But Rechmann is a friend of your parents.'

'They might know, but I certainly don't.'

'How do you find him? What do you think of him?'

'He's hard-working, amiable, mildly interested in music. Seems an OK guy to me.'

'Paul Rechmann was a major in the *Wehrmacht* but nobody ever mentions it now.'

'Why not? That's nothing to be ashamed of.'

'It depends on what you were up to of course.'

'Like what?'

'Rechmann was one of von Gehlen's men in *Fremde Heere Ost*. Working against the Russians. In charge of the groups operating against the so-called partisans. I'm told that Rechmann was a bitter Russian-hater. And still is.'

'There are plenty of those around, Otto. Anyone who was in Berlin when the Red army came in has things to remember.'

'Agreed. But if your trade is international it's better to have been a simple soldier than the man in charge of the thugs who killed Russian patriots. It gets in the way. It confuses the issue. It's better to lock it in the closet and keep it locked. With Bonn playing footsie with Moscow it's best to keep the temperature down.'

'Was he a party member?'

'No but there are rumours that the company paid tens of thousands into local party funds. The old man was made a *Wehrwirtschaftsführer* and you didn't get that for spitting in Adolf's eye.' Prahl looked at his watch. 'Gentlemen, it's after midnight and I need my sleep.'

After he had left the two of them sat there finishing the whisky.

'Was it any help, Jake?'

'What do you think?'

Fischer shrugged, his face despondent. 'Another piece in the jigsaw puzzle, but no use to us.'

'It's that kind of operation, Heinz. Just plugging away.'

'What next?'

'See what you can find out about the chap in Goslar. The retired judge.'

Heinz Fischer phoned from Goslar. He had traced the judge. His name was Lemke. Gustav Lemke. He had retired from the *Landesgericht* a year ago. He was a widower with no children.

'What is he, Heinz? Left wing or right wing?'

'Doesn't belong to any party, Jake. And he wasn't a member of the Nazi Party, either.'

'That's not possible, Heinz. He could never have had the education and training to be a lawyer without being a member.'

'He wasn't, Jake,' Heinz said softly. 'He was in a camp for six years.'

'Which camp?'

'Sachsenhausen.'

'Is he a Jew?'

'No.'

'Do you know why he was in the camp?'

'Yes. I've got a press cutting. He announced in open court that he would not accept the Nuremberg Race Laws in his court. That was in November 1938. He was arrested as he left the court and went first to Buchenwald and ended up in Sachsenhausen. Refused any post-war compensation on the grounds that he was only doing his duty as a German citizen. He was offered an Order of Merit by Bonn in 1951 and refused that too.'

'Sounds incredible. But he doesn't seem to fit in these groups in any way. A man like that wouldn't be seen dead with synagogue daubers.'

'There is a connection, believe it or not. I showed the local police a photograph of Amos Meyer. He has stayed in a local hotel a number of times. I've checked at the hotel and they confirmed this. I also checked with the taxi driver who does most of the hotel work. He remembers taking Meyer to see the judge a couple of times in the last few weeks.'

'Anything else?'

'Yes. Lauterbacher from Hamburg telexed me at HQ to say that Meyer had booked a suite at the Atlantic. He's due to arrive on Friday morning.'

'You'd better come back, Heinz, and we'll fly up to Hamburg tomorrow.'

They took a taxi from the airport to Lauterbacher's office. He gave them the number of Meyer's suite at the hotel and they booked the double room adjoining. But when Malik asked for Meyer's suite to be bugged, Lauterbacher was adamant.

99

If they wanted that they would have to apply for a warrant and give a judge in chambers good reason. Or get the BKA to sponsor their application.

In the hotel Malik checked the lock on their door and opened the soft brown leather wallet that Fischer had seen at the *Waldhaus*. One after the other he tried the odd-shaped bits of steel until one turned the heavy spring bolt of the lock. Then as Fischer watched, Malik slid a small metal sleeve along the steel rod and walked into the corridor. Slowly and carefully he slid the rod into the lock of Meyer's suite and turned it slowly. Fischer heard the soft thud as the bolt turned back into the lock. With his free hand Malik turned the knob and slightly opened the heavy door. A few seconds later the lock was closed again and Fischer followed Malik back into their own room.

'Check what time the plane from London gets in, Heinz. If it's after midday try the Paris one. And check if Meyer's on the passenger list.'

The airport had refused to give the information and Malik had to wait until Fischer contacted Lauterbacher to find out for them. He came back in ten minutes. Amos Meyer was a passenger on the London plane and his point of departure was Tel Aviv. The London plane had landed on time twenty minutes earlier.

At two-fifteen Meyer was let into his suite and Malik waited anxiously, looking at his watch from time to time. If Meyer was a practising Jew he would go to the synagogue soon so that he could be back in his rooms before dusk.

'When he leaves his room, Heinz, you follow him. Check that he actually leaves the hotel and then phone me from the lobby. Then stay down there and wait until he comes back. As soon as you see him, ring *his* room number. Let it ring just twice. Even if I'm still in there I shan't answer. Then ring our number and check with me.'

'What do you expect to find?'

Malik shrugged. 'God knows. It's just a fishing expedition.'

And as he spoke they heard Meyer's door slam to and the rattle of keys. Fischer opened their door carefully, looked out, nodded to Malik and closed the door behind him as he walked into the corridor. Ten minutes later Fischer phoned. Meyer had left the hotel.

There was a large sitting room to Meyer's suite and a double bedroom with two single beds. One tan leather case lay open on one of the beds and a black briefcase with a brass zip was on the bedside table. In an old-fashioned silver frame propped up against the bedside lamp was a faded photograph of a pretty girl holding a cat cradled in her arms as she smiled into the camera.

He checked the wardrobe first. There was one blue suit on a hanger and nothing in any of its pockets. There were four white shirts with Marks and Spencer's labels in the top drawer. Three pairs of cotton pants and several pairs of socks in the second drawer, and the third drawer was empty.

In the case there were several magazines. A paperback n Hebrew and two in English. One was the Penguin edition of Montaigne's *Essays* and the other was Lionel Davidson's *A Long Way to Shiloh*. A plastic bag held an electric razor, a bottle of pre-shave, a pack of tissues and an unused flannel. There were two blue denim shirts and a pair of faded khaki shorts wrapped round a pair of well-worn sandals.

Malik picked up the black briefcase and unzipped it. There was Meyer's Israeli passport. A first-class El Al return ticket: Tel Aviv–London–Hamburg–Berlin–Brussels–Tel Aviv. A small diary with few entries, and all of them in Hebrew, an American Express card, and a Timex stop-watch. In a plastic folder were half a dozen business letters and memos, all concerning expenditure on engineering equipment and buildings. Inside an inner flap was a hand-written letter in German. Malik read it several times.

Dear M,

When one sees what has happened in only the last few months, I feel we must hasten our programme. With Nixon sent packing, Mozambique, Angola, the Russians in Ethiopia, Greece pulling out of NATO; it's a catalogue of turmoil that sadly confirms our worst fears.

What is, perhaps, even more concern to us, is that

instead of one of our two interests supporting the other we may both be involved at the same time. That would weaken our position tactically if not practically.

The four of us should meet quite quickly. We have the funds, the plan, and the facilities, but our time schedule was wrong. If we have to take risks we should do so. Unless we are *all* in place soon we could be too late. We must look to your people. Remember Judges 20 verse 1 and Judges 21 verse 25.

von B.

Then the phone rang twice. Malik put everything back in its place, locked the outer door and went back to their room. The phone was already ringing.

'He's just waiting for the lift, Jake. Von Busch is with him. He's been waiting for him down here in the foyer.'

'OK. Watch him into the lift and come up in about five minutes.'

Back in their room Malik scribbled down the chapters and verses and then opened the drawer. A red-bound Gideon Bible was in the drawer of the bedside table with the local telephone directory.

He leafed through for Judges and read both references carefully, and wrote them out.

Judges Chapter 20, verse 1

Then all the children of Israel went out, and the congregation was gathered together as one man, from Dan even to Beer-sheba, with the land of Gilead, unto the Lord in Mizpeh.

Judges Chapter 21, verse 25

In those days there was no king in Israel: every man did that which was right in his own eyes.

When Fischer came into the room he said, 'Anything interesting?'

'I've got his address in Tel Aviv and the name of his main company. I think that we ought to have a look at his set-up in Israel.'

'I wouldn't be allowed to go.'

'Why not?'

'There's an unofficial agreement between Bonn and the Israelis. Political police and intelligence people only go there at the Israelis' specific request.' He smiled. 'They've never requested anyone yet. Mossad don't like German secret service people in Israel.'

'But I've met Mossad liaison officers at joint intelligence meetings here in Hamburg. Several times.'

'It's a one-way traffic, Jake. We don't object to *them*, but they do object to us. They cooperate in most ways but they won't have us on the ground. I guess it's understandable.'

'Can't you apply for leave and we could go as tourists?'

Fischer smiled. 'West Germans have to apply for visas at the point of entry. I'd never be given one. They'll have my name on some file or other. If you're German and born before 1928 you won't get a visa whoever you are. Unless you're a Jew, of course.'

Malik stood up and walked over to the window. There were pleasure boats tied up at the marina on the far side of the Alster and dinghies racing a course round a dozen orange buoys. He had known that Heinz Fischer would never be allowed into Israel but he didn't want to make his move too obvious. And if he were truthful there was just the faintest touch of *schadenfreude* from the fact that he would be welcome while Fischer was banned. He could fix Lisa's visa himself.

He turned, smiling. 'Maybe a week's leave would do me good. Lisa might like to come too. It would give me a chance to do a bit of checking on our friend Meyer.'

'See what she says, Jake. She'd probably jump at the chance.'

And Malik was momentarily ashamed at his deception in the face of such an amiable and trusting response from the man he was deceiving. Because he knew now that he was deceiving Fischer. And meant to go on deceiving him until he had cleared the doubt in his own mind. One thing he knew now for certain. They had been piecing together the wrong pieces for the wrong jigsaw. They were way off beam. Not that he knew where they should be, but at least he could go back to square one and start again with an open mind. There were ominous warning bells ringing in his mind but they were very faint and far away.

Chapter 11

As THE taxi drove off Lisa stood looking at the house. Malik had never described it to her but in some strange way it was exactly what she had imagined. Not in any particular detail, but in its aura. It reminded her of the houses in novels by Thomas Mann. Old-fashioned and solid, as if its red bricks had absorbed the warmth and strength of decades of summer sun. Not a warmth of the spirit, but the russet-faced self-assurance that country people have. The stained-glass panels above the front door, the elongated, square-edged bays with their net curtains and stone lintels had a kind of mild aggression that could have come from the Bauhaus; and the worn concave centres to the three stone steps to the front door looked better for not having been levelled.

Malik picked up their bags and they walked together up the short garden path. Tall thistles almost up to their shoulders and bindweed everywhere.

As Malik unlocked the door and she walked inside, the close, hot air was overwhelming, and there was an odour of floor-polish and dust. And as he walked through the house with her, showing her the rooms, she knew exactly what it would have been like to grow up in that house. All it needed was a vignetted sepia portrait of the Kaiser or Pilsudski, and the sound of a child practising scales on a piano and it could have been in Europe rather than Hampstead. It was the kind of house the Maliks would have had in Warsaw once Abraham Malik had established himself.

They went out that evening to eat at a small local restaurant and when they got back to the house she made them coffee, and as they sat drinking it she said, 'What kind of people do you like, Jake?'

He leaned forward and put his empty cup on the table before he spoke.

'I think I ought to do what the Mafia do and plead the Fifth Amendment.'

'Why?'

'Present company and your family excepted I don't think I like people at all.'

'No heroes?'

'No, none.'

'Nobody you've ever loved?'

'Just my father, but even that was more affection than love.'

'But you read poetry and like music.'

Malik shrugged and smiled. 'I like flowers, too, and sunsets. But none of those things are people.'

'But you're very perceptive about people.'

'That doesn't make me like them.' He sighed and shrugged. 'I don't belong, Lisa. There's me and there's the rest of the world. I just want to survive.

'And you're never lonely?'

'No. Nobody can hurt me that way.'

'What way?'

'By leaving me, turning me down.' Malik looked at her half-smiling. 'Tell me what you don't like about me.'

She frowned. 'I don't understand.'

'Tell me something bad about me. Something that irritates you. Or embarrasses you.'

'There isn't anything, Jake.'

'Nothing at all?'

'No. Nothing at all.'

'So what do you like about me?'

'Everything.'

He laughed. 'That's impossible.'

'What don't you like about *me*?'

He turned away from her, towards the window. For long minutes he sat there in silence and then he turned to look at her face again.

'There's nothing I don't like about you.'

'Is that because you don't think about me much?'

He sighed. 'No. I think about you a lot.'

'Nice thoughts?'

'Always.'

'I love you, Jake,' she said softly.

He opened his mouth to speak, hesitated and then closed it and she said, 'Say it Jake. Whatever it was.'

He turned in his chair to face her. 'It's just that it's terribly complicated. I don't know how to explain it. I don't understand it myself, so I don't know how to say it.'

'Tell me, Jake. Try. Please.'

He sat with his head back in the chair, his eyes closed.

'I would like to say that I love you too, Lisa. But I don't really know what love is. My father loved me, but that's a different kind of love. One or two girls . . . women . . . have liked me but I didn't feel any involvement with them. None at all. I've always taken for granted that my background from when I was a child would always get in the way. I've wondered sometimes if I'm not actually mad, insane. And my thoughts about those days, my nightmares, are always there in the background, like wild animals in a forest waiting to come out and devour me. I never deliberately think about those days, but now and again something will remind me and trigger it off. Small things, ridiculous things. I used to think it would go, but it doesn't. Sometimes I think it gets worse. Because you're a very kind and gentle person, you sympathise with me, but I'd always be afraid that in the end the sympathy would be worn out. You'd get tired of it, bored with it. You'd wonder why loving you and being loved by you didn't compensate for all that. It would always seem like I had a separate part of my life away from you. And because of my job it would seem even worse.'

He opened his eyes and looked at her face. He saw the tears on her cheeks.

'And now I've made you unhappy.'

'You haven't, Jake. The tears are for you. I understand very well what you mean, but there's no way I can prove to you that I would rather be with you, exactly as you are, than anyone else. Even my family.'

Malik looked at the girl's face for a long time and she saw him take a deep breath before he spoke.

'My momma was twenty-six or seven when we went in the camp. She was very pretty. Every night she was taken to the guard hut, and I went with her. I guess I was about seven then, and she was afraid that something would happen to me if she left me in the big hut. And every night I sat there and watched. There were always three SS guards on standby, and the three of them would have her. Have sex with her. And when they'd finished we sat at the guard room table and we had a plate of soup and some bread. I didn't know then what they were doing to her but I know now. So I hate Germans. I haven't ever eaten soup since, wooden huts frighten me, and I disappointed my father because I refused to believe in the One True God who could let those things happen. And I could never tell him why.'

'What happened to your Momma?'

'They got tired of her and put her in the gas chambers.'

'I could help you, Jake,' she said softly.

'How?'

'I'll remember those things with you. It won't be just you on your own.'

'You won't tell your family or Heinz about my momma, will you?'

She shook her head. 'No.' She paused. 'You've got a paperback book you read. Palgrave's *Golden Treasury*. Have you read all of it?'

'A lot. But not all.'

'You left it in the house one night and I read it in bed and there was a verse in a poem that made me think of you and me.'

'What was it? Shakespeare?'

'No. It was by a poet I've never heard of. The Earl of Stirling and it was called "To Aurora".'

'Can you remember it?'

She nodded, and said softly,

'Then all my thoughts should in thy visage shine,
And if that aught mischanced thou shouldst not moan
Nor bear the burden of thy griefs alone;
No, I would have my share in what were thine:
And whilst we thus should make our sorrows one,
This happy harmony would make them none.'

He reached over and pulled her to him, his mouth on hers, passionately at first, and then gently. Then putting his cheek against hers he said, 'I love you, Lisa. I hope it's going to be all right.'

She reached out and touched his hand. 'It'll be all right, Jake. I do understand. Nobody could survive all that without being affected.'

She saw from the look on Malik's face that it was time to change the subject. But he interrupted her thought.

'I'll be going in to town tomorrow. Provided they can fix it we could fly to Israel on Monday.'

'Does it excite you, the thought of being in Israel?'

'No. And don't you run away with the idea that the streets of Tel Aviv are crowded with Jews playing fiddles and cellos.'

She laughed. 'You try to sound like a hardened cynic, my love, but you're not. You've just got a better disguise than most people.'

Malik stood up, taking her hand as she stood up too.

'I'll put your bags in the back bedroom. It's quieter in there.'

'Was that your bedroom?'

'Yes. I'll do you some hot chocolate to relax you. I'll bring it up.'

When Malik came in with the glass of hot chocolate and a biscuit on an old-fashioned tray it was like being a child again for the girl.

She patted the bed beside her and, smiling, she said, 'Are you going to tell me a story?'

'It was good of your parents to let you come with me.'

'I'm twenty-three, Jake, nearly twenty-four. I'm glad they said yes but I should have come anyway, if that was what you wanted.'

'I want it to work, Lisa, so much.'

Her blue eyes looked at him. 'D'you want to sleep with me, Jake?'

'Of course I do. But I'm not going to. Not until we're married.'

'Why not? Is it because of what those animals did to your mother?'

109

'Partly. There's several reasons. And that's the least part of what you mean to me.'

'What *do* I mean to you, Jake?' she said quietly.

He looked away from her face towards the window, and for several moments he sat in silence, her hand in his, before he turned his head to look at her again.

'You mean a great change in my life. I feel you have quietly opened a door for me that had always been closed. You've put a third dimension in my life because you're gentle and understanding. And beautiful. You understand me and I think I understand you. I just love you, Lisa.'

He bent to kiss her gently and her arms went round him. It was a long time before he stood up and left her.

Some sound woke her early, and when she looked at her watch she saw that it was barely five o'clock. She slipped out of bed and walked over to the window.

The ground fell away sharply so that all she could see were the tops of the trees and, in the far distance, what she guessed must be Hampstead Heath. She turned and looked around the room. Jake Malik's room.

It was a strange room, lacking any indication of its owner. The walls were papered with a heavy flock paper of plum-red, unidentifiable flowers, the furniture solid but old-fashioned. There were no pictures or photographs, no decorative objects. It was almost monastic. More impersonal than the bedroom of a cheap hotel. The rest of the house was much the same. It was the home of two men who didn't want to remember, anything. It wasn't just Abraham Malik who existed rather than lived. Jacob Malik was just the same. For a brief moment before she got back into bed she closed her eyes and prayed that she really could make a difference.

Chapter 12

JENKINS SEEMED barely to conceal his impatience and indifference as Malik told him briefly of what he and Fischer had done. He gave no details or names, and refrained from any speculation.

'Is your German cooperating, Jake?'

'Yes.'

'No other problems?'

'Just the lack of anything positive.'

Jenkins stood up. 'It's probably some low-key group of cranks. Just keep plugging away.'

'You got my application for leave, sir?'

'Your what . . . ah yes . . . application for leave. Of course. How long would you like?'

'Up to three weeks if I may, but I may come back earlier.'

'Of course. You need a rest, my boy. Where are you going?'

'To Israel.'

'Ah, yes. I see. Good idea.'

Jenkins could barely conceal his embarrassment. He was in no way anti-Jewish. He just wished that they'd keep it to themselves. He felt exactly the same way about homosexuals. He wouldn't ever knowingly employ them, because it made them doubly vulnerable, but he accepted their existence. Providing they didn't flaunt it. All this 'coming out' business was just self-indulgent exhibitionism. There were excellent Jews, but there was no need to emphasise one's religion. To Jenkins it was just bad taste. A lack of feeling for others.

He walked with Malik to the door. 'Gordon can help you with flights and that sort of thing. Don't hesitate to use him.'

The security check had been time-consuming and thorough. Lisa, with her BRD passport, had taken even longer, but

111

when they were together again there was still half an hour before their flight call was due.

They bought cigarettes and soap at the duty-free shop, half a dozen magazines and a couple of paperbacks each.

'I don't think I'll be able to read, Jake, I'm so excited. I feel I ought to have a bucket and spade.'

Malik smiled. 'Let's have a coffee while we're waiting.'

As they sat at the table sipping the scalding coffee she said, 'Mama told me to give you her love when I phoned. She's trying not to be worried.'

'About what?'

'Me, a German, going to Israel.'

He laughed. 'At least ten per cent of the population were Germans before they became Israelis.' And it was the first time she had seen him laugh.

'What are you looking forward to most?'

'Some sunshine. And you?'

'Oh, meeting people who care about music and literature, and seeing all the things they've done. Making a country out of a desert.'

Malik turned his head, listening. 'That's us, sweetie. They're calling us early. You take the boarding cards and tickets and I'll take our hand-luggage.'

They were lucky and had been able to arrange double seats together on the starboard aisle. Lisa had the window seat and Malik passed her a couple of the magazines. But she ignored them, watching intently as the ground staff rolled the passenger steps away and the hoses were stowed away on the drinking-water truck. And then they were taxiing slowly along the feeder, the wide wings undulating as the plane rolled forward. Ten minutes later the undercarriages thudded into place and the billowing cumulus clouds were awash with the vivid colours of the midday sun.

Malik had been amused when the girl insisted on the kosher meals, but even before they were crossing the Swiss Alps he was asleep. And as he slept she looked at his face. There was nothing Jewish about it except the tanned skin, and that could have been Spanish or Italian. He didn't gesticulate as Jews were supposed to do and he never used those Yiddish or

112

Hebrew words that even Germans sometimes used. But she suspected that inside was a flood of Jewish emotion waiting to be released. Even in the time she had known him he had changed a lot. He actually smiled sometimes, and he was prepared to talk to her about his father and himself. Something that would have been impossible when she first knew him. And the music he liked was all hearts-on-the-sleeve music. Violins and cellos, from Bach Partitas to Viennese schmaltz.

Heinz had warned her not to expect too much and had hinted gently that there was a danger that she could be indulging in wishful thinking. Heinz was often right about people, but she had wondered sometimes if there wasn't just a faint touch of jealousy in his warnings about Jake. Heinz was so obviously the junior in whatever it was they were doing together. And Jake Malik was like rock to her brother's crystal glass.

Her father liked Malik, although he was not the kind of man he would normally take to. Malik was too masculine in many ways. Too tough, too sure of himself in physical ways, to appeal to Helmut Fischer. She wasn't sure of her mother's opinion. She seldom passed comments on other people, even to her family. She had seen her mother smiling affectionately sometimes as she looked at Malik when he was unaware of her glance. When she asked her mother what she thought of him she had been noncommittal. 'Everybody has problems. Your Jake has more than most. But you seem to be doing him good.' Lisa had glowed at 'your Jake' and dismissed the rest as mere motherly caution. Of course he had problems, but she would help him get rid of them.

She slept soundly until Malik woke her to say that they were landing in fifteen minutes, and even as he spoke the warning lights went on and she felt the jolt as the under-carriages came down.

As they walked from the plane to the terminal she was thrilled to see the sign that said: Ben Gurion International Airport – Welcome to Israel.

The welcome started right at the airport when Malik managed to get them a taxi to themselves. The driver was a New York

113

Jew who had lived in Israel for ten years. They heard the whole family saga. He had owned his own garage and workshop in the Bronx and was making twenty grand a year clear. But always there had been the pull of Israel. There had been family meetings every few weeks. Everybody over eighteen was for going. Everybody under eighteen was for staying. Boyfriends, girlfriends, football teams, drama classes and even New York itself suddenly became beautiful and desirable. Grandmothers, as always, had made the decision. When there was twenty-five grand in the bank on top of fares and moving expenses they would go. And a year after the money was there they had booked their passages for two months later after the youngest boy had been bar-mitzvahed. Never a day's regret. Driving a cab in Tel Aviv produced nothing much in the way of extras but all the children were doing well. All of them earning except the boy in the army.

He dropped them at the Tourist Information Service and as Malik gave him the fare the man saw the tattoo on his wrist. He looked at Malik's face, and waved the money away.

'No way, pal. I'm not taking no bread from you. That number on your arm beats twenty Purple Hearts as far as I'm concerned. Where you going now?'

'We're going to find a hotel at the Tourist Office.'

'Forget it. I'm taking you to the City. It's not too expensive, it's clean, it's got decent food. Near the beach and right in town. Let's go.'

Smiling, they got back into the taxi and minutes later they were at the hotel. The driver insisted that he carried in their bags and launched into an energetic dialogue in Hebrew with the receptionist. He stood waiting until they had their rooms and waved peremptorily to the bell-hop to take their luggage.

He held out his hand. 'Tonight at nine o'clock I'm coming back here for you and you're eating with my family.'

Despite Malik's protestations he brushed aside all excuses. He phoned his wife from the reception desk as if he owned the place.

The Brodskys, mother, father, two grandmothers and two daughters kept them amused for the whole of the meal with

114

the gossip of Tel Aviv. Politicians, the more extreme religious groups, rabbis and business were all fair game, and it was obvious that if there was an Israeli style of humour it had been transplanted from New York. They made a special fuss of Lisa. Praising her good looks, agreeing with everything she said. The last half hour was spent with a street map on the dining-room table while Brodsky laid out a programme of sightseeing that would have taken a year.

When he eventually drove them back to the hotel he told them that he was at their disposal. Anytime, every day. It was an honour to please them, he said.

It was the same everywhere they went. Helpful directions when they lost their way, and mild-looking ladies breaking out into tirades when they were being over-charged by the peddlers in the market at Shuk Hacarmel.

They spent most of their mornings on the beach. Lisa swimming and Malik just watching. In the afternoon they explored the city. Malik was amazed at its size and the traffic. It was easier and quicker to walk than take a taxi. Even the loyal Brodsky admitted that.

On the evening of the third day they were discussing the others they had met. A journalist who had talked to them in the bank when they were changing traveller's cheques and had had a coffee with them afterwards, and the businessman who had insisted on escorting them when they asked the way to the old City Hall. Not only walk there with them but show them and explain the exhibits that were housed there now that it was a museum.

'I've never seen you looking so relaxed, Jake.'

Malik smiled. 'I guess I am relaxed. I don't know what it is.'

Lisa laughed softly. 'You do know. You're at home here. You like it, don't you?'

'Yes I do, but I still don't know why. How about you? Are you disappointed that everybody isn't playing violins in the street?'

'I love it, but it *is* funny about the music.'

'In what way?'

'I always felt that because my favourite performers are all Jews, that every Jew was musical. But they're not. A lot of

115

people we've met aren't the slightest bit interested in music, and they'd never heard of some internationally famous Jewish performers. It was only Menuhin, Ashkenazy and Perlman they knew of. And even then they saw them more as show-biz stars than musicians. It's their success they admire rather than their playing. And I find that sad.'

Malik shrugged. 'It just means that Jews are much the same as everyone else. If the experts say it's good, applaud it. And if it's a Jew who's doing it then you pay good money to see him do his stuff. And you cheer like mad because he's a Jew and the rest of the world are impressed, so he's making being a Jew OK.'

'But Jews aren't ordinary. They really are special.'

'What *don't* you like about Israel?'

'Nothing. But I think I'd prefer Jerusalem to Tel Aviv. Tel Aviv is fine for a visit but it's a bit too American for me. Maybe Joppa would be ideal. Not Tel Aviv proper, but near. What do you like about Israel?'

'Like I said. I don't really know. But for the first time in my life I feel that being a Jew does matter.' Smiling he held up his hand. 'No. I *don't* mean I'm proud of being a Jew. That's racism or nationalism. I'm suddenly aware of all the sad sacrifices that have been made for centuries just so that this small country can exist. A sanctuary for Jews.' He laughed. 'Somebody once said that home is the place where, when you go there, they have to take you in. I guess this is home.'

By the fifth day he had brought himself out of his Israeli mental warm bath and had checked Amos Meyer's number in the directory. There was no company listed under that name and when he phoned the home number a servant told him that Mr Meyer was at his office and gave him the number.

When he rang the number the telephonist had replied, 'Litvak Enterprises Holdings,' and he had hung up.

Only because he spoke Polish had they been able to book a table at Lipski's for the last day of Lisa's stay. He had told her

116

before they came that he would have to stay on for some days on things connected with his work.

They walked along the sea road to Joppa and kept straight on to Yefet Street and Lipski's. As so often in Israel the tattoo had been noticed but not remarked on, except by Mrs Lipski herself, who did the cooking for the five tables, coming over to talk to them as her husband served the *krupnik* soup. They lingered over the *pierogi* and finished with lemon sorbet and real coffee. And when they left Lipski produced from somewhere a red rose for Lisa. They walked back to the hotel through the soft night air.

Malik hadn't used Brodsky to take them to Ben Gurion. He didn't want to explain why he was staying on alone. When her flight was called he walked with her to the door and handed her the small leather box that was not to be opened until she was airborne. The elaborate security checks had meant a long wait in the visitors' lounge, but eventually she was walking across the tarmac with the others. She stopped and turned to look for him and when she saw him she waved and blew him a kiss. He waved back and smiled. His little *shiksa* was more Jewish than he was. He waited until the plane took off and wondered if she was already opening the small box. It was a gold medallion on a fine gold necklace, and on its face was the Hebrew for Joppa, and his note that said, "Yafo is the Hebrew for Jaffa – Yafo means beautiful. I love you. J.M."

Malik rented a car at the airport and drove back into the city to the Embassy on Ha-yarqon. He sat in the information room and noted down all the details given in their commercial review of Israeli companies. Litvak Enterprises Holdings controlled nine companies and had minority shareholdings in half a dozen others. The holding company was registered in Vaduz, and the issued capital of the group companies was seventeen million dollars.

He wrote down the addresses and telephone numbers of all the companies actually in Israel. There were only two that really interested him: one was called Precision Products

with an address at Bat Yam just outside Joppa, the other was
Project Engineering which had no telephone number given,
and just Beersheba as its address. It was a Friday and Malik
was sure that Meyer would keep the Sabbath.

Meyer's home address was on the hill near the park at Gan
Ha'atzmaut on the other side of the road from the big hotels;
Malik parked his car and waited.

Half an hour later he saw the black Mercedes turn into the
drive of Meyer's fine house. And Meyer was at the wheel.
Malik noted its registration number and then went back to
the hotel.

He drove out that evening to Bat Yam. Apart from its
beautiful beach and the giant new hotel there was nothing,
certainly nothing that looked like a small engineering plant.
But a barman told him of an industrial estate at Holon and it
was there that he found it. It was small and surrounded by
other small industrial plants, too small to be what he vaguely
had in mind. But what he had in mind didn't fit most of the
established facts. He would have to check out the place at
Beersheba the following day.

As Malik drove down the coast road to Beersheba he thought
of all those times his father had talked about the city. His
father had never been there but he never tired of talking
about it because it had been the home of Isaac, Jacob and
Abraham. And the long arguments with his father's friends
about its name. The Well of the Seven; some said, because
Abraham took an oath there to set aside the seven ewe lambs.
But the Hebrew word for seven was virtually the same as the
word for oath and the scholars had argued ever since. Malik
parked his car near the empty camel market. And as he stood
there for a moment in the blazing sun he realised for the first
time that Israel was the Middle East. Tel Aviv was Europe
and it gave the wrong impression. This was the Old
Testament. All of them, Arabs and Jews, were Semites. The
acrid stench of the camels, the rotting fruit, the raised voices
of the Bedouin. No wonder people said that the Jews wore
their hearts on their sleeves. Like the Arabs they were easy to

118

rouse. It didn't take much to strip off the European veneer and make them tribesmen again.

As Malik walked around the town he was aware of its strong contrasts. The beautiful new campus of the University of the Negev and a few miles away the desert. That bland-looking grave of the Bedouin; the grim acres of sand where so many Israeli soldiers had died. The heat was almost unbearable in the midday sun and the air was so dry that his throat was parched in minutes. He went to one of the smaller cafés and sipped slowly at a long glass of iced orange juice. He asked the Arab proprietor if he knew where Project Engineering was located. He had never heard of it. Shrugging, he said that Beersheba was a place for university people, desalination experts and the Bedouin. There were a few struggling kibbutzim just off the desert road but engineering workers he had never heard of. But when Malik ordered another drink the man sent his young son to talk to the Bedouin who were loading a ramshackle truck with unsold goods for the journey back to the desert.

The boy came back fifteen minutes later and stood talking volubly to his father who eventually brought him across to Malik at his table. The Bedouin had seen a place in the desert where a track had been established. It was to the east of the road between Tel Malha and Mishlat Ma'ahaz. They were scared to talk about it because they thought it was something to do with *Chail Avir*, the Israeli Air Force.

The Bedouin said it was built out of sand and was protected with barbed wire. They had seen trucks there and sometimes a helicopter. And a bus which took workers home at night and brought them back in the morning. They had not seen men in uniform and that was why they thought it was a secret armed forces installation.

Malik gave the boy a small tip and ordered another drink as he looked at his map. He set off back again the way he had come, driving slowly as he watched for a track leading off the road that was worn enough and wide enough to be the one the Bedouin had described.

He almost missed it. It was just past the third kilometre stone from Tel Malha and as he turned off he could see the

119

tyre marks of heavy vehicles, but a few kilometres from the road the ruts in the sand were too deep for the wheels of his car to take. The steering wheel fought his hands and the car slowly juddered to a halt. It was like driving in deep hard-packed snow, and it took him an hour to turn the car and get back to the road.

As soon as he was back in Tel Aviv he checked in the car and rented an ancient Willys-Knight jeep complete with spare petrol container and sand grids. The hotel made up a basket of food for him and he bought a pair of second-hand Leitz field-glasses in the Shuk.

He was on the road at four o'clock the next morning, and thirty metres north of the track he stopped the jeep and jacked up the rear axle and took off the nearside wheel. As the sun came up there were a few trucks from the fruit farms heading north with their scarce products, and one or two military vehicles.

The bus had taken him by surprise. He had expected it to come from the south, from Beersheba, but it came from the north, a sand-coloured diesel bus carrying a dozen or so passengers. As far as he could see they were all men, and all Israelis.

He bolted on the wheel again and waited another ten minutes to let the bus get well ahead. He would be able to see its dust trail for miles across the desert.

As he drove from the road on to the track, the hard springing in the jeep kept it high off the ground but it was an uncomfortable ride. In places the ruts and tyre marks were packed as hard as rocks, and after fifteen minutes every muscle in his body ached from the pounding and bouncing of the jeep. Everything metallic was too hot to touch and his blue denim shirt was black with sweat.

But way ahead he could see the dust cloud from the bus. The glare from the sand strained his eyes and ten minutes later he realised that he had lost sight of the tell-tale dust clouds. And he discovered too that deserts are not all flat. Not even rolling sensual dunes. No more than a kilometre ahead of him was a range of rocky hills. Red in the morning sun. When he came to the fork in the tracks he took the one

120

that was marked with stones, and minutes later he was in the cool shadow of the sandstone hills.

After two kilometres he stopped and got out to look at the tracks. The sand was looser and the tyre marks were no more than light trucks would make. He realised that he had taken the wrong fork. The stones had been put there by the Bedouin for their truck drivers at night.

He stood there looking up at the hill and guessed that from the top he could probably see for miles. He slung his field glasses round his neck and tucked them inside his shirt, buttoning it to keep them from swinging.

It was easier to climb to the top than he had expected, and as he straightened up at the top of the ridge he crouched down immediately. It was there, in sight, and no more than half a kilometre away. He unbuttoned his shirt and slid out the binoculars, pulling out the matt-black lens hoods.

As far as he could see the desert shimmered in the heat until it met the grey blue mountains in the far distance. Small bushes of camel-thorn were dotted sparsely across the landscape and only the vehicle tracks led his eyes to the buildings.

They were perfectly camouflaged, the flat roofs covered with sand, and the sloping sides were so widely raked that they cast no shadow. As he looked through the glasses he could just make out the shape of vehicles under camouflage nets that were near perfect. There was no sign of people. He lay there in the rocks until the heat of the sun was too great to bear and then moved to the shadow of a cave to recover. At ten-minute intervals he went back to watch the buildings and after half an hour he stumbled back down the rocks to the jeep. The water from the can was hot and acrid, too foul to swallow but enough to ease the burning in his throat and mouth.

He drove the jeep into the shadow of an overhanging rock and slowly ate a couple of sandwiches from the hotel pack. Even in the shadows the heat was almost unbearable. And the silence was total. As he wondered if it might not be a wild goose chase and more sensible to go back to Tel Aviv some instinct or stubborness made him stay, and he stumbled back up to the crest of the ridge and lay down.

121

For three hours the silence was only broken once. By a trio of Israeli Air Force jets streaking northwards across the sky. Just once he thought he heard the faint sound of artillery fire from the distant hills. When dark came it came quickly.

As the sun went down he could see faint shadows from the buildings, and the ruts left by the vehicles looked black from the oblique angle of the setting sun, and here and there the wind was beginning to stir the sand in small spirals. Twenty minutes later he could see nothing. The deep blue of the night-sky glittered with stars, but the moon was still behind the mountains. And now he was shivering with cold. He went back to the jeep for his anorak and the blankets, and settled as best he could on the outcrop of rock.

He was half asleep when he heard the noise of the truck and as he lifted his head he saw that it was at least a mile away, its headlights shafting through the darkness. As it approached the site it turned slowly, and as it pulled up Malik could see the orange light at the head of a mobile crane. A door opened, flooding the sand with a long tapering rectangle of light, and a tractor came out towing a flat-bed carrier. And on the flat-bed were two large wooden crates. Malik lifted the glasses to his eyes and focused on the crates, and the short hairs on the back of his neck rose as he saw the shape and size of the wooden packing cases. He had seen cases like those before. Outside the piano factory in Cologne.

Malik watched as they hooked up the chains, and one after the other the two crates were swung up onto the articulated lorry. Four men covered them with canvas covers before they were chained and roped to the truck. It was barely half an hour before the lorry moved off, turning in a narrow half-circle back to the track from where it had come. The moon was up now and Malik stayed to watch as the light on the crane was doused and the door in the huge building was shut. And in the stillness of the night he could just hear the beat of a generator. Like a submarine, they used the night to clear the air. And very faintly he could hear the sound of metal on metal. A ringing sound like a hammer on a pipe.

He stood up slowly and awkwardly, suddenly aware of the stiffness of his joints. For a few moments he stood there

122

looking through the glasses, but there was nothing to be seen. The desert looked white in the moonlight as if it were frost or snow rather than the yellow sand.

Malik climbed back into the jeep, switched on the sidelights and started the engine. As he came out of the rocky mountain track towards the main truck road northwards he felt the steering behaving oddly and clouds of sand rose up around the jeep, the canvas hood billowing madly, straining at the ropes that held it to the body. When he could no longer see the track for the swirling dust he stopped the jeep and switched off the lights. And only then did he hear the noise of the helicopter. He got out of the cab and looked up to where it swung in slow circles above him. He could see two faces at the lighted windows, both peering down at him, one of them with binoculars. And as he looked, a searchlight in the chopper's belly came on, blinding him momentarily, and as he shaded his eyes to look up again the helicopter lifted and swung, turning slowly on its own axis and heading back towards the camouflaged site. It was one of Aerospatiale's Alouette IIIs. One of the 1964 all-weather models with its Doppler radar clearly visible at the rear of the cabin. It was camouflaged in sand and dark green but he hadn't been able to make out its markings.

As he climbed back in the jeep he guessed that somewhere there had been a look-out, but they hadn't spotted him until he stood up on the rock as the truck left. He had had the shades pulled forward on the binoculars but maybe even they had not prevented a reflection from the moon. It had been a stupid thing to do. But they couldn't possibly have identified him from that height nor have read the numberplate on the jeep.

He switched on the headlights and started the engine. He could go flat out now with the headlights on, and he could probably catch up with the articulated before it got to the main road at Kiryat Gat. He held the wheel loosely as the jeep juddered its way along the stone-littered track. It took nearly twenty minutes to reach the main road, a distance of little more than seven kilometres, but there had been no sign of the articulated. He stopped short of the main road and knelt down to check the tyres. They were as hard as iron because of the build up of air pressure from the heat and the rough going. He unscrewed the caps and pressed the valves to release the excess pressure, and the stench of the hot rubber smell was overwhelming. He walked away from the jeep and took deep breaths of the cold night air.

Just past Kiryat Mal'akhi there was a road-block, red and white poles across the road. An Israeli sergeant walked over to him and asked him for his identity card. He showed his passport and the sergeant looked at every page before handing it back. And then he saw the reason for the road-block. Soldiers were removing the poles and he saw the lights of vehicles. A long line of them moving quite slowly. Tanks and armoured fighting vehicles, two staff cars and then a dozen or more troop carriers. It took twenty minutes for them to pass and he knew then that there was no chance of catching up with the articulated. All he could do was to head straight back for Tel-Aviv.

Malik turned off the road at the junction before Bene Re'em and took the road to Gedeva, and it was beginning to get light as he approached Rehovot. As he went through the town people were already at work. There were workers spraying in the orange groves and men were filling farm lorries at a petrol station. It looked peaceful and pastoral in the early morning light. Chaim Weizmann had worked and died there.

It was twenty-three kilometres to Tel Aviv, and by the time he got into the outskirts the roads were busy with cars and buses, and he pulled up at a stall for a fruit drink. He stood sipping the drink and watching the stream of cars. The crates had been export crates. Too elaborate and too expensive for domestic use and that must mean Haifa. He would hand over the jeep and hire a car. He could be there before midday.

Malik stopped for a break just outside Haifa, stretching his arms and legs as he looked across to Mount Carmel. He took off his shirt and laid it on the bonnet of the car to dry out the

124

black patches of sweat, and five minutes later it was dry. He drove the rest of the way to the city in just his shorts; he wanted to save his dry shirt for when he walked round the docks.

In Ha'atzma'uth Road he was stuck in a long line of lorries queueing for the docks, and it was half an hour before he turned into the dock road itself.

He parked the BMW between the first and second warehouses. There were two big merchant ships tied up alongside. One was discharging and the other was loading. The one discharging was French and the other was Greek. He walked slowly down to where the lorries were parked. There were just over twenty but none of them was the yellow articulated. Slowly and meticulously he checked each of the warehouses. There were sacks of grain, drums of chemicals, forty-gallon drums of petrol, wooden crates, hundreds of tins of paint, stacks of timber, and all the things that you could expect at an international port. But there were no signs of the two crates.

Malik called in at one of the shipping offices and asked how he could trace a consignment of pianos and was told that unless he knew who was consigning them or where they were going there was no way to trace them.

He sat on a bollard on the dock side and lit a cigarette. There was no way the crates could have been loaded on a boat before he arrived. They had told him that the average clearing time was eight hours and that loading could be another day or two. The ship that was loading was only taking on ballast. The only other place he could think of was Joppa and that didn't make sense. Whatever was in those crates wasn't pianos. You don't make pianos in camouflaged buildings in the middle of a desert in Israel. And to unload them and load them onto a ship at Joppa would pull as many spectators as a football match. But Malik was a professional and he walked back to the car and headed back down the coast road to Tel Aviv and Joppa.

On Japhet Street he turned down to the jetty and slowly cruised along. There was no boat there larger than a pleasure boat, no crane and no trucks. He was on his way back up

125

Eilat Street when he noticed the El Al poster in a travel agency window and he cursed softly, turned into a side street and stopped the car. He reached into the glove shelf for the street map.

It took him two hours and a lot of lies to get what he wanted at the airport and he walked slowly back from the Freight Office to the cafeteria. As he sat drinking his grape juice he made notes of the details stencilled on the two crates. Instinct and experience were telling him that it wasn't what it seemed. There was no logic to it. Something they were doing was wrong. In some way he and Fischer were kidding themselves. They were listening to the music and ignoring the words.

There was always a point in any operation when it seemed to hang in the balance. A time when the team got together and looked at what they'd got. And inevitably they plodded on. And equally inevitably, in weeks or months, and sometimes years, something happened. Just one thing that pulled aside the curtain and they knew what had to be done. But there was no team. Just him and Heinz Fischer. And no operations director who could keep out of the detail and look down dispassionately from above and help them to avoid every blind alley in the maze.

He walked back to the security hut and one of the guards unlocked the small door to the car park and let him in. At the main guardhouse they checked him and the car again thoroughly. Taking their time with probes and stethoscopes, leaving nothing unchecked. Even if he had been an Israeli they would have done exactly the same.

As he drove back to Tel Aviv he realised what a burden it must be that these hard-working, lively people should have to live under such conditions. Surely to God the gas chambers had been enough. Did they still have to face the threat of bombs and war and terrorists every day of their lives? They had been given so little and they had made it so much. Their supporters were unreliable and the United Nations who had given them back their land now saw world events through

126

Arab eyes. Dependent on Gulf oil and eager to supply their enemies with modern weapons, Israel's 'allies' were politically inept, and their minds more on catching the Jewish vote than on the facts of Middle East life. Claiming to have been horrified by the Holocaust they didn't mind when the slaughter was just a dozen a day. The same victims, just a different generation. Almost every day innocent women and children were blown to pieces somewhere in the country, and forgotten by the world the next day. Israelis were fair game, they were tough, they could look after themselves and there was no close season. Shooting sitting ducks was bad form. Shooting women and children was OK. Maybe Lisa was right and they should live here and be part of it. He felt at home here. He never needed to think about being a Jew. There was nothing to explain. Not even Auschwitz. There were hundreds of others with numbers tattooed on their arms or shiny pink scars where the tattoos had been surgically removed. You didn't need to talk about it. They already knew. Even those who had not been in camps understood by a kind of osmosis. No longer would he have to try to fit in or be the department's statutory Jew. And Tel Aviv was too urgent and too alive to let those skeleton memories parade through his skull at night.

'British Embassy.'
   'I want to speak to Mr Morris.'
   'Which Mr Morris is that?'
   'John Morris.'
   'Can I ask what it's about?'
   'Just put me through, please.'
   'Just a moment.'
   It was a couple of minutes before the clicks came and he was put through.
   'Johnny. This is Malik. I'd like to see you.'
   'Jake. Fine. How about you come in for lunch tomorrow?'
   'I need to see you right away.'
   'Business or pleasure?'
   'Business.'

127

'We're closed officially and the front's locked up. I'll wait outside for you. Better still, do you know Café Rowal in Rehov Dizengoff?'

'Yes.'

'I'll go over there now and wait for you.'

'OK. See you.'

Morris was sitting at a table already when Malik arrived, four glasses of orange juice arrayed on the table.

'*Shalom*,' Morris said.

'*Shalom*.'

'What's eating you, pal?'

'Technically I'm on holiday, Johnny.'

'Of course. Of course. And technically I'm Embassy librarian, I'll have you know.'

'There are two crates going out from the airport tomorrow afternoon. I need to know where they're going. I think it's Germany. It's a private air-freight company and I need to know where the crates end up, and any stops the plane makes on the way. Authorised and unauthorised stops.'

'What do you mean by unauthorised?'

'Stops that aren't on the normal route and landings on private airstrips. That sort of thing.'

'Have you got details of the consignor and details of the crates?'

Malik pulled out a sheet of paper and passed it to Morris who sat reading it, slowly sipping his orange juice. Then he folded it up and slid it into the pocket of his shirt.

'How Brit is this?'

'What do you mean?'

'Can I use Interpol Air Liaison?'

'What do you have to tell them?'

'Nothing that matters. Any cover story you like. Drugs, old masters, fraud. You name it.'

'If we say terrorism will they want to probe?'

'God. No. It's too common to raise any interest. They're bureaucrats. As long as they aren't heading your way you wave it on. As long as it's not PLO, of course.'

'It's not PLO.'

'What are you doing tonight?'

'I'll just get some sleep. I'm flying out tomorrow provided you can lay on the surveillance.'

'Don't worry about that. When you called I asked over a couple of friends for dinner tonight. I'll go back to the Embassy and fix this thing for you and then I'll pick you up and you can eat with us. No suits. No ties. Just a snack and some chit-chat. OK?'

'OK.'

Johnny Morris left his car at the bottom of the drive and they walked together slowly up the steep incline to the house. Morris turned to look back towards Tel Aviv and the setting sun. He and his wife had rented the house at Ramat Gan rather than take one of the Embassy houses. Ambassadors and senior Embassy staff seldom accepted their SIS man as part of the family. They too often caused diplomatic disturbances – that was the general reason given; but nearer the truth was the fact that His Excellency was not privy to their reports to London and all too often the SIS man's report on local current affairs was at odds with the official version.

The house at Ramat Gan was set on the hillside that gave the suburb its name. It was as isolated as a house in the city could be but still within easy commuting distance of the Embassy by car.

The garden, like most of the gardens on the hill, was flooded with bougainvillea, and there was a sweet heavy smell from a long herbaceous border.

'Do you grow oranges here, Johnny?'

'No. Why?'

'I thought I could smell oranges.'

Morris laughed. 'That's different. And we don't call it a smell in these parts. It's a fragrance. It comes from the Assis processing plant, and we rather like it. Let's go in. The Levys are already here, I can see their car by the garage. You'll like them, they're a nice couple.'

There were lights on in the house already and Adele Morris stood at the door.

'It's lovely to see you, Jake. Come in.'

She kissed his cheek and turned to the couple who were standing, glasses in hand, by the big fireplace.

'Helen and David Levy . . . Jacob Malik.'

They shook hands and said their '*shaloms*' and Johnny Morris led them all to the comfortable armchairs ranged around a low, circular, glass-topped table. There were cold meats and fish, and salad and fruit, and as she handed round the plates Adele Morris looked at Malik.

'Are you here for business or pleasure? Or shouldn't I ask?'

'A bit of both. My girlfriend was with me for the first week but she's gone back now.'

Adele Morris leaned back, smiling. 'A girlfriend. Jake Malik with a girlfriend. I can't believe it. Tell me more.'

'There's nothing to tell. I'm going to ask her to marry me when my present assignment's finished.'

'What's her name? Come on. Don't be a tease.'

'Her name's Lisa Fischer. She's twenty-three and she's a musician. And she's German.'

Adele Morris noticed the faint touch of defiance in Malik's voice.

'You should have called us and brought her up for a meal.' She turned to look at the Levys. 'You've heard of guys who love them and leave them, well this fellow just leaves them.'

David Levy smiled and said quietly, 'We're dark horses, us Jews.'

Adele Morris smiled. 'But Jake isn't . . .' and she turned to look at Malik who said, 'I am, Adele. The only Jew in SIS. They're still looking round for the statutory negro.'

Adele looked at her husband. 'Did you know, Johnny?'

'No. And I don't know who's a Catholic and who isn't.' He stood up to break up the talk. 'I'm famished, kid. What have we got?'

Adele Morris recovered quickly, standing up, smiling at Malik.

'Do you keep to *kashrut*, Jake?'

'I'm happy to, Adele, whatever you've done will do me.'

She nodded and turned to the Levys. 'Help yourselves, you two.'

As they sat eating and the others chatted Malik looked at

David Levy. He was in his late thirties, well-built and quite handsome. But what was probably most attractive was his smile. He was a ready smiler and the big strong white teeth under the black moustache gave him a faintly swashbuckling air that matched his broad shoulders and well-muscled legs and arms. And as he was watching him Levy turned and looked at him.

'Is this your first trip to Israel, Jake?'

'Yes.'

'How do you like it?'

'It's strange in a way.'

'How come?'

'I was born a Jew, but I don't live as a Jew. I'm not proud of being a Jew, or ashamed of it for that matter. I'm just me. Jacob Malik. To me Israel was a place for fanatics and refugees. But there's something odd about this place. I feel more alive here. Almost glad to be a Jew.'

'Do you get hassled much as a Jew in London?'

'Very few people know that I am a Jew. And there's no hassle that I've noticed.'

'So why do you feel different here?'

'I honestly don't know. Maybe in a way it's that things that used to put me down don't have any effect on me here. Other people have had what I had. Lots of them. It helps somehow.'

Levy said quietly. 'Do you mean things to do with that number on your arm?'

'Yes.'

Levy leaned forward. 'Try and think, Jake, what's different? It matters, you know, to us Israelis. We forget what it was like outside.'

Malik sighed. 'It will sound crazy. You won't understand. But if I heard a band playing the Horst Wessel Lied in Tel Aviv I don't think it would affect me.'

Levy looked at Johnny Morris. 'You know, that's one of the oddest compliments this country's ever had. But to me it's better than a poem.' He turned to Malik again. 'How long are you staying?'

'I'm leaving tomorrow morning.'

131

'Have you thought of coming back here?'

'My girlfriend would like us to live here. She was in love with the place before we came.'

'Where's she from?'

'Like I said. She's German, and she's not Jewish.'

Levy laughed. 'You'd better marry before you get here. The Rabbis are hell on mixed marriages. Thank God I married this *shiksa* of mine in Sydney before we came over.' Levy smiled at Morris and Malik. 'I got into a terrible argument with Rabbi Letz about mixed marriages and conversions and all that. He said how can Helen want to become a Jew just to marry me. It can't be genuine, he said. I asked him why not, and he said, "If you were an Arab, my son, then she'd have become a Muslim to marry you. Who do you think you are – Jehovah?" There's something in it of course. Those old boys know most of the answers.'

Morris, eager to change the subject, said softly, looking at Levy, 'What's going to happen on the West Bank, David?'

'We shall keep it, I've no doubt of that.'

'And colonise it?'

'That's not the word I would have used. But yes.'

'Wouldn't it be better to hand it back, so that it's out of the way once and for all? A gesture to the Arabs, for peace, that the whole world can see.'

Levy sighed and glanced at his wife. 'They don't understand, do they? I don't think you people ever will. Because you never listen to what's said. It doesn't matter *what* we give the Arabs. Land, money, economic or industrial help, it would make no difference. They will never recognise Israel. They have said so, in public, a dozen times. They have said that they will sweep us into the sea. Kill us, every man, woman, and child. But you don't believe it. You think that people don't really do those things. But they do, my friend. Hitler said what he was going to do. You had the warning but you didn't believe it. But he did it. By God, he did it. Six million Jews were exterminated for this. For Israel. And nobody, Arab, American, French or whatever, is going to make us give up one grain of sand. No matter who promises what. The Americans won't risk their oil supplies for us

132

despite the Jewish vote in New York. The UN is a paper tiger and Europe just wants a quiet life to sell arms to Israel and arms to the Arabs.'

Morris raised his eyebrows. 'I'm sorry, David. I obviously touched a raw nerve.'

'Forget it, Johnny. You're in good company. Even Kissinger would sell us down the Jordan if it won the next election for his lot.'

Malik diverted the lightning. 'How much would a house cost me in Tel Aviv? Or an apartment?'

The big brown eyes looked at him. 'Are you serious?'

'Yes.'

Levy said, 'What would you do for work?'

'We can both play the fiddle. Lisa's a professional performer and teacher.'

Levy laughed. 'You could get a place in Jaffa. You have to be an artist of some kind or they won't let you buy anything down there. It would still cost, mind you. At least forty thousand sterling. And you wouldn't get much for that.'

It was just before midnight when Johnny Morris drove him back to the hotel.

As they sat in the car at the bottom of Mapu Street, Morris said, 'I fixed what you wanted. They just called me back. On the manifest it says the crates are going to Hamburg and they're down as upright pianos for repair. What's it all about, Jake?'

'I'm not sure, Johnny. It's just part of an operation.'

'OK. Have a good flight and let me know if I can help at this end.'

In his room he put a call through to Heinz Fischer and told him what he wanted him to do. Suddenly Malik's hunter instinct was working. He had been aware for the past weeks that his mind had only been partially engaged by the investigation. With no pressure or apparent interest from Century House, no pattern to the sparse information they had gathered, the operation had become unreal. They needed all the resources of men and facilities that one or both of the two Intelligence services would normally have made available to weave together the hundreds of threads that such operations always revealed. What they had been doing had irked Malik; it fitted neither his character nor his experience. He realised that without his relationship with Lisa Fischer he would probably have asked London to replace him. But instinct told him that the operation was beginning to harden.

He phoned the airport and booked himself a flight for the next morning. When he looked at his watch he was surprised that it was already one o'clock. For a moment he hesitated, and then he put on his jacket and walked down to the street. There were still people about as he headed for the beach. An army jeep patrol stopped him as he crossed the main road. They checked his passport and warned him not to go down on to the beach itself.

He stayed on the promenade, leaning against the balustrade looking out towards the sea. On the horizon he could see an Aldis light blinking a Morse message to the shore, and away to the north he could see a haze of light where Haifa jutted into the Mediterranean. And from one of the big hotels behind him he could hear, faintly, the strains of a dance band. They were playing 'Somewhere over the rainbow', and it seemed oddly appropriate. For several million people Israel *was* the mythical country over the rainbow. Maybe even for Lisa and himself.

He closed his eyes. Trying once again to decide whether they really should settle in Israel. He felt strangely at home. For the first time in his life it didn't matter that he was a Jew. He was quite honest when he said that he was neither proud nor ashamed of being a Jew. It was other people who seemed to think it mattered. One way or the other. It was other people who reminded him that he was a Jew. He had met older survivors from concentration camps who were more deeply religious because of the experience. Seeing their survival as one more proof that the One True God existed. But for Malik the things he had seen made the idea of God controlling men's destinies anathema. It wasn't reasons of religion that would make him live in Israel, but almost the opposite. In Israel he could relax and just be a man.

134

Chapter 13

THE FLAT in Cologne had become just a place to live in. He put his bags alongside his bed and reached for the telephone. It was Frau Fischer who answered. Lisa was giving a music lesson at one of the schools. She'd be back at five in the evening. Frau Fischer was as friendly and welcoming as always but he thought he detected just a shade of distance in her voice. But he was tired and on the edge of one of his moods. Maybe he had imagined it. She didn't know where Heinz was.

Malik was dialling the police number when Heinz came in. He looked surprised to see Malik.

'What brings you back so early, Jake? I thought you'd be there at least another week.'

'Did you get a report from Interpol?'

'Yes, it came through early this morning. I couldn't understand what it was about.'

'Where is it?'

'On the desk in the other room. By the telephone.'

Malik walked into the small room that served as an office and picked up the two sheets of flimsy paper that were stapled together. It was all in capitals, the original off the police teleprinter.

EX INPOL PARIS. MALIK, KÖLN. INF. MORRIS TEL AVIV. NUMBER 74193 AIRFREIGHTER REG NO. D1047 LANDED APPROX 51 FIGURES DEGREES 8 FIGURES SECONDS BY 7 FIGURES DEGREES 28 FIGURES SECONDS AREA EAST OF KÖLN. AT 21 FIGURES HOURS 15 FIGURES MINUTES SAME DAY STOP. PROCEEDED TO WAHN AIRPORT 2 FIGURES HOURS LATER STOP NO FURTHER MOVEMENT STOP MESSAGE ENDS.

Malik walked back into the sitting room, but Fischer was in the small kitchen making them coffee. Malik leaned against the door.

'Who do you know at the airport, Heinz?'

Fischer shrugged. 'Practically everybody.'

'Who do you know on the freight side?'

'The manager and his two assistants. His secretary. A girl clerk . . .'

Malik smiled. 'OK. I get the message. I want to check two crates that came in early this morning. I want to know what's inside them.'

'I can phone and get Karl to check the manifest.'

'No. I want to actually see inside them. See for myself. A manifest can be phony.'

Fischer looked doubtful. 'They wouldn't do that as a personal favour, Jake. I'd have to use my police authority.'

'But they wouldn't inform the consignee or anyone else?'

'Not if I gave them official instructions not to.'

Malik gave Fischer the telex message and said, 'Have we got a local map that gives latitudes and longitudes? So that we can identify this first landing place?'

'Sure. I'll get it.'

They spread the large scale map on the table and carefully drew the two lines. One vertical and one horizontal. And where they crossed was a big patch of green indicating woodlands and parkland. The intersection was almost exactly the centre-point of Rechmann's estate.

'What's it all about, Jake?'

'I don't know, Heinz. But this plane is owned by a private independent freight company. The crates it was carrying are exactly the same as those we saw coming out of the piano factory. They were sent from overseas. The freight note said they were going to Hamburg. But they end up in Cologne. Why? And why did the plane touch down at Rechmann's place?'

'Maybe he radioed him to land to get instructions about the diversion.'

'Interpol would have recorded that if it had happened.'

'That's not much to go on, Jake.'

136

'Why use a private freight company when an airline could do it cheaper?'

'Maybe speed, or convenience.'

'What's all the hurry about a couple of pianos? And why are they coming in, not going out?'

'Reconditioning or repairs maybe.'

'Two at once? Why not get them done locally? There's nothing all that technical about repairing a piano.'

'What country did they come from?'

Malik hesitated for only a second. 'I'm not sure. Somewhere in the Middle East I think.'

'Do you want me to try and get them opened?'

'Yes. As soon as possible in case they get shifted somewhere else.'

'OK. Let's go.'

Karl Oetker, the freight manager, sat at his teak desk, his chin cupped in his hand.

'If you want to know what's inside the crates I'll accept your authority, but our insurance wouldn't cover damage caused in these circumstances.'

'We'll accept responsibility for that.'

Oetker frowned. 'I don't like it, Heinz, but if you say it's necessary then you can go ahead. They're due to collect them sometime tomorrow.'

'Can your people open the crates while we watch?'

'If you want it that way, yes.'

Oetker led Malik and Fischer over to the freight bay and signalled to one of his men and told him to open the crates. The man hammered the splayed end of the crowbar under each of the thick planks and eased them away from the main frame. Then after the other end had been prised away he hammered the planks free. Inside was a brand-new upright piano. When the second crate was opened and that too held a piano Malik asked for a screwdriver. He wanted the backs off both pianos. Oetker refused, but agreed that one of his joiners should take them off.

When the backs were removed Malik knelt and went

carefully over every part of both pianos, tapping the iron frames, checking each key and its individual action, sniffing, pressing and touching every accessible part. Eventually he stood up and turned to Fischer.

'Do the airport police have dogs for sniffing out drugs?'

'Yes.'

'Can you get one and its handler over here?'

'I'll phone the main office. There shouldn't be a problem.'

Ten minutes later the handler and the dog came over to the warehouse but there was no positive response. The dog sniffed without interest and returned to his handler.

Malik thanked Oetker and he and Fischer walked back to the car. They were on their way back to the flat when Malik said, 'I want to take some photographs, Heinz. I need a chopper and an infra-red camera. How do we get hold of them?'

'We've got the helicopters that do the traffic surveys and any camera will do for infra-red photographs, it's only the film and the focusing that's different. When do you want to do this, and where?'

'As soon as possible, and I want to cover the whole of Rechmann's estate. Where can we get the film processed and printed?'

'The police lab can do it for us.'

'I don't want anyone official to see the results.'

'Let me make some enquiries when I ask for the chopper and the camera.'

'The main thing is to adjust the focusing back to this red mark to allow for infra-red light waves being longer than light in the normal spectrum. And we can only use black and white or this Kodak colour film, Ektachrome X. And we can use either this special infra-red filter over the lens or the orange one if we want to eliminate the colour cast. There are typed recommendations with the camera operating instructions.'

'When can we have the chopper?'

'As soon as they've finished the autobahn control tomorrow morning.'

'Any information on how we can get the film processed?'

138

'There's a specialist photo-lab in town that can do both black and white and colour the same day. They process most of the scientific stuff for the university.'

'Write down the name and address for me, will you.'

'Do you want me in the chopper with you?'

Malik sat silent for several seconds, and Fischer realised that Malik's face had that closed-in look that it had had when he first came to Cologne.

'I want you to do something else, Heinz.'

'What?'

'I want you to check as far back as you can go on Rechmann's family and see if there is any indication of a Jew among them. And the same for his wife and her family.'

The cups and saucers and glasses had been cleared from the canteen table and Malik showed the pilot the area that he wanted to photograph. He had outlined the squares in red. It was a large area and he asked the pilot how long he would need.

'It depends on how much ground you cover with each frame. I can go as slow as you want.' He smiled. 'What's the focal length of your lens? We can do a bit of elementary trigonometry.'

'Five centimetres.'

'Have you got a motor-drive?'

'Yes.'

'How many frames a second?'

'Five. But I'll only use it at one frame a second.'

The pilot turned over the map and took out a pencil. A few minutes later he said, 'How much detail do you want? What's the size of the smallest object you want to show clearly?'

'About two metres, a car for instance.'

The man went back to his calculations and Malik read through the operational instruction for the Olympus OM2 yet again. Then the pilot straightened up.

'If we go up and down the long axis it will take five sweeps. Say twenty minutes.'

'I'd like to do it twice.'

139

'That's OK.'

'Are you ready to go now?'

'I'll file my trip with Air Control and come back here for you.'

Ten minutes later the pilot came back into the office. 'Air Control asked me what it was all about. I referred them to Heinz Fischer – is that OK?'

'That's fine.'

As they walked across the helicopter parking area Malik said, 'Is it easy to photograph from the chopper?'

'Yes. The TV stations use it regularly for video stuff. We can keep the sun on my side for three of the sweeps so that there's no risk of flare.'

And then they were at the pad. It was a Fairchild Hiller in white and black police livery. Up-to-date and well stabilised.

The pilot circled the area once so that Malik could focus the camera and stop down the aperture to allow for some fluctuation on infinity, and then he was ready.

The camera held film for 250 frames and there were only two spare packs and half a dozen bulk cassettes of both black and white and Ektachrome X, and Malik had to make quick changes in the loops at the end of each run. Despite the calculations it had only taken twenty-four minutes for the two coverages.

He drove straight from Wahn to the processing laboratory and asked for immediate processing, including contacts of the black and white infra-red film. The colour film would come back as continuous strips of positives. They wanted three hours and he parked the car and walked back to the flat.

The telephone was ringing as he walked in. It was Heinz Fischer.

'I'm at HQ. I've just had Traffic on the phone. They put Rechmann's estate manager on to me, Jake, asking about the chopper. I told him they were testing the gyro-compasses. He hinted that Rechmann was likely to lodge a complaint.'

'On what grounds?'

'Disturbing the livestock. He mentioned his pedigree Friesian herd.'

140

'Can you deal with it if he does complain?'

'I should think so. At least he knows me.'

'Anything else?'

'I'm working on the genealogy stuff for you. It's not easy because so many records were destroyed in the war. There are no indications of what you were looking for so far. But I'll keep trying.'

'There's one other thing I'd like you to check. The airfreight company. Who owns it and any background material you can get.'

'OK.'

On his way back to the photo-lab Malik looked at the diamond rings in a jeweller's windows and spent twenty minutes inside looking at half-a-dozen rings. He couldn't make up his mind between one large solitaire diamond and a setting of five smaller ones. In the end he chose the solitaire.

At the photo-lab he handed in his ticket and a couple of minutes later one of the technicians came from the laboratory to the reception counter.

'We've just finished the contact prints. Have you got any way of examining them? An enlarger maybe?'

'No. Maybe I can hire one.'

'I can put the colour strips through our projector if you've got the time. The black and white stuff will be wrong way round of course but it will give you an idea of whether you've got what you want or not. They're very slightly over-exposed but I doubt if you'll be able to tell with the naked eye.'

Malik sat in the darkness of the projection theatre and watched the colour frames one by one as they came up on the big screen. They had an eerie reddish purple cast but it wasn't until the second roll that he pressed the button and the theatre lights came up and the assistant's voice came over the speaker system.

'Can I help you?'

'Can you hear me?'

'Yes. The seats are wired for sound.'

'What's the red fuzzy line across the last two frames?'

'Drains. What they call mole drains. This looks like farmland and mole drains are common.'

'How deep in the ground are they?'
'Between two and two point five metres usually.'
'Thanks.'
'Shall I carry on?'
'Yes please.'

The lights dimmed and the frames passed through again. And on the third roll of exposures he saw it. Even in the warm theatre he felt suddenly cold. He just sat there repeating the frame number. 139.

On the black and white film it was frame number 141 and even clearer. When the lights finally went up again he asked for half-a-dozen enlargements of both the colour and the black and white frames. They would be available from the overnight shift and could be collected any time after nine the next morning.

Heinz Fischer was waiting for him at the flat.

'I've got something, Jake, on the air-freight company.'

'Tell me.'

'It's not a German company. It just operates here out of Berlin, Cologne and Hamburg. The general manager and the staff are all German. But guess where it's registered?'

'I've no idea.'

'In Israel. In Tel Aviv. And guess who the owner is?'

'Rechmann?'

'No.'

'Tell me.'

'Amos Meyer. It's a subsidiary of his group holding company. Wholly owned. And Amos Meyer holds all the shares in the airline company except one which is owned by von Busch.'

Malik smiled. 'We're beginning to get there, Heinz. Well done.'

'I just did the routine, Jake. How was your trip?'

'Not so interesting as your stuff.'

'I'm going to pick up Ruth if you don't need me right now.'

'That's fine. Where will you be?'

'I'm meeting her at home.'

'Have a good time.'

Malik walked back into the sitting room and ten minutes later the phone rang. It was the Cologne Police HQ. The man wanted to speak to Fischer. He gave him Heinz's home number. Ten minutes later Heinz phoned himself.

'Jake, I've just had the central records guy on the phone. I've been putting all the names we get through central records computer system. They've just come back with something. You remember the girl from Humboldt University, Anna Bauer?

'Yes?'

'One of the men she meets regularly in West Berlin is an Erich Deissner.'

'Who is he?'

'He's the general manager and senior pilot of the air-freight company.'

'Have they got details of dates and where he sees her?'

'Berlin may have. They'll send them through if we want them.'

'We want them.'

'OK. I'll notify them.'

Lisa's parents were out when he picked her up and they went to the cinema to see a re-run of *Guess Who's Coming to Dinner*. Neither of them had seen it before and after ten minutes Malik looked surreptitiously at Lisa's face. But she was already looking at him and they both laughed softly at the obvious parallel. Change negro to Jew and it was almost their story.

They had a snack in a café afterwards and argued amiably about the two parents in the film and whether the happy ending was justified. They decided it was.

Malik took the small cube from his pocket and put it on the table in front of her. Her fingers trembled as she tore off the paper and when she turned back the lid she gazed at the ring without taking it out of the velvet base.

When she looked up at Malik's face to speak he said, 'Maybe I should ask your father first.' And as he said it he was ashamed that he couldn't say the words he should have said.

She said softly, 'We can tell them when we go back. They'll be happy for me. And for you too . . . if you *are* happy?' She raised her eyebrows as she smiled at him.

'I just don't want to let you down, Lisa.'

'You won't, my love. Why should you?'

'Not the usual ways men let down women. Just that . . .' He shrugged. '. . . I'm not used to permanent relationships with people . . . a girl.'

'Don't worry, Jake. We'll be all right. Just relax.'

Malik nodded. 'We'll have to wait a few weeks until I've finished this assignment.'

'How long will it be, Jake?'

'I don't know, sweetie. A month. Could be longer.'

'Can I tell my parents?'

'We'll both tell them.'

'When?'

'Will they be at home now?'

'I think so.'

'I think they know already. But I want them to be happy about it. Let's go and see them now.'

The Fischers were saying goodbye to one of their friends as Malik and Lisa walked from the garage to the front of the house and they went together into the music room.

'Where did you two go in the end?' Herr Fischer asked.

'We went to the cinema.' Malik paused and took a deep breath. 'We wanted to have a word with you, if it's convenient.'

Herr Fischer pointed to the settee. 'Of course it is. Sit down, both of you. How about a drink?'

'Not for me, thank you.'

'Nor me,' said Lisa quietly.

Herr Fischer poured himself a whisky and sat down by his wife. He smiled and raised his glass.

'The answer, of course, is yes.'

Malik smiled. 'You knew already.'

'We wondered. We should have had to be deaf and blind not to have seen how things are. We both hope you'll be very happy. The pair of you.'

'There is one other thing.'

'What's that?'

'We're probably going to live in Israel.'

Malik saw the smile fade from Herr Fischer's face and then the trembling lips as he gallantly tried to recover and bring back some semblance of a smile. He glanced at his wife but she didn't respond. He turned his head back to look at Malik and his daughter.

'I'm sure you've thought about it very carefully.'

'We have, papa. We both know that we'll be happier there than in London.'

Herr Fischer slowly absorbed the fact that the choice was between London and Israel, not Germany and Israel, and Malik felt a sudden compassion for this man who so loved his daughter that he tried to look cheerful in his unhappiness. As his own father had done.

He said, 'We hope you'll spend all the time you can with us and we shall be back here frequently I'm sure.'

Herr Fischer nodded and stood up. 'We must celebrate. I'll find our one and only bottle of champagne.'

And both Lisa and Malik saw Herr Fischer furtively wipe the tears from his eyes as he walked over to the small drinks cabinet. He slowly arranged the glasses and the bottle on a silver tray and carried it over to the coffee table. His hands trembled as he peeled off the gold foil and the wire cradle over the bulbous cork. As the champagne foamed from the neck of the bottle he filled their glasses.

'Well. Here's to both of you. Every happiness. We will have a real celebration so that all our friends can be there. And Heidi. And Heinz of course. Does he know about all this already?'

Malik shook his head. 'He's probably guessed how it would end but we wanted to tell you first.'

'What date have you got in mind, Lisa?' It was the first time Frau Fischer had spoken, and although her smile was friendly there was an edge to her voice that alerted Malik.

145

And she had obliquely excluded him from the question as if his view was not necessary.

'We haven't decided yet, Mama. It will depend on the work Jake is doing at the moment.'

'You must let us know dear, when you've decided.'

There was some desultory chat about the concert the Fischers had been to and then Lisa walked with Malik to his car. As they stood there in the bright moonlight she said, 'Like you always say. No problem.'

Malik shrugged. 'I thought your mother was a bit subdued.'

'I expect that was for Papa's benefit. She tries to be the practical one who has to worry about dates and arrangements and all that.'

'Are you teaching tomorrow?'

'Only until midday. Phone me when you can and I'll be ready whenever you want.'

He kissed her gently and then got into his car. She stood there in the moonlight and waved back to him as he drove off, and he was depressed enough to wonder if there was any significance in the fact that she hadn't done what she usually did and walk back to the light of the front porch to wave to him. Was staying by the garage a sign that she was identifying with him, or was not walking back to the porch a subconscious excluding of him from her family? And for the first time for weeks he wondered as he wondered so often, if he was insane.

Chapter 14

MALIK DROVE over the bridge at Marlow and at the end of the High Street he turned onto the Henley road. About five miles out of Marlow he turned off the road to the entrance of the RAF station. A guard stopped him before he got to the concrete guard room.

'I've got an appointment with Squadron Leader Fowler.'

'Can I have your name, sir?'

'Malik. Jacob Malik.'

'Will you switch off your car engine and give me the keys, Mr Malik, and we'll walk over to the guard room.'

Malik switched off, got out of the car and handed over the keys. He was given a striped celluloid card in exchange and he followed the RAF sergeant to the guard room. A flight-lieutenant asked him if he had anything to identify himself with and he handed over his SIS card. The officer looked at the photograph and back at Malik's face as he reached for a telephone that had a bank of fifty or more touch-buttons. He tapped five of them and waited, then two more.

'Tideway, this is Phantom. I have an MI6 card with serial number 4791032. I'd like a trace.' He looked at Malik as he listened. Then nodded to himself and hung up.

'I'll keep the card, Mr Malik, and issue you an internal pass.'

As he handed Malik a second plastic card the officer reached for the blue phone and dialled four numbers.

'Squadron Leader Fowler? I see . . . will you tell him his visitor is in the guard room . . . thanks.'

A few minutes later Fowler drew up in a Range Rover with RAF roundels on the side and waved Malik over.

'Jump in, Jake. I'm over the other side.'

Fowler turned the vehicle and they followed a tarmac road past a series of buildings; a hangar, a couple of Westland helicopters and then they were at a small concrete building.

They had to use both their passes for Malik to enter, and inside the lighting was artificial but bright and almost like sunshine.

Fowler led him to his own room which was a mass of electronics and photographic equipment. Fowler took off his cap, smiling.

'Sorry about all the bullshit but you're probably used to it. Nice to see you again.'

'Nice to see you too, and thanks for finding time to see me.'

'Not at all. What can I do for you?'

Malik reached into his jacket pocket, took out a plain brown envelope and handed it to Fowler.

'Have a look at that. And tell me what it is.'

Fowler tapped the photograph out of the envelope and held it carefully by its edges. He looked at it, holding it so that it caught the light, and then he looked at Malik before he walked with the print over to a white topped desk.

'Is the scale correct, Jake, or just a guess?'

'The scale was built in on the camera.'

Fowler put it down on the inspection desk and swung over a magnifying lens. Then he reached up and directed a circle of light onto the photograph. For long minutes he looked through the lens, then he turned to look at Malik.

'Where did you get this, Jake?' he asked softly.

Malik shook his head. 'Tell me what it is.'

Fowler frowned. 'You must know roughly what it is.'

Malik half-smiled. 'It's a weapon. I want you to tell me exactly what it is.'

'Can I keep a copy?'

'Afraid not.'

'Can I put in an official request? We haven't got an actual record of one on a site.'

Malik shook his head. 'You'd be told we didn't know what you're on about. Maybe in a few weeks time you can have that print provided you leave it at that for now and don't ask for any more information. Anyway, what the hell is it?'

'I can't give you a precise answer because I don't know. But I can give you a fair idea of what it is. It's a bastard version of a Soviet IRBM that NATO calls Scapegoat. Its proper designation is the SS-14. We know very little about SS-14s and it's too mobile to even appear on satellite pictures.'

'Tell me more.'

'What can I tell you? It's just over thirty-five feet long and it's got a range of just under 2500 miles. It's solid fuel and can be launched easily from an IS-3 chassis.'

'Where have they been used?'

'That I can't tell you. Apart from test launches we've never had evidence that they have been used operationally. But they've been deployed all over the place. You can put them in silos but they're so flexible you don't really need to. The launchers are totally mobile. You can plant one in woods, in buildings, you can trundle it away in a matter of minutes and deploy it somewhere else. It's almost as mobile as a heavy-goods vehicle.'

'What makes you think this is a bastardised version?'

'There's what looks like an extra body unit.'

'What would that do?'

'The only thing I can think of was that they wanted to try making them in smaller plants where the equipment had to produce shorter lengths. It won't affect the performance one way or another.'

'And the warhead?'

'Oh, nuclear.'

'Accurate?'

'Yes. Inertial guidance system. They could MIRV it at some stage and give it two or three warheads.'

'A big bang when it lands?'

Fowler shrugged. 'They're all big bangs these days, Jake. This would be Hiroshima times four or five I'd guess.'

'What kind of crews do they have?'

'God knows. The only sightings have been by the Americans. They saw two SS-14s at the Soviet test centre for ICBMs at Tyuratim. It was a verbal report. Their camera was out of action. I'd guess maybe a technician and a driver would do. They would vector on instructions from a command

149

post. They could be linked in clusters of course if they were permanent sites and the targets weren't changed.'

'What does that mean – linked?'

'You could fire them by remote control in pairs or clusters from a single control point. They would be fired like that, by radio, at Tyuratim.'

Malik held out his hand for the photograph but Fowler was reluctant to hand it over.

'How the hell did the reconnaisance plane get so low, Jake?'

'Who says it was low?'

'If this was satellite or even a U2 the grain would be far worse. This must have been taken at under a thousand feet. And there's almost no atmospheric interference.'

Malik waved his hand for the photograph and Fowler handed it back.

Malik smiled. 'I'll have it nicely framed and you can have it for Christmas.'

Fowler wasn't amused. 'Let's go over to the Mess for a drink.'

'I haven't got time, Freddy.'

'OK. Let me take you back to the gate.'

The applause went on long after the lights had gone up in the concert hall and Ashkenazy came back for the sixth and seventh time. It was rapturous to the point of embarrassment, and Malik did not notice Heinz Fischer standing a few feet away at the end of the row vainly trying to attract his attention. It was Lisa who noticed him; she tugged at Malik's arm.

'Heinz wants you, Jake.'

Malik made his apologies as he pushed his way past the rapt faces to the aisle.

'I've just had a call from Lauterbacher. He seems to be doing his stuff for us. He says Meyer is booked into the same hotel in Hamburg the day after tomorrow if we're still interested.'

'Have you tried to book us on a flight yet?'

'No.'

'See what you can do. As early as possible.'

'Are you taking Lisa home after this?'

'Yes.'

'I'll phone you there.'

It was nearly midnight when Heinz Fischer phoned. He had been unable to get them on the early morning flight but using his police muscle he had arranged for them to fly up on a freighter that was leaving at five a.m.

They were at the hotel in Hamburg by seven-thirty but they had not been able to book into the suite next door to Meyer. The best they could do was to be on the same corridor on the same floor.

When they were in their suite Malik said, 'I'm going to pick up Meyer, Heinz. I don't have any choice, and there's no time to play it slowly even if I knew how to go about it. D'you want to stay out of it?'

'Does he end up the same way as Loeb?'

Malik half-smiled. 'I shouldn't think so. Meyer isn't stupid, and I know a hell of a lot more about the background this time.'

'When do *I* get to know about the background?'

'I'd rather you heard it as it comes out. Anyway I don't really know all that much. And I could be way off beam. But I *do* know that it's far and away more serious than we thought. Just how serious remains to be seen.'

'OK. I'll stay.'

'Rent me another house then, Heinz. Somewhere really isolated and not too big.'

'How long for?'

'Same as before. A couple of months.'

In the late afternoon Malik went with Fischer to see the house he had rented deep in the forest of Sachsenwald. He checked it over thoroughly, room by room. It was well furnished and of a size that would be reasonably easy to control.

151

Back at the hotel Malik rehearsed his plan with Fischer, checking again and again the timings from their suite to Meyer's suite, and then the long journey down the stairs to the last section of the fire escape and the emergency doors that led to the yard serving the kitchens and boiler-house. Malik tested the lock a dozen times. There was no way to drug Meyer and remove him once he was insensible. He either cooperated or they had to guard him in his suite and then take him by force in the early hours of the morning. They covered variations on both methods until Malik was satisfied that both plans could work unless something totally unexpected happened.

Heinz phoned Ruth, and Malik phoned Lisa. She had heard from one of her old schoolfriends that another girl in their class was now a teacher at a kibbutz near Ramla. She had also told the principal at the music school where she taught that she would be leaving before the end of the year. He was giving her a glowing reference and two introductions that could be helpful in getting a job. She was quite sure that those were all obvious signals from the good Lord that everything was going to be fine.

They ate together in their suite and went early to bed. As Malik lay quietly in the darkness his mind went over the things he knew. Remembering the small clues that had been there all the while like minute specks of gold in a prospector's sludge. Loeb and his electronics experience with army control systems. The girl from Humboldt and her talk with the journalist that had wandered off into nuclear missiles and the Israelis. The camouflaged place in the Negev. The crates that he now knew had brought a missile or parts of a missile to Rechmann's estate where they had been unloaded and the pianos substituted. The infra-red photograph of that pencil shape that was a missile in an underground silo. But what the hell were they going to do with a missile? And what in God's name could have brought Jews and Germans together in such an unholy alliance? There was no sense in it. Was there a chance that one or both governments were involved? And if so, why? And what kind of crazy set-up brought together a German

152

piano manufacturer, and a wealthy Israeli industrialist? And why was Meyer's airline chief pilot sleeping with the pretty blonde from East Berlin who was also sleeping with a KGB man? Nothing about it gave off the smell of a KGB operation, but it was the KGB bit that had brought MI6 into it in the first place. And as the flotsam swirled in his mind he realised that he had missed an elementary point. In what direction was Rechmann's missile pointing? He had completely over-looked the obvious fact that missiles on fixed sites have a permanent target. And the photographs wouldn't help unless they were all accurately pasted down and orientated on a smaller scale map. He could get it done if necessary but it would take a couple of days.

In the darkness he pressed the light button on his watch. It was past one o'clock. He closed his eyes and pulled the blanket over his head.

The old crone was like the witch in his story book of Hansel and Gretel. She had a shrunken face, the skin like parchment stretched over a skull, yellow and mottled with suppurating patches of eczema. She was sitting on the bottom bunk, her wiry grey hair like a roughly made bird's nest, the whites of her eyes stained with brown patches, her hands trembling as they rested on her bony legs. It was their third day in Auschwitz.

The old woman's voice quavered as she spoke, her eyes intent on his mother's face.

'You need trousers for the boy, missus. I tell you how to get them.'

'But he's got trousers.'

The old witch cackled. 'With short trousers they say he is a child and then in two days he is in the gas chamber. With long trousers he is a man. A small man. But they want men to work before they die.'

'You mean they kill children without reason?'

The old woman made strange, horrifying noises as she laughed. 'He's a Jew, you stupid cow. That is a reason to them. Where you been all these years?'

'Where can I get long trousers for him?'

The old woman leaned forward, cupping her bony hands round her mouth as she whispered.

153

'The Kapo in hut thirty-one has seen the boy. He wants him for himself. He's in for hundred and sixty-five. Done four years already.'

'I don't understand. What's hundred and sixty-five?'

The old woman smiled, her mouth quite toothless.

'He's a homo. He fancies him.'

For a moment his mother sat there paralysed and then she reached for his hand as she stood up unsteadily. The old woman clawed at her dress, holding her there.

'There's another way, sweetheart, an easier way.'

'What's that?'

'Old Schmidt.' She pointed to the man on the bunk in the corner. He wore a kapo's armband. He was an old man, with a beard and whiskers like a rabbi, but he wasn't a rabbi. He was one of the early inmates from when the prisoners were actual criminals. The old woman was stroking his mother's leg. 'He can still get it hard, missus. You open your legs for him and he'll get you the trousers. You tell him I told you. Tell him to remember old Friedl.'

He looked up at his mother's face. Her eyes were closed and her hands were clasped, and as he saw her lips moving he knew she was praying. She had told him to sit on the bunk and wait for her.

He had been asleep when she came back but he woke, trembling as she stuffed the filthy pair of cut-down long trousers under his blanket. He pulled the thin blanket over his head to hide from the world of grown-ups.

Chapter 15

MALIK SENT Heinz Fischer to buy food and take it to the house at Sachsenwald. Meyer was not due at the airport until midday. When Fischer got back they checked the stairways and the fire-escape again, and at one o'clock, just before Meyer was due at the hotel, Fischer drove the car round to the hotel's service area at the back and parked it alongside the boiler-room. The only eventuality that he couldn't plan for was if Meyer was not alone when he booked in at the hotel. Malik was afraid that if they weren't able to pick up Meyer quickly he might have visitors or phone someone so that his disappearance would be noticed too quickly.

Fischer moved down the lobby so that he could phone up when Meyer arrived. When Meyer had not arrived by three o'clock Malik gave it another ten minutes. He was just reaching to telephone the lobby when Fischer rang. Meyer had booked in and was just walking over to the lift with the porter.

Malik walked into the corridor and saw the porter standing to one side as Meyer walked into his suite. He saw Fischer come out of the furthest lift and hold the gates as the porter came out of Meyer's door, and then they were alone in the corridor. He waited for a couple of minutes.

Fischer held his breath as Malik slid the skeleton key into the lock and quietly turned the knob. The sitting room was empty and Fischer closed the door carefully as Malik walked across to the half-open bedroom door.

Meyer was sitting on his bed, loosening his tie, his jacket on the bed beside him. He half-smiled as Malik walked into the bedroom.

'You've got the wrong room, I'm afraid. The porter must have left the door open by mistake.'

'Amos Meyer?'

155

The half-smile faded but Meyer didn't look alarmed.

'Why yes. Who are you? I don't understand.'

'I want you to come with me, Herr Meyer. I want to talk to you. You won't get hurt if you do as I ask.'

Meyer was reaching for the bedside phone when Malik pulled out the Walther. Meyer withdrew his hand from the telephone but he looked quite composed.

'I don't know who you are, but you're being very silly. Now what is it you want?'

'My name is Malik, Herr Meyer, and I told you what I want. I want you to come with me and answer some questions.'

'Are you some sort of policeman, or what?'

'Put your jacket on, Meyer. I have a colleague in the other room. He'll bring your bags.'

'If it's money you want, it's in my wallet.'

Malik waved the pistol. 'Come on, Meyer, you're wasting time,' he said sharply.

Then, as Meyer's hand darted towards the room-service call-button, Malik chopped at Meyer's neck with his hand. The blow knocked him sideways on the bed but its force had been relieved by his collar and tie. He was still conscious, his eyes turned sideways to look at Malik. He sat up slowly and tentatively, as if half-expecting another blow. He opened his mouth to speak but Malik cut in.

'Stand up, Meyer, and put on your jacket.'

Meyer stood up, and his hands shook as he pulled on his jacket. Malik guessed that the trembling was more from shock than actual fear. Meyer looked cautious but not scared.

'Now walk out into the sitting room.'

Malik nodded to Fischer who went into the bedroom and came out a couple of minutes later with Meyer's bag and briefcase. He opened the outer door, looked out and nodded. Malik slid the pistol into his jacket pocket and motioned to Meyer to follow Fischer into the corridor.

They passed an elderly couple heading for the lifts. The man nodded in their general direction as they passed by. Fischer led the way and they walked down ten double flights of carpeted stairs to the emergency door on the mezzanine floor. Fischer pushed on the metal roller and the two doors grated open. There was nobody in the yard as they walked down the iron fire-escape and Malik kept close to Meyer as they made their way through the hotel staff's cars to the BMW. As Malik bent to open the passenger door he saw Meyer turn and he stood up, ramming the pistol hard into Meyer's kidneys. The man's angry eyes looked for a moment at Malik's grim face and then he bent to get into the passenger seat. Malik pushed the door to, waited until Fischer had started the car then slid quickly into the rear seat and the car jerked forward as he was closing the door.

Malik took the pistol out of his pocket. 'Don't do anything stupid, Meyer,' and he reached forward, the nose of the pistol just touching Meyer's neck as they made their way through the city traffic towards the autobahn.

There was heavy traffic until they got to the city boundary just beyond the Youth Hostel at Horn. Fischer took them off the highway at Öjendorf Park and by the time they were passing through Oststeinbrek the traffic was lighter, and by Schönningstedt they were alone. At the Friedrich's Museum Fischer switched on the sidelights as they turned onto the forest road. Ten minutes later the car turned off the road down the hard, rutted track that led to the house.

Malik got out and opened the white wooden gates and Fischer drove up to the small garage. Meyer looked around as they stood waiting for Malik to come. Once they were all inside the house Malik switched on the lights and drew the curtains. He turned to look at Meyer and pointed to one of the armchairs.

'Sit down, Herr Meyer.'

Meyer sat down awkwardly. His face was impassive and he sat there without speaking. Almost dignified.

'Tell me about it, Meyer. All of it.'

'I don't know who you are, or what you want. But I'd better warn you that I have meetings arranged with important people. When I don't arrive there will be immediate enquiries.'

'Who are the important meetings with, Meyer?'

'That's my business.'

'I don't want to hurt you, Meyer.'

Meyer half-smiled. 'You won't hurt me, my friend. I spent two years in one of your concentration camps. There's nothing you can do that will frighten me.'

'Which concentration camp was that?'

'Sachsenhausen.'

'Show me your mark.'

Meyer pushed forward his hands and Malik saw where the tattoo had been removed. There was just a patch of shiny tissue, wrinkled and raw.

He leaned forward and unlocked the handcuffs, sliding them into his jacket pocket. Then he sat back in his chair.

'My name is Malik, Herr Meyer, Jacob Malik. I am a British Intelligence officer and I'm investigating, in conjunction with the German Political Police, the outbreaks of anti-Semitic daubings on synagogues and other Jewish buildings. I believe you are connected with those groups. I don't understand why. Maybe you could tell me.'

'I'm a Jew, Herr Malik, an Israeli citizen. I'm hardly likely to be connected with that sort of activity.'

Malik sighed. 'Neither is Baron von Busch, or Herr Rechmann in Cologne, or the judge in Goslar. Nevertheless they are connected with these groups and you know it.'

For the first time Meyer looked agitated. His hand went to his shirt collar, unbuttoning it and loosening his tie. Then, looking at Malik he said, 'I'm afraid I can't help you.'

'Would you rather I filed my report with Bonn and London?'

'That's up to you.'

Malik reached inside his jacket and pulled out one of the postcard-sized colour prints, handing it to Meyer.

'Are you sure you mean that?'

Meyer looked at the photograph and his hand trembled as he handed it back to Malik. For a moment or two Meyer sat with his eyes closed as if he were praying, then lifting his eyes slowly to look at Malik he said, 'I'll talk to you alone, Herr Malik.'

Malik looked across at Fischer and nodded, and the German stood up and walked out of the room. Malik turned his head to look back at Meyer.

'You realise that if you try to get away not only are you likely to get hurt but everything you've been doing will be exposed.'

'You are a Jew, aren't you, Herr Malik?'

'Yes.'

'How much do you know already?'

Malik shook his head. 'Just tell me your story. I'm not here to answer your questions.'

'How many people have you informed?'

'None. Neither London nor Bonn know yet what I have discovered.'

'But Herr Fischer knows?'

'No. Just me.'

'We could cause another Holocaust, you and I, if we are not very wise.'

'Maybe you should have thought of that before you started.'

'Do you care about what happened to us Jews, Herr Malik?' Meyer saw the anger in Malik's eyes but he went on. 'Everything I have planned, everything I have done, has been to protect my country. I beg of you to believe me.'

'If I believed you, Meyer, I should think you ought to be in a mental hospital.'

'Let me explain and you will understand.'

'That's what I've been asking you to do.'

'It's going to take a long time.'

Malik shrugged and sat down. Meyer leaned forward.

'Maybe it'll be easier if I just answer your questions.'

'OK. Who's in with you apart from von Busch, Rechmann and the old judge?'

'There's two Israelis. Halberstein and Cohen. And one other German.'

'Is there anybody above you?'

'No. I put it together and I run it.'

'How many missiles are there?'

'Ten.'

'Where are they?'

159

'Five in Germany and five in Israel.'

'Are they armed?'

'Yes.'

'What with?'

'Single nuclear warheads.'

'How are they controlled?'

'Electronic synchroniser and radio.'

'The missile at Rechmann's place. Where is it aimed? And the others.'

'I'll give you a list. They're all aimed at Soviet cities.'

'Who controls the firing?'

'I do, but von Busch could too if I passed him the code.'

'Does he know it?'

'No.'

Malik stood up, looking at Meyer's face. He said softly, 'You must be out of your mind.'

He walked to the door and turned to look at Meyer. 'Don't move, Meyer. If you make any move you'll get hurt.'

Malik walked into the hall and called out.

'Heinz.'

Fischer came out of the kitchen, a half-eaten sandwich in his hand.

'What is it, Jake? Is he talking?'

'Can you put a round-the-clock surveillance on Rechmann and von Busch?'

'I'd have to give a damn good reason. They're both important men in their communities. That wouldn't stop a surveillance, but I'd have to give chapter and verse.'

'I can't do that.'

'Why not?'

Malik shook his head. 'It's better you don't know.' He looked at Heinz Fischer's face. 'You probably wouldn't believe it anyway.'

'What do you want me to do?'

'What time is it?'

Fischer looked at his watch. 'Just past ten.'

'Forget the surveillance. Get some sleep, Heinz. I'll wake you about three. I want you to watch Meyer when he's sleeping. I'll relieve you about seven.'

160

'Do you want something to eat?'

'What have you got?'

'I can do beef sandwiches, cheese, tomatoes and apples.'

'Bring in a few beef sandwiches and tomatoes. And a flask of coffee.'

'Milk and sugar in the coffee?'

'No milk. He's kosher. And no cheese either for the same reason.'

'I'll be about fifteen minutes.'

'OK. Knock before you come in.'

'Is he likely to try and do a bolt?'

'No. More likely to cut his throat.'

Malik turned and walked back into the sitting room. Meyer was sitting with his head in his hands but he looked up as soon as Malik walked in.

'I don't think you understand, Herr Malik. You've got the wrong impression. This is for defence, not attack.'

'What was a man like Loeb used for?'

'Loeb?' Meyer looked puzzled.

'He worked for von Busch. Played guitar in a club.'

'He was killed.'

'I know. What was he used for?'

'I think he knew about electronics. He was controlled by von Busch.'

'Why the swastikas on the synagogues?'

Meyer sighed and shrugged. 'We thought that the KGB had information about our intentions. We wanted to provide a cover. A diversion. Something to put them off our tracks. We paid a few hooligans to do all that.'

'How many people are in your groups?'

'There are no groups. Just the four of us in Germany. Two in Israel and myself. We have used people for certain things but they didn't know anything about what we were doing.'

'And what the hell *were* you doing?'

'Were you German originally, Herr Malik?'

'No. I was born in Poland.'

Meyer frowned. 'How did you . . .' He stopped as Malik uncovered his wrist for a moment. He looked amazed. 'You were in a camp.'

Malik nodded and Meyer sighed. 'Thank God. Thank God. At least you'll understand.'

Malik shook his head. 'I won't, Meyer. I assure you I won't. I'm not just a Jew, I'm also an intelligence officer and I don't give a damn whether criminals are Jews, Catholics or atheists.'

'Do you care about being a Jew? Do you care about us? Do you care about Israel and all it means?'

Malik took off his jacket and Meyer heard the metallic thud of the gun in the jacket pocket as Malik dropped it onto the floor as he sat down facing Meyer.

'Let me warn you, Herr Meyer, that you have committed a dozen or more criminal acts. Criminal offences under German law, Israeli law and the laws of every civilised country in the world. You must consider yourself as already being under arrest. Anything you tell me I shall report to the authorities, and what you tell me will be used in evidence when you come to trial. Do not, I repeat, do not, imagine for a moment that because I am a Jew, or because I was in Auschwitz, or that because you are a Jew and an Israeli, that it will make any difference. There are Jews in jail tonight in Tel Aviv and Jerusalem because they are criminals as well as Jews. You are a criminal too. Don't make any mistake about that.'

'Are your father and mother still living, Herr Malik?'

'Forget my father and mother. Tell me what you were planning.'

'What do you want to know?'

'For Christ's sake, Meyer. What were you trying to do?'

'To save the peace.'

'Cut out the bullshit. What were you trying to do with ten atomic missiles?'

Meyer opened his mouth to speak and then closed it as Fischer came in with a tray and put it down on the low table between Meyer and Malik.

'You know where I am if you want me, Jake.'

'OK. I'll be around for some time.'

Malik waved towards the sandwiches and Meyer.

'Help yourself. It's not kosher but it's all we've got.'

162

Meyer shook his head, taking a deep breath as he leaned back in his chair. His mottled hands were clasped together and a nerve quivered at one side of his mouth. And there were beads of perspiration on his forehead and his upper lip.

'It's difficult, Herr Malik, to explain in a few minutes something that I have thought about for years. Especially something as complex as this.'

Meyer waited for a response but when Malik ignored the pause Meyer shrugged and went on.

'I tried to plan for the day when our enemies attacked us and our allies deserted us. I feared that that day would come. I fear now that it is very near. The Soviet Union is openly anti-Semitic. It persecutes our people and supports the Arabs who want to wipe out Israel.

'Because of the Jewish vote and natural generosity the United States has helped us with money, arms, technology, and in the United Nations. But when God gave us Israel he forgot to give us oil. And the Americans need oil. Only the Arabs have oil. Before long the Americans will be forced into deciding whether they want oil or Israel. I fear that they will choose oil. I don't criticise them for that. Without enough oil their whole economy would disintegrate.

'When this happens we shall be open to attack from all sides. Egypt, the Lebanon, Syria, Iran, Iraq, Jordan . . . all the quarrelling Arabs will suddenly be allies. We should fight, of course, but in the end we should be wiped out. All of us. Men, women and children. Just like they always said they would do. The Soviet Union would encourage and assist them. Our friends in America would be shocked and angry. They would raise hell in the Security Council and when we were all dead the United Nations would pass a vote of censure on the Soviet Union. But the Cadillacs and the trucks would still have gas.'

Meyer waited for Malik to respond. But there was no response.

'Germany is in the same position as Israel. They have allies too. NATO and the United States. They have the same old enemy . . . the Soviet Union. And just as the Russians can use their Arab stooges to attack Israel the Russians have

163

their Warsaw Pact stooges to attack West Germany. NATO couldn't stop the Warsaw Pact forces. They may not even try. Especially if the Russians declare on day one that they undertake to go no further than the Rhine. The French and the British are not going to declare war on the Soviet Union for the sake of half of Germany. It would be all over in three or four days. By the time the Americans had called on the UN it would be all over. This is the scenario I imagined, and every week in the last two years has seen it become more likely. When I originally explained it to my colleagues they agreed with its logic but couldn't believe that it would happen. When they saw what was happening, they believed, and we went ahead.' Meyer looked at Malik's grim face and said, hesitantly, 'And I guess you know the rest.'

'You tell me, Meyer. You tell me.'

'We made a pact, the seven of us. We accepted that if either Israel or West Germany was attacked, no government action, no diplomacy, no United Nations would be able to stop the attack. While presidents and prime ministers were consulting their experts, and the diplomats were beating on the doors of the UN, it would be half over, and by the time they decided what to do it would be too late.

'My plan is – was – that on the first move over the frontiers of either country we should inform the media all over the world by anonymous phone calls that somewhere in the world, within striking distance of ten named Soviet cities, are nuclear missiles trained on those cities which would be launched within six hours of our statement.

'We should not announce who we are, our motives, our nationalities . . . absolutely nothing. We should make clear that no organisation or government on either side was responsible. There would be nobody for the Russians to negotiate with, and no time for us to be discovered. We could be in South America, anywhere, for all they knew. They would not be able to accuse any country. Their own citizens would know that they were being sacrificed because their leaders were trying to destroy West Germany or Israel. They would have a simple choice. No ifs and buts. They would withdraw within the six hours or their cities would be destroyed.

164

The messages to all the media would be given in Spanish, and no Spanish-speaking country has a nuclear missile capacity.'

Meyer spread his arms in a typically resigned Jewish gesture and said, 'They wouldn't have risked it. Who would they retaliate against? You only start a world war when you've planned it. Not on the spur of the moment, under pressure. They would have withdrawn. The missiles would not have been fired and the world would have been warned of Soviet intentions.'

'And if they *had* ignored the threat?'

Meyer shook his head. 'You're going back into the thinking of planners. What will *they* do if we do this? What shall we do if they do that? They are all hamstrung. They have to go on looking in crystal balls and playing never-ending guessing games. All their thinking is based on "We'll press the button as soon as they attack us. But we press no buttons for other countries." And that's why they are weak. The Russians don't want a world war. There would be nothing left for the winners. Just a heap of radioactive rubble. You don't imagine Brezhnev wants to spend two years down an underground shelter from the moment when the KGB man comes in to tell him that they've won but there's nothing left, anywhere, including the Soviet Union. They want their cars and the pretty girls from the Bolshoi, and all the rest of it. They want power over people, not over cinders and corpses. And what do they lose by withdrawing from inside Israel or West Germany? Nothing. The prize isn't worth the risk. They'll withdraw, Herr Malik. They have no choice.' Meyer leaned forward, looking intently at Malik's face. 'They couldn't withdraw so readily if the threat was from a government. But from an anonymous, independent, uncaring and indifferent source. That's different.'

Malik stood up and walked slowly over to the window, pulling the curtains to one side, looking out to where the half-moon hung in the sky just above the tops of the forest trees. He could see the dark patches on the moon's surface that made it look much like the earth, and even its emptiness gave it a peace and serenity that its companion planet, Earth, seemed to lack. And intentionally or unintentionally Meyer had now handed over to him his can of writhing worms.

He would need time to sort out in his mind what to do. If Meyer's plan was exposed the Germans and the Israelis would be pariahs in the eyes of the whole world. Nobody would believe that they hadn't some knowledge of what was going on. But how did you get ten nuclear missiles into launching sites without anyone knowing? How did you get ten nuclear missiles, period? London, Bonn and Tel Aviv thought they had problems, but this thing was in a league of its own. Each would blame the other for lack of control and security. Each would suspect the other of knowing something. And each would certainly blame the other. London would blame both Bonn and Tel Aviv. After all, the missiles were on their territory.

And yet there was a real validity to Meyer's crazy thinking. It could have worked. But it wouldn't work now and it wouldn't ever be possible to try it again. He tried to imagine Jenkins' reaction when he told him. The hand reaching for the red phone marked 'Foreign Secretary', then the hesitation and withdrawal as he worked out the effect on his inevitable knighthood of being the bearer of such disastrous news. All that diplomatic dancing around in the cause of 'detente' would have been proved to be wasted effort. Down the pan with all the rest of the diplomatic charades that keep ordinary Russians, Britishers, and Israelis from knowing what was really going on behind the scenes. And Washington would go berserk at the thought of its two proteges, West Germany and Israel, going it alone and asking a cynical world to believe that the United States didn't know a thing about it. The words 'trust' and 'loyalty' would be in every White House statement for years. And after that the New York bar-mitzvahs would have to be held behind locked doors.

Malik turned to look at Meyer.

'Where did you get the missiles, Meyer?'

'They were missiles left behind awaiting transport when the Russians were kicked out of Egypt. The warheads were intact but parts of the guidance and firing equipment had been removed. They came under control of an Israeli army

166

unit during the 1973 war. I bought them clandestinely. I implied that I was acting for the government for special security reasons. We made the missing equipment parts ourselves. And the launchers.'

'Where, for God's sake?'

'When you break them all down into bits and pieces nobody except an expert could recognise what they are. The electronics were done at Rechmann's factory and the other parts were made all over Europe.'

'And you assembled them at the place in the Negev?'

'How did you know about that?' Then he nodded. 'You must have been the man in the jeep.'

'But who assembled them?'

'Engineers. They are used to working in odd places on secret devices for *Tsahal* . . . the army. We don't have to explain.'

'Have you got map references for the ten sites?'

'Yes.'

Malik took a deep breath. 'You'd better get some sleep, Meyer. You're going to have a busy time.'

'It will destroy West Germany and Israel if this comes out, Herr Malik. Nobody will believe that Bonn and Tel Aviv were not involved.'

Malik watched Meyer's face as he spoke. 'Maybe they are.'

'I swear to you that they are not. I swear on my life, on my loved ones who were murdered in the camps. Nobody knew but the seven of us.'

'I'll take you up to your room.'

Malik sat staring with his red-rimmed, tired eyes at the picture on the wall, trying to collect his thoughts. It was a painting of some mediaeval German town. He guessed it was either Göttingen or Hildesheim. He shook his head to clear it from such distractions.

There was a variety of moves he could make. He could take Meyer to London, report what he knew and leave them to sort it out. He could tell Fischer and let Bonn sort it out, and

167

leave London clean-handed. Or he could tell the Israelis and they could bring their guile to the problem. He tried not to let the other alternative gel in his mind.

If he landed the shambles in London's lap they would think he was out of his mind. And they would be right. The responsibility lay anywhere but in London. But hand it over to Bonn or Israel and it would be disaster. Once the bureaucrats were involved it would be leaked by somebody. Any newspaper in the Western world would pay a fortune for the story. And Moscow would pay even more. It would be the end of all credibility that Israel and West Germany could be trusted as responsible states. It could lead to the very situation that Meyer had forecast.

Malik put his head back in the armchair and closed his eyes to think. Two minutes later he was asleep.

From far away Malik could hear Fischer's voice and he clawed his way painfully out of the long tunnel of sleep. His eyes focused slowly on Fischer's face.

'Jake. Wake up, Jake.'

'What is it, Heinz? What time is it?'

'Drink this coffee; it'll help you wake up.'

Malik wiped his face and eyes with his hands then reached for the mug of coffee that Fischer held out for him. He had drunk half of it when Fischer said, 'We've got a problem, Jake.'

Malik didn't look up. 'What is it?'

'A man came to the door and asked for you.'

Malik frowned as he looked up at Fischer's face.

'But nobody knows I'm here.'

'This guy does, he asked for you by name. Jake Malik.'

'Who is he? What did you say?'

'I told him that he'd made a mistake and that there was nobody here of that name.'

'Then what?'

'He just said, "Tell him I'm waiting for him in my car." And he walked away. He's sitting in a white BMW outside the gate.'

'What does he look like?'

'Big-built. Tanned. He said his name was Johnny Morris.'

'Jesus. What the hell's he doing here?'

'Who is he?'

'He's the SIS guy in Tel Aviv. But how can he know I'm here?'

'Do you want me to get him in?'

'What's Meyer doing?'

'He's asleep. He's been tossing and turning but he isn't going to wake for a long while.'

Malik took a deep breath and struggled out of the armchair.

'Go and watch Meyer, Heinz. If he wakes and I'm still outside, keep him in his room . . . in fact keep him in his room anyway. I'll call you when I need you.'

Malik looked at his watch as he opened the door of the cottage. It was ten-fifteen and a sunny morning. He could just see the top of the white BMW as he walked down the flagged pathway to the wicket gate. He wondered how Johnny Morris could have traced him. How could he have known that he was in Germany, let alone Hamburg? Nobody knew but himself and Heinz.

As he walked across the grass verge to the car he saw the window being wound down and when he bent down to speak to Morris the shock was almost like a physical blow. It wasn't Johnny Morris. He recognised the face but he couldn't place it. The man in the driving seat had a Luger resting on his arm, its muzzle only just visible against his rough tweed jacket.

'Get in the back, Jake. It's loaded, and the safety catch is off.'

And then the voice, added to the face, took him back. Back to Johnny Morris's house that last night in Tel Aviv. And David Levy. The smiling, amiable David Levy. But his face looked grim enough now.

As Malik opened the rear door and clambered into the car Levy stepped out and joined him on the back seat, pulling the door to behind him.

'D'you remember me, Jake?'

'Yes.'

'Can we talk?'

'I guess I'm not in a position to stop you.'

Levy nodded. 'Where's Meyer? Is he in the house?'

'Who's Meyer?'

Levy's big brown eyes looked at Malik. 'We haven't got time for bullshit, Jake. You'd better level with me.'

'About what?'

'Jake. I'm liaison officer between Mossad and *Shin Beth*. Israel's a small country. You came in as a tourist and you had your girlfriend with you. Maybe you *were* on holiday but you were doing some ferreting at the same time. We picked up your name when you came through immigration. We did a bit of quick checking in London and confirmed that you had applied for leave and had been granted leave. But that could have been just SIS being efficiently deceptive. So we kept an eye on you.

'We watched you tagging Meyer and we watched you drive in the jeep off the Beersheba road into the desert. There was no way we could follow you without either you seeing us, or Meyer seeing both vehicles, so we waited for you to come back. Air Force electronic surveillance saw a chopper go up and land but that was about all we got.

'We also found out that Johnny Morris had been doing some prowling for you at the airport. We've been keeping close tabs on Amos Meyer ourselves, and lo and behold he pays a visit to Hamburg and books in at the Atlantic. And you and the German book in on the same floor. I took it you must be in cahoots with him on whatever he was up to. But no. An unhappy-looking Meyer, and you and your Kraut, troop out of the hotel and end up in this little hideaway.' Levy smiled grimly. 'I just want to know what's going on.'

'What else do you know?'

'A bit. Not much.'

'Tell me the bit.'

'Later my friend. You tell me your bit first.'

'What makes you think I should discuss anything I'm doing with a Mossad officer. What's it got to do with you?'

'Anything that involves an intelligence officer of another

170

country stalking an important Israeli citizen inside Israel and eventually kidnapping him in Germany concerns me.'

'Your superiors wouldn't be very happy if I told you what it's all about.'

'They'll be a damn sight more unhappy if you don't, my friend.'

'You said that Meyer is an important citizen. In what way is he important?'

'In one company or another he employs nearly a thousand people. Apart from that he has given money generously to a number of government sponsored projects. He has contacts with most of the top brass in government and politics. They wouldn't like him to get lost in the wash.'

'Can I ask you what rank you have in Mossad?'

'Yes. *Sgan Aloof.* Lieutenant Colonel.'

'What have you reported to your people?'

'Very little. There was nothing worth reporting until you laid hands on Meyer. Maybe you were both just old friends.'

'It wasn't an accident that you were at the Morrises' that night?'

'Not exactly. But Johnny knows I'm Mossad and we cooperate whenever we can. I'd told him we knew of an SIS guy on holiday in Tel Aviv. I told him your name. He said he knew you well and I said I'd like to meet you. He invited us over and said he'd try and contact you. It turned out that you contacted him first. So we met. He doesn't know that it was anything more than just me wanting to get to know one more SIS officer. He told me later that he wasn't even sure that you were a Jew, and he definitely didn't know that you'd been in a camp.'

'Would it be possible for you and me to talk off the record? Genuinely and permanently off the record?'

'It depends on what it's about, Jake.'

'What would make it possible?'

Levy shrugged. 'If it was some purely commercial jiggery-pokery that you were up to. Something that doesn't affect security. I'd even go as far as ignoring something that was more the concern of the police than Mossad.'

171

'What if it was political but it would be more embarrassing for Tel Aviv to know than not know?'

'There ain't no such scenario, Jake. We're used to being embarrassed. Everything we do or say angers somebody somewhere.'

'Tell me the other bit you know.'

'OK. We ran a photographic reconnaisance over the desert area we reckoned you'd been to. We discovered there was a secret plant there that we hadn't been informed about.'

'Making what?'

'High technology electronics for weapons and control systems.'

'What did you do about it?'

Levy shrugged. 'Nothing. We checked with the Defence Ministry. The plant was authorised by a senior official who had omitted to notify us. There are dozens of plants like that.'

'Who was the authorising official?'

'I don't remember.'

'Would you recognise the name if you heard it?'

'I guess so.'

'Was it Cohen?'

'No.'

'Was it Halberstein?'

'Yes. It was.' Levy looked at Malik. 'You'd better tell me what's going on, Jake.'

'Let's go back to the cottage.'

Levy smiled. 'No way, sweetheart. I didn't sit out here for the fresh air and the view.'

Malik turned away and looked out of the car windows. It was close and hot inside the car, and outside the tall trees of the forest looked cool in the hot summer sun. Two girls rode by on sleek ponies, an elderly German Shepherd tagging along behind them, and wood-pigeons cooed in the quiet of the forest. Malik turned to Levy.

'I've got a problem, Levy. If I do the wrong thing, your people in Tel Aviv are going to curse the day I was born. If I tell *you* it could maybe help avoid the problem. But if you were stupid it could make it even worse.'

'Maybe you've got an inflated idea of your own importance,

172

my friend. One SIS man and one Israeli businessman couldn't do anything that would make the Cabinet lose five minutes sleep.'

'What about five nuclear missiles in Israel and five in West Germany? All vectored on Soviet cities and all armed. And all in private hands.'

Levy's face showed first disbelief and then caution. He shook his head slowly. 'It's not possible.' But there was doubt in his eyes. 'You don't mean this, Jake. You're talking about some wild plan.'

'I'm not. They're in place. In secret, and in certain circumstances they'll be fired.'

'You're kidding.'

Malik shook his head. 'I'll do a deal with you, Levy. I'll tell you the whole thing provided that you guarantee that it's off the record. I'll tell you how I intend dealing with it. If you don't agree with my plan I'll come back with you to Tel Aviv and tell your people myself. And leave them to sort it out. They'll curse us both for telling them but there's no other way.'

'Who knows about all this?'

'I do. Fischer, my German; Amos Meyer; three other Germans and two other Israelis.'

'Who's in charge of your investigation? You or the Kraut?'

'Me.'

'How did you get involved in it?'

'The Germans in this crazy group used anti-Semitic daubings on synagogues to put up a smokescreen. I came here because London thought it was genuine.'

'Do London know what you've just told me?'

'No.'

'Why not?'

'I've only just discovered what it's all about.'

'When are you reporting to them?'

'Providing you'll cooperate I don't intend telling them. And I'd be grateful if you'd put that catch back on safety.'

Levy pushed the catch back to 'safety' and slid the Luger into his jacket pocket, butt first. For a few moments he sat thinking with his eyes closed. Then, sighing, he said, 'OK.

173

'I'll go along with your deal. I guess I don't have much choice. But if half what you say is true I don't think you and I can solve the problem.'

And as they sat there Malik told him everything he had learned that was relevant.

'How reliable is your Kraut?' Levy asked.

'He's a nice enough guy. Lisa, my girlfriend, is his sister. We're getting married when this lot's over.'

'He'll want to play it by the book. Germans always do. Orders are orders and all that crap.'

'Not these days. He's a very sensible guy.'

'What were you planning to do?'

'I've changed my thinking now you're here. Let's go back in the cottage and I'll put Heinz in the picture and we'll discuss my ideas.'

Heinz Fischer sat in silence while Malik told him what he had discovered, and what Meyer had told him. He saw the same look of disbelief and doubt give way to concern and anxiety. Fischer had asked sensible questions and when Malik had answered his questions Fischer asked what Malik was going to do next. Malik looked first at Levy and then back at Fischer.

'If we tell London or Bonn or Tel Aviv it will be a disaster for West Germany and for Israel. Do you both agree with that? Nobody would believe their denials of responsibility. It would seem too much, too outlandish, for them to have known nothing. Do you agree?'

'If you missed London out, maybe Bonn and Tel Aviv could bury it together,' said Levy.

'How? They've got to locate and destroy the missiles. Fill in the sites. And then they've got four Germans and three Israelis who still know all about it. And us of course. And who do they use to dismantle the weapons and fill the sites? It's going to take dozens of men. Men who'll talk. And the experts who disarm the missiles, they'll talk too.'

Fischer shrugged. 'Meyer's people did it, Jake.'

'It was done over many months, Heinz. Pieces were made all over Europe, not recognisable as to what they were or what they would be. The sites would be dug by farm hands

174

as underground stores. Maybe even casual labourers who didn't know or care why or what they were digging. Maybe one other person saw the final results and that was Loeb. And he's dead.

'If we tell Bonn and Tel Aviv it also means that it's on the record. It's official. It's recorded. There will be minutes of meetings. It will be there for all time.'

Fischer looked at Malik. 'So you mean we tell London only?'

'No. We don't tell London.'

Fischer frowned. 'So who do we tell?'

'We don't tell anybody.'

'You mean we leave these madmen to get on with it?'

'No. We make them undo what they've done.'

The two others sat digesting what Malik had said. Fischer looking unimpressed and Levy's face impassive. And as Malik sat watching them, waiting for an answer, the door opened and Meyer walked in, dishevelled and pale, his sparse hair askew, and his pale blue eyes trying to take in what he saw. Instinctively he looked at Malik and said, like a child. 'I've only just woken up.'

Malik nodded to Fischer. 'Take him, Heinz. Fix him something to eat and stick with him.'

Fischer led Meyer away and Malik realised that Meyer no longer looked like the wealthy and successful businessman, but just an old and weary Jew with bent shoulders and stumbling feet. When the door closed behind them Levy stood up.

'How about we walk out to the garden. We can talk easier there.'

'OK. Are you hungry?'

Levy shrugged. 'I was, but I'm not now.'

There was a wrought-iron garden bench painted white. Its decorations and curlicues uncomfortable to sit on but it was under a willow tree in the far corner of the lawn and they sat there together.

'I'd go along with some of your thinking, Jake. Not all of it.'

'What would you go along with?'

175

'That we don't tell London, Bonn or Tel Aviv. You're right about it leaking. It's inevitable. But I wouldn't leave it to these people to do it.'

'Why not?'

'It's a weak move. It leaves them in a morally strong position. It's kind of putting ourselves in with them. I wouldn't go along with that. And it leaves too many loose ends.'

'So who disposes of the hardware and fills in the sites?'

'The sites don't matter; they're just holes in the bloody ground. We can fill those in if we've got time but it's the missiles that have to be removed. Every trace of them.'

'And how do we do that?'

'Would you trust me to put a team together to do that?'

'I'd trust you, David. But how would we trust your team?'

'My people are used to doing as they're told without knowing what it's all about. It's the way we operate and the way we live. They wouldn't know the background. They wouldn't know a damn thing. I'd plan it with you and they'd do it. And that would be the end of it.'

'How long would it take?'

Levy closed his eyes and was silent for a few moments and then he said. 'The rest of today for you and me to work out the basics. A night for me to get back. A day or maybe two to bring my people together. A day to get back and say four days or five to do it. How long's that?'

'Say ten days.'

Levy sighed. 'It's too long, but that's it. How about it?'

'I wonder if Fischer will agree?'

'To hell with Fischer. You're in charge of your end, I'm in charge of mine. You don't ask him, you tell him.'

'But he's the one who's got to guarantee that the three Germans keep quiet.'

'I can deal with that too. If you want me to.'

'What do you mean?'

'You know what I mean, fella. You and I don't need to play games with one another. I'll deal with the two Israelis as well.'

'These people had the right idea you know, David. They

176

may be crazy but it could have worked. The idea wasn't crazy, it was putting it into practice that made it crazy. It was Meyer's idea. He talked the others into it. Would you kill Meyer too?'

'Sure I would. And I don't give a damn whether it would have worked or not. If it had been exposed by the KGB or anyone else you could have said '*shalom*', and our allies would have been among the first to send us down the pike. They may not be brilliant but it's for governments to decide about how we defend ourselves. It can be as dirty as you like and I'll do it. But it's not for private enterprise. That's anarchy gone mad.'

'I need time to think about it, David. But we haven't got time. How about we do it in stages. Deal with the hardware first and then work out what we do with the people.'

Levy shrugged. 'OK. If that's how you want it, I'll go along with it. But I shan't alter my views.'

'But I get final say on the people.'

'OK. Now let's talk about the first part. I think we've got to dump the stuff at sea. Somewhere pretty deep. Take them out whole, not in bits and pieces.'

'That means a ship or a plane.'

'It means a plane. It would take too long to get a ship up here. Where are the bloody things anyway?'

'Meyer has got a list of map references. One will be in Cologne, I guess, one in Hamburg, and I've no idea about the others.'

'Doesn't matter. The next thing is a place we can land a plane. A big one.'

'I'll have to get Heinz Fischer on to that. Maybe we could use a normal airport and crate the stuff like they did. But we don't have time to do it in pieces which was how they did it. Fischer could probably fiddle us through Customs.'

'OK. I'll give you three numbers where you can contact me in Israel. You'll have two days to fix something before I need to know. D'you speak Hebrew?'

'No.'

'We'll use English then, not German. And talk about pianos. And when you've settled on a place or an airport give me the map reference. Give it me the wrong way round. Eastings first and northings second. Minutes first degrees second. OK?'

'OK.'

'I'll get on my way. Give me some paper and I'll write out the phone numbers. And give me your number here and the number in Cologne. And don't tell Fischer more than you need to. He may be a lovely guy but he's still a Kraut, and now the chips are down he'll be looking out for them not us.'

Chapter 16

HEINZ FISCHER had reservations about the plan. But when Malik pressed him about which of the alternatives he preferred he shrugged hopelessly and agreed that Malik's was the only way. Malik gave him a list of things to check on while he talked to Meyer.

Meyer had shaved and tidied himself up and he looked in control of himself again as Malik pointed to a chair. When he had sat down Malik started.

'I want your cooperation, Meyer. I'm arranging for the missiles you and your collaborators have collected to be removed and destroyed. I'm doing this so that neither Bonn nor Tel Aviv learn of your crazy scheme, and are not involved. If you cooperate fully I shall bear that in mind when I consider how to deal with you and your colleagues. Do you understand?'

'I assure you that I only had . . .'

Malik held up his hand. 'Do you understand, Meyer?'

Meyer nodded, and said quietly, 'Yes, I understand. And I'll cooperate any way you want.'

Malik reached for the pad on the coffee table.

'Write down this list of questions I want answered.' He waited for Meyer to take a pen from his inside pocket. 'The map references of all the missiles. Dimensions and weight. The basic operations code and any relevant pre-firing procedures. Any code words you have with your friends. Any details necessary for disarming the missiles. And the names, addresses and telephone numbers of your group. All of them, Israelis and Germans. When you've done that, come and see me. I'll be with Herr Fischer in the next room.'

Meyer nodded and set the pad in front of him, sighing as he looked at the blank page.

179

It was almost an hour later when Meyer knocked on the door and came into the side room that Malik and Fischer were using as an office. Malik took the pages and said, 'Sit down, Meyer,' as he read the careful old-fashioned Gothic script. At the top of the second page was one heart-stopping figure and he closed his eyes for a moment before he read on. When he had read every page he turned to Meyer.

'The weight you give . . . twelve thousand kilos. That's for a single missile?'

'Yes. That's the loaded weight.'

'About ten tons?'

'Yes.'

Malik moved to stand up and then relaxed back onto the chair.

'Will your people carry out your orders?'

'Of course.'

'Without argument?'

'Will you let me explain it to them?'

'We'll see. Are they expecting to see you?'

'They were expecting me but I hadn't contacted them. They don't know I'm in Hamburg yet.'

'What about the two in Israel?'

'We don't have much contact unless we have a reason.'

'Is there anyone expecting to hear from you? Your family or business associates, maybe?'

'No. I often go away on business trips. I contact them when I get there.'

'Are you sure?'

'Yes. Why do you ask if I'm sure?'

'There was a photograph of a young woman in your room at the hotel. What about her?'

Meyer shook his head. 'There's no problem there.'

'Who is she?'

'She's dead. She was my wife. She died in Ravensbrück.'

Malik looked at Meyer's drawn face, at the trembling lips, and tried to think of something to say. Something real. But he knew there wasn't anything to say. Or maybe not enough time to say it in.

'You know that there's no point in trying to get away

180

or anything stupid like that? You know it's all over and finished?'

Meyer nodded. 'I recognise that.'

'I won't put you under guard then, Meyer. But keep to the house.'

'You think it was a mistake, my scheme?'

'It was crazy, my friend, not just a mistake.'

'But you understand?'

For a moment Malik hesitated, then, sighing deeply, he said softly, 'Yes. I understand.'

He phoned the Tel Aviv number that Levy had given him and left his name, and asked for Levy to phone him as soon as he arrived. It was four o'clock in the morning when Levy called.

'What's the matter, Jake?'

'We can forget the plane. Those things weigh ten tons.'

'That's OK.'

'Each.'

'Jesus. That's different.'

'Have you got a boat up this way?'

'I've no idea. I'll have to check. But even if there is it won't be easy.

'Why not?'

'Too many documents, too many formalities.'

'We can cope with those at this end.'

'Let me do some checking first. I'll phone you back.'

Fischer had shaken him awake and it was ten o'clock.

'Tel Aviv on the phone for you, Jake. They're hanging on.'

Levy had sounded dog-tired but he had done his checking. There were two Israeli merchant ships in dock at Hamburg. One waiting for a cargo of steel tubing and engineering spares, the other looking for a cargo before taking on ballast. They were negotiating a mixed cargo from Rotterdam. He was going to have a couple of hours' sleep and then fly straight back to Hamburg.

Chapter 17

THEY SAT at the table looking at the maps. Large scale maps of Hamburg, Hanover and Cologne, a map covering the whole of northern Germany, and a map of the Harz mountains.

Malik looked at Levy and Fischer. 'Any views on where we go first?'

Levy shrugged. 'I don't think it matters. Maybe Hamburg last because we've got two to deal with here. I think it's more a matter of choosing the right site to do our first lift. It'll be experience for the others. The easiest one first, I'd say.'

'Heinz?'

Fischer looked embarrassed. 'I'd like to leave the Cologne one way down the list because so many people could recognise me. And Rechmann's going to be a permanent problem if he knows I know what he's been up to.'

'Maybe it's better if you don't get involved in Cologne. Or maybe best of all if you leave it to me and Jake,' said Levy.

Fischer's face was impassive but his voice was harsh and touched with suppressed anger. 'It's up to Jake.'

Malik shook his head. 'We're going to need your help, Heinz. I'll want you riding with every load. We could be stopped by the transport police. But we can keep you away from Rechmann. He doesn't ever need to know that you were involved.'

Levy looked directly at Fischer. 'How about you check on Meyer for ten minutes or so and let Jake and me have a chat?'

Fischer's face was flushed with anger as he turned to look at Malik.

'Is that what you want?'

Malik nodded. 'Maybe. Ten minutes will be long enough.'

As the heavy door slammed to behind Fischer, Malik said, 'You seem to go out of your way to antagonise him, David. He's part of the operation. He's entitled to be in on our discussions.'

'He's not, Jake. Your operation is over. We're in a different ball-game now and the less he knows the better.'

'Why?'

'He's a German, for God's sake. I wouldn't trust any German as far as I could chuck one of Rechmann's pianos. What he doesn't know he can't talk about.'

'But his country is just as much involved as yours.'

'That's rubbish, Jake. The West Germans are vulnerable to the Soviets but they're not surrounded by fanatical enemies. France and Holland and Austria aren't just waiting for the moment when they can slaughter every German. Even the bloody Russians are more interested in territory than killing Germans.' He banged his fist on the table. 'The Arabs don't just want territory and you know it. They want to kill the lot of us. I don't want to let the bastards have even the slightest excuse. And I don't want Israel left without a friend in the world because a stupid oaf like Meyer fancies playing God. He may be a Jew and an Israeli, but for me he's an enemy, whatever his motives were. All I care about is putting the clock back so that it can be as if this crazy dream of Meyer's had never happened.'

'Antagonising Fischer won't help do that.'

Levy sighed. 'Maybe you're right, but I want you to know how I stand on all this.'

'OK, David, but don't rock the boat. Until this is all cleared up I'm still in charge.'

Malik was well aware that Levy's shrug cancelled out his nod and that he had only reluctantly gone along with his attitude.

Fischer had not come back after half an hour and Malik had found him playing chess with Meyer and ostentatiously more interested in the game than in joining him and Levy.

When the three of them were round the table again Malik reckoned it was time to make it clear that he was in charge.

'We'll do the site at Hildesheim first. Then Goslar.' He

looked at Levy. 'Do you think we could risk doing two at the same time?'

Levy shook his head. 'No. It's too risky. We need to be in and out of each site as quickly as possible.'

'OK. After Goslar, Cologne; and then we come up to Hamburg.'

Fischer said, 'Where are we going to store the first three while we are getting the last two?'

'We can rent warehouse space at the docks.'

Fischer shook his head. 'No way. There are regular checks of all cargo left in store, by the dock police and the Kripo anti-terrorist squads.'

Malik half-smiled at Fischer's proof of them needing him. 'Where do you suggest?'

'Hire warehouse space outside the city. A furniture depository or maybe an outbuilding on a farm. There are plenty of empty barns at this time of the year before they get the harvest in. We aren't even concerned with protection against the weather. We can just tarpaulin them.'

Levy nodded. 'Could you recce a place for us, Heinz?'

'Yes. How soon and for how long, and what cover story? What do we say is in them?'

Malik shrugged. 'Just heavy machinery. Printing machinery would do fine.' He turned to look at Levy. 'What sort of people have you got in your team?'

'Two carpenters. Two electronics experts. A welder. Four precision engineering experts. An armourer. And the rest are just strong lads.'

'How many altogether?'

'Twenty-two. And one girl. A radio expert. I've borrowed four sets from our people in . . .' Both Malik and Fischer noticed the hiatus. '. . . our people who are over here for other reasons.'

Malik smiled. 'OK. Heinz, you get moving on storage, and maybe before that you could hire the transporters and the hoists.' Malik turned to Levy. 'Have your men got licences to drive articulateds and operate hoists?'

Levy nodded. 'German documents. Current, and almost genuine.'

Malik turned to Fischer. 'How long will it take you, Heinz?'

'The rest of today. Maybe tomorrow. Depends on what luck I have.'

'I want you to go over all our documents before we start. Check that we've got everything we need, and that it's in order.'

Fischer stood up, nodded to the other two and left them.

They started just after midnight and were on the autobahn in less than half an hour. Levy was in the white Mercedes convertible with two of his men, behind the BMW driven by Fischer with Meyer, Malik and the Israeli signals girl as passengers. Next came the two long mobile homes, and they were followed by the two yellow articulated transporters and finally the two mobile hoists, lagging well behind because of their speed restrictions.

They pulled into the lay-by just before Fallingbostel to wait for the hoists to catch up. By the time they were at the northern outskirts of Hanover the dawn clouds were lifting and there was a pale hint of sun on the horizon. There was a heat mist rising from the fields as they turned off the autobahn for Hildesheim, and when they pulled into the lay-by just outside the town the sun was hot on Malik's back as he stood beside the road drinking coffee from one of the big flasks. Levy and Fischer were with him and Meyer stood alone a few yards away. As Malik tossed away the last drops of coffee from the enamelled mug he beckoned to Meyer who hurried over.

'You're quite sure that he'll be there, Meyer?'

'Quite sure. I told him it was vitally important.'

'Where are we meeting him?'

'At the brickworks.'

'What time?'

'I told him to be there at eight o'clock.'

'Alone?'

'Yes. The workpeople are not there on Saturdays. Just a watchman and a dog. Herr Hoffman will have dismissed him for the day.'

185

'You remember what you tell him?'

'Yes. I understand. I shan't give any explanation.'

'And you make clear to him that if he talks to anyone his life is in danger.'

'He won't talk, I assure you. None of them will. They trust me.' He looked with his pale blue eyes at Malik's face. 'Even when I am betraying them they trust me.'

Malik opened his mouth to reply but decided to stay silent. They drove through Hildesheim and took the road to Bad Salzdetfurth, but after two kilometres they turned into a side road and the BMW left the main convoy and went on for another two kilometres. And then they saw the buildings, and the big sign that said: *Siegelei und Baustoff Werke Hoffman*.

Malik got out with Meyer and they walked across the dusty area in front of the big double gates. As they approached the long brick building a door opened and a small man came out. His head almost completely bald but held stiffly erect. He wore a formal black suit, and despite the heat of the day, a waistcoat with a gold chain looped across its front.

He held out his hand to Meyer. 'Good to see you, Amos. You've brought a fine day with you. Let's go inside.'

Hoffman glanced at Malik then turned and led them into a narrow corridor. There was a small office at the far end and when they were all inside Meyer wasted no time.

'I've had to alter our plans, Johann. I've brought my people to remove our . . . our weapon.'

Hoffman frowned. 'But why, Amos, why?'

'It's only a temporary move, my friend. I can't say more at the moment.'

Hoffman half turned, shoving some papers aside on his desk before he sat on it. He pulled out a handkerchief and wiped the sweat from his brow.

'I don't understand, Amos. The calculations, the fine adjustments . . . all wasted. Are you sure it's necessary?'

'Quite sure. We can't waste time, my friend. My companion here is responsible for the removal operation. Take us over to the site.'

Hoffman shrugged submissively and raised himself from the desk. 'I'll open the gates and we can go in your car.'

186

'Open them both, Johann, so that the other vehicles can come inside.'

When both the big gates had been pushed aside Malik told Fischer to walk back to the convoy, get them inside the plant and close the gates.

Malik drove the BMW. Past row on row of circular kilns and tall chimneys. Hoffman gave him new directions from time to time until they were almost a kilometre from the entrance. They came to a fence of tall wooden posts with barbed wire laced between them. Long, close horizontal strands carefully criss-crossed up to a wide metal gate.

Hoffman got out and they watched as he unlocked a series of locks and bolts, struggling to open the heavy gate. A notice said simply: *Forschungs Zone – Eintritt Verboten.*

As they walked inside Malik could hear the rumble of the convoy in the distance. A hundred metres or so from the metal gates were three low structures. Too low for a man to enter. They followed Hoffman to the furthest of the three and then Malik saw the metal steps leading down into the ground.

The locks on the steel door were not elaborate, just two long metal bars with hasps and padlocks. As he walked down the steps and through the open door Malik felt the cool draught from an air-conditioner and then Hoffman switched on the fluorescent lights.

It was an almost incredible sight. The long, comparatively narrow underground room. Tiled like a hospital operating theatre. Dustless, stark and silent, except for the faint beat of an electric motor. And the missile itself looked no more elaborate or dangerous than some giant cigar as it lay cradled in the launcher.

The casing of the missile was olive-green except for the final stage at its tip which was matt black. At its base were the three funnelled exhausts all set at the same angle, but slightly splayed; their metal shrouds looked like untreated gun-metal. The launching cradle went from a large tripod-like front structure to a channel just wide enough to hold the last stage of the rocket. Behind was a huge pit, whose outer face seemed to be clad with baked clay or firebrick, and on a metal trolley linked with heavy cables was a panel of instruments, with a

187

red-figured digital display, its last two digits moving so fast that they were almost unreadable. And two raised buttons. One white and one red.

Then David Levy and two of his men in white overalls clambered down into the chamber. Levy tried to hide his reaction but it wasn't easy. The rocket had a kind of beauty. In its shape, in its size and its inevitability. It was hard to actually encompass its destructive power.

Meyer took Levy and his two men to the control panel and they stood there talking, nodding and pointing until eventually Levy turned and nodded to Malik who walked out of the emplacement back to the BMW and poured himself another coffee. As he stood there, mug in hand, he looked across the flat landscape of the brick-field. It stretched out on every side as far as the eye could see. Still and silent, small wisps of blue-grey smoke winding from the cones of the drying-kilns to be quickly lost in the hazy blue of the summer sky.

It was like the landscape on another planet, a setting for some science-fiction film. And in that vault-like underground emplacement, that smooth surrealist tube, so beautifully made, so precisely engineered. The piece of weaponry they called an SS-14. He had seen the designation in reports and evaluations, and had read details of its destructive power; but weaponry and war were not part of his service life. But there was something especially horrific about a nuclear missile and he wondered if that was the reason that NATO always gave them those jolly code names that they normally gave to Soviet nuclear weapons. Names like Scapegoat, Scamp; Scarp and Scrooge; Sand and Frog. Surface-to-surface nuclear missile number 14. Just two letters and a number, in a combination that made even the missile experts lower their voices. It was like a rare stamp whose reproduction every philatelist knew by heart but had never seen. A Shakespeare Folio, too precious in its air-conditioned vault to be seen by others than its guardian. And all you had to do was press the white button and the red button at the same time. And minutes later, in this particular case, the city of Kiev would shudder for a micro-second in silence before one glowing

188

mushroom cloud grew out of another, again and again as the molecules of half a million human bodies mingled with the molecules of the Cinerama on Rustaveli Ulitsa and Yaroslav the Wise's Golden Gate.

It was an hour before Levy came out, and as he stood with Malik, smoking a cigarette, he seemed full of confidence.

'We've got all the electrical connections unhooked and they're dismantling the guidance system and that's the whole damn thing disarmed.' He turned to look back at the equipment. 'We're going to have to take the roof off. It won't be too bad here but it's going to mean hiring a digger for the others if there's ten foot of earth on top.'

'How long will it take to finish this one?'

Levy looked at his watch. 'We'll have it out in three hours, maybe four. But my carpenters will need at least five hours to crate it.'

'Would it help to dismantle one of the stages?'

'Yes. But we don't know enough to risk it. Meyer destroyed the drawings that were made and the circuit diagrams. I'd rather take it as it is.'

'Is there anything I can do to help?'

Levy smiled. 'Yes. Look like you think I know what I'm doing . . . but say a little prayer as well.'

As Levy walked over to his men Malik knew that although the Israeli was no diplomat he was as much on top of the removal operation as any layman could be.

He turned the car so that he could sit and watch Levy's men hacking at the roof and sides of the emplacement. Despite their overalls they still looked like soldiers, and Malik wondered how Levy could lay his hands on so many men at such short notice. But that was typically Mossad. SIS would have needed God knows how many committee meetings to get a couple of men let alone a couple of dozen.

There had been no break for a meal. Fischer had driven to Hildesheim and come back with the big coffee flasks refilled and boxes of sandwiches. The men ate as they worked.

The shadows were long when Levy walked over to the car and bent down to talk to Malik.

'We're practically finished, Jake, but I don't want to take

189

the last layer off while it's still light. There are too many planes going over. The crates are ready except for fitting up, so I'm going to stand my boys down for a couple of hours sleep. Then we can work through the night at Goslar if it looks like being necessary. OK?'

'That's fine, David. They're a good team.'

Levy smiled. 'These guys have just come back from putting a tunnel under the Nile. Half-way across.'

'What's it for?'

'An electronic listening post. We can even pick up the sound of a rubber dinghy on the far side. Even a swimmer. I'd better go and stand them down.'

Before the team was stood down the two mobile hoists had been manoeuvred into place alongside the emplacement, and alongside them was one of the transporters with the framework of the crate already in place.

Meyer came back to sit in the car with Malik. Subdued and unhappy as he saw his handiwork reduced almost to rubble. Ten minutes later the older man was asleep, his head back on the seat of the car, his hand supporting his cheek, the tattoo scar clearly visible, the skin puckered like a deflated child's balloon. Despite the tan his face looked older than his actual years, and it reminded Malik of his father's face when he was dying. All hope gone, all courage gone, the open, wet-lipped mouth, the hollow cheeks and the ragged breathing. He shuddered at the memory and got quickly out of the car.

It was after midnight when they were finished and Malik decided that it was better to leave the loaded transporter inside the locked gates of the brickfield rather than take it on to Goslar. A driver was left with it and one of the radios. The rest of the convoy headed for Goslar, just over 50 kilometres to the south-east of Hildesheim.

Malik stopped the convoy ten kilometres before Goslar and checked the map with Meyer. A string of heavy vehicles rumbling through the mediaeval town in the early hours of a Sunday morning would fetch out half the population to check that it wasn't the East Germans coming over the border. But there was no way of avoiding the town completely. They took the outer road and went through two at a time at ten-minute intervals and turned up the steep road to Ramseck.

The gate in the stone wall was already wide open but although it was wide Malik guessed that the bigger vehicles would find it difficult to turn in because the road was too narrow to allow a wide turn to the gate.

Gerichtspräsident Gustav Lemke owned an 800-acre estate on the stark mountainside. Farmers had long ago given up trying to eke out a living with sheep on the craggy outcrops of granite with its thin bracken-covered top-soil. But its woods and streams could support roe deer and rabbits and a host of game birds which enabled the judge to indulge in his favourite sport, and to glean a regular addition to his State pension by letting the estate to a sporting syndicate for half the year. The big house that had once been the owner's home stood gaunt, its empty windows sprouting willow-herb, its walls half collapsed, covered in lichen and mosses. The retired judge lived in the stone-built lodge just inside the gate.

At three in the morning the old man was sleeping soundly and the convoy passed the lodge without waking him. It was seven-thirty before Malik and Meyer saw the closed curtains pulled aside as the judge looked down, surprised, at the BMW parked in his drive.

As he stood at the open door in his dressing-gown Malik was aware of the man's inherent dignity. He was tall and thin, his feet in sandals and for a moment he didn't seem to recognise Amos Meyer.

'Amos, my boy, what brings you here?'

'Can I come inside, Gustav, with my friend?'

'Of course. Come along in.'

They followed him into a pleasant room. Flowers in brass vases, chintz-covered armchairs and a cat asleep on the windowsill.

'Shall I make us all some coffee, Amos? Or do you want to talk first?'

'I've come to remove the . . . apparatus, Gustav. There is a problem It will have to be postponed.'

191

'What kind of problem could make that necessary, Amos?'

'I don't feel it would be wise to explain. I just wanted to let you know.'

Lemke pointed a long finger at Malik.

'Who is this? Is he your problem?'

'His name is Jacob. No, he's not the problem. He is a friend.'

'But how on earth can you remove our little thing. I would take dozens of men. And machinery.'

'We have that, Gustav. I've sent them up to the old house. We've been here for some time. I've told them what to do. They will have already started work.'

'So much effort, so much money, all gone to waste, my old friend?'

'Let's leave it, Gustav. I want you to forget all about it, as if it never happened.'

The old man leaned back in his chair. 'It seems a long time ago when you first came to see me. All those long talks and subtle questions to test me out. And then our meetings. You and the others. Seven men for peace. To prevent another holocaust. What will prevent it now?'

Malik said softly. 'The weapons, all of them, *are* the holocaust, Judge. The new holocaust. First the millions of Jews were killed. Coldly, economically by the standards of the day. Some buildings, a bit of barbed wire, a few sub-machine guns and just a little Zyclon B gas. Only three minutes of gas because prussic acid crystals are expensive. And those who aren't dead in three minutes will be dead in ten.

'And now we have nuclear weapons. They have no point except to kill hundreds of thousands of people in a second or two. If that wasn't their only purpose they might just as well be filled with ice cream. They are not even weapons of war. They won't kill soldiers. They can only be used to kill innocent people, civilians. In their beds, sleeping or making love, shopping, playing music, playing with children. People are the targets, not tanks and guns. The only difference this time is that they won't only be Jews.'

The old man pursed his lips, looking down at his gnarled

192

bony hands as he held them together, then he looked at Malik.

'I'm afraid I've forgotten your name.'

'Jacob. Jake.'

'I gather that you're a pacifist, Jake? Anti-war?'

Malik smiled. 'Even Brezhnev is anti-war. No, I'm not a pacifist. Just a war-preventer if it's possible.'

The old man's hand slapped his bony knee.

'Exactly. That's exactly what we were too. Preventers. Not aggressors.'

Malik shook his head slowly. 'I want you to forget all about it, Judge. Your friends' lives could be in danger.'

'You mean that seriously?'

'Indeed I do.'

Lemke sighed and looked at Meyer. 'Let me get us some coffee.'

Half an hour later Malik and Meyer were standing with Levy and Fischer. Great mounds of earth rose up the stone sides of the building and a dozen men were smashing concrete with huge sledgehammers.

Levy wiped the sweat from his eyes. 'We could have done with pneumatic drills but it's going to be easier than the first one. We disarmed it in twenty minutes and it suddenly dawned on me that after that we don't need to give it cotton-wool treatment. We'll have it uncovered and out in a couple of hours. But I think my guys are gonna need a day's rest before we tackle the next one.'

'We'll all go back to Hamburg. Store the two crates and leave one of your men to keep an eye on them. Then Heinz and Meyer and I will go down to Cologne and get things ready.'

'They can take my electronics guys and the armourer. They can disarm it, and then all we'll have to do is get the bastard out.' Levy looked at Meyer. 'What's the construction in Cologne, Meyer?'

'The same as here. Earth over concrete. It's the same in Hamburg.'

'Great. We know what we're doing now. If we had to pre-serve them it would have taken at least three days apiece.'

But Levy had been over-optimistic. It was eleven o'clock that night before the crate was on the transporter. The weight of one of the hoists under load had caused it to break through the foundations of the derelict house so that its rear wheels were wedged into a cellar in the basement. It had taken careful manoeuvring with the second transporter to tow it out without collapsing the hoist completely.

Fischer had driven down to Goslar for extra food but the best he had been able to do on a Sunday was cartons of cold cooked sausages and two dozen loaves of bread with two kilos of butter. But there had been no complaints from the hungry men.

They had to back all the vehicles down the steep path as there was no room for even the cars to turn, and it had taken two hours before they were heading back to Hildesheim and the autobahn.

Fischer had gone with Levy to guide them to the warehouse he had rented for them just outside Hamburg at Lohbrügge.

It was dawn when they arrived but the sky was overcast and as Fischer took the padlocks off the high wooden doors it was beginning to drizzle. The ramshackle building had lain empty for two years but it was high enough and big enough to take all the vehicles. Levy had insisted that the crates were unloaded before they left for the city centre. He was sending his men to a hotel to make sure they were properly rested for the longer journey down to Cologne. Fischer, Meyer and Malik were flying down on the early plane.

Fischer had taken a taxi home and Malik had taken a bus to the city centre and walked to the flat with Amos Meyer. Meyer was no problem now, he wouldn't do anything stupid, and he needed all the sleep he could get. He looked exhausted and near the end of his tether.

Chapter 18

MALIK HAD sat with Meyer as he phoned Rechmann's home but was told that he was already at the works. An hour later they drove into the works and the doorkeeper pointed to the visitors' parking spaces. Malik parked alongside a big black Mercedes that he guessed was Rechmann's.

The receptionist phoned through Meyer's name to Rechmann's secretary and almost immediately Rechmann himself came into the reception area. The smile fading from his face as he saw that Meyer was not alone. But his outstretched hand was too far committed to withdraw.

'Well this is a surprise, Herr Meyer.' Rechmann turned to look at Malik. 'Franz Rechmann, glad to meet you.'

'This is my friend Jacob, Franz. Could you spare us a little of your time?'

'Certainly. Let's go into the boardroom – or would you prefer my office?'

'I think your office, Franz.'

As they walked down the corridor Rechmann glanced at Malik. 'You know, I'm sure I've met you before. Are you musical at all?'

'I'm afraid not.'

'You live in Cologne?'

'No. I spend most of my time overseas.'

'Ah well. It's a small world,' he said briskly. 'And getting smaller every day.'

Malik remembered what Lisa had once said about Rechmann. That despite the fact that he had made a fortune from making pianos he couldn't tell Tchaikowsky from Delibes unless it was printed in the programme, and that she and her friends sometimes had small bets on how many clichés he would use in an hour.

195

Rechmann's office was modern and well-furnished, Swedish style, and he sat down briskly at his desk pointing to the two green leather chairs in front of him.

'Now, Amos. What can I do for you?'

'I need to go to your estate, Franz. It may take a couple of days, starting tomorrow. Can you keep your people away for that time?'

Rechmann leaned back in his chair. The astonished businessman, thought Malik. The negotiator doing his stuff. Shocked at the suggestion of an extra discount. He looked as though he had done it a hundred times before. He glanced briefly at Malik and then back at Meyer.

'I've misunderstood, Amos. Obviously I've misunderstood.'

'No, Franz. You haven't.'

'Isn't this something you and I should discuss in private?'

'I'm afraid there's nothing to discuss. The decision has been taken. I can't delay.'

'Has it been . . .' He looked at Malik. He smiled a businessman's smile. Mouth but not eyes. 'I wonder if I could ask you to step outside for a couple of minutes while two old friends have a chat?'

'I'm afraid not, Herr Rechmann. Herr Meyer is acting under my orders.'

Rechmann leaned forward his elbows on his desk with overtly feigned deference.

'Tell me more. Who *are* you, for instance?'

'You don't need to know who I am, Herr Rechmann, and this is not a business negotiation, it's a matter of life and death. It could be *your* death if you waste time.'

Rechmann shifted the leather blotter to one side, trying not to look concerned about the threat. Malik could see that he was concerned all right. But he'd got the problem of how to back down and not lose face.

Malik said softly, 'Herr Meyer assured me that you were entirely reliable, Herr Rechmann, and entirely loyal to your friends. They have cooperated with him without question. He is relying on you for all the assistance he needs.'

Rechmann stared back at Malik, his fingers drumming on

the blotter. His head nodding as if he were digesting and agreeing with Malik's comments. Finally he turned to Meyer.

'Just tell me how I can help, Amos. I'm at your disposal.'

'I need the combination, Franz, and nobody in that area for tomorrow and the next day.'

Rechmann smiled benignly. 'It's a letter combination-lock, my friend. A five-letter word dear to my heart.' He smiled. 'And to yours.'

Malik guessed what it was immediately. With a mind like Rechmann's it was obvious. But he sat silently. To say it would rob the actor of his punch-line.

Meyer shook his head. 'Tell me, Franz.'

'M-E-Y-E-R. A good Jewish name, eh?' He smacked his hand on his desk, beaming. Then he stood up and walked round his desk, putting an arm round Meyer's shoulders. 'And as from six o'clock this evening the whole area will be clear of staff. For two whole days. How's that?'

'Thank you, Franz. That's fine.'

Rechmann walked with them back to reception. The businessman once more. An awkward negotiation successfully concluded. Nothing given away that didn't have to be given, and now back to the grindstone. Or words to that effect, thought Malik.

They went out to Wahn in the afternoon to pick up Levy's three men, and hired them a car at the airport. Meyer was going with them out to Rechmann's place at seven and Levy would book them into the Dom.

Malik phoned Lisa and Heinz answered the phone. He said that Lisa was not at home. Almost peremptorily he had suggested that Malik phone the music school. He hadn't bothered to give Malik the number and had hung up before he could ask.

He eventually contacted her at the school and arranged to pick her up at six o'clock when her classes finished.

'Why didn't you want to see me at home, Jake?'

'No particular reason, I just wanted to be on our own.'

And her heart sank because she knew instinctively that for

197

the first time since she had known him he had told her a half-truth or maybe a lie. Suddenly she was an outsider, kept out of his private thoughts.

'How's your work going?'

'What made you ask that?'

She smiled. 'Mainly because I wondered how long it would be before we are married.'

'You said "mainly". What was the other reason?'

She reached out and picked a daisy, looking at it before she looked back at Malik.

'Heinz seems terribly on edge since you both got back. I asked him how you were and he just snapped my head off and told me to ask you myself. I asked him if anything was wrong between you two and he said something odd.'

'What did he say?'

'He said, "Jake's treating me as a German; maybe he'll do the same to you one day."'

Malik sighed and was silent for a moment, then he said, 'It isn't that, Lisa. It's just that I'm in charge of this particular operation and Heinz doesn't like some of my decisions. I think he resents that it's got to a stage when I have to give orders and he has to carry them out whether he agrees or not.'

'It's not like Heinz.'

'It will be over soon; meantime he'll just have to put up with it like the rest of us.'

'Even you sound cross with me, Jake.'

He smiled. 'I'm sorry, sweetie. I don't mean to. I was looking forward to seeing you.'

'Let's forget about Heinz and his problems and enjoy the nice evening.'

'Tell me what you've been doing.'

'Practising, giving some lessons. We had a musical evening you would have liked. Brahms and Schubert. We went over to the Rechmanns' one evening to hear his new hi-fi.'

Malik looked away. 'What's he like . . . Rechmann?'

'I like him. He's a bit stiff. Very much the gentleman. He ought to have lived in the Weimar Republic. I don't think he likes the modern world too much.'

'What's his family like?'

'His wife's very different. A great charmer. She sings very well – musical comedy stuff. She's old-fashioned too in a different sort of way. Mildly flirtatious and she must have been terribly pretty when they married.'

'Children?'

'Two daughters. One married and very happy. And one unmarried and very happy. Daddy's girl.' She laughed. 'No. That's a bit unfair. She just gets more attention because she's still at home. They were both very good parents. Kind, and sensibly indulgent. You must meet them.'

'What would you have done if you hadn't met me?'

'How do you mean? I don't understand.'

'What kind of man would you have married? What would you have done with your life?'

She sat in silence, one slim finger probing at the buckle on her shoe.

'I don't know, Jake. I didn't have any sort of plans. Life just went on. I guess things happened to me rather than me making them happen. Somebody might have come eventually whom I'd marry, but it wouldn't have been like with us.'

'What would be different?'

'Oh everything. He would have been somebody from the family's sort of background. Pleasant and routine would have been the best I could hope for.'

'And now?'

She smiled. 'My love, even you must know in your heart that you're one of a kind. You landed on me like an unexploded bomb that not only exploded but has kept on exploding. And I guess you'll go on being like that. It will take longer than we both live for me to peel all the onion skins off you and find what's really inside. When I first knew you that's what I wanted to do. But not any more. I'm just happy to be with you however you are and whatever you do.'

'What would I have to do to stop you loving me?'

'There isn't anything. If you did something I would know that it had to be done.'

'If I say I love you more than I've ever loved anyone it's not much of a compliment because you know that I've never

199

loved anyone even slightly, ever. Except for my father, and that was a poor sort of love when I look back on it.'

She reached out her hand for his. 'I feel so safe and secure with you, Jake. Even my father doesn't seem quite the same since you came along.'

Malik leaned back, resting his head on her shoulder.

'What shall I do for work when we're married?'

'Won't you carry on with your police job?'

Malik turned up his face to look at Lisa. 'I'm not a policeman, Lisa. I'm an Intelligence officer. I work for MI6. I wouldn't be able to stay on.'

'Why not?' She said softly.

'If we're going to live in Israel there's no chance of me getting a posting there. They wouldn't say so but they wouldn't trust a Jew doing their work in Israel. And if MI6 people marry foreigners there's always a suspicion about them. Put those two factors together and I might as well resign. I'd get a bit more than half-pension so we wouldn't starve.'

'How would you feel about giving up your work?'

He smiled up at her. 'Perfectly happy provided I had you.'

She kissed him gently on the forehead, one hand touching his cheek.

'What would you like to do in Israel?'

'I've no idea. I've no qualifications.'

'You could teach violin, you could teach English.'

'I'm not a musician, honey. I can play the fiddle but it's by ear not from music and I've no teaching qualifications for either music or English. Let's not worry about it. I'll get something.'

'When do you think we shall be able to get married?'

'I'd guess in a month. Six weeks at the outside.'

'Will I be able to see you tomorrow?'

'I don't think so, I think I may have to go back to Hamburg. Wherever I am I'll phone you as often as I can. Let's go and eat somewhere, it's getting late.'

When they were driving back towards the city she put her hand on his leg. 'Heinz told me you'd had one of your nightmares again. Was it because of your work?'

'I guess so. It's hard to say.'

'I love you, Jake. I love you so much.'

He smiled. 'I love you too, sweetie.'

David Levy had had a brainwave and hired a 35-mm film camera, an Arriflex with a lighting set-up, and when the convoy rolled through the gates at Rechmann's estate and up to the site at the edge of the woods they had some semblance of a film unit on location. It also gave them an excuse for using lights if they needed to work in the dark.

Rechmann himself drove up to the site to watch. He didn't stay long and he didn't speak to any of them, not even Meyer. He just watched, his face disapproving, his hands in his pockets as he rocked gently on his heels as the mounds of rich soil built up around the pit. He shook his head slowly as he walked back to his car. A sane man witnessing lunatics at their work, vandals destroying a work of art.

Levy was standing with Malik as Rechmann watched the work going on, and when Rechmann went back to his car Levy said, 'How have these birds been taking it, Jake?'

Malik shrugged. 'Mild protests but not for long. Meyer was obviously the organiser. They were willing collaborators but I'd guess that now the chips are down they're glad to be out of it. They're not young and they've got other things to put their minds to.'

'How did Rechmann behave?'

'He was the toughest so far. Not really tough. Just self-important and faintly bloody-minded.' Malik smiled. 'Nothing to worry about. He took maybe ten minutes where the others took five.'

'Do you think they'll talk?'

'God knows. That's the thing that worries me. It's why I want the bloody things out of the way quickly. A hole in the ground doesn't prove anything and we could deny the whole thing. Anyway there's no reason for them to talk. They've nothing to gain.'

'I wouldn't trust Rechmann, he looks a tricky bastard.'

'How long will you need here, David?'

'I'd say we could be gone soon after lunch. We know what we're doing now so it's much easier. And it's good loam here, none of those bloody rocks. Do you want us to go straight back to Hamburg?'

'Yes. The sooner the better.'

Levy smiled. 'You're getting edgy, my boy.'

Malik shrugged. 'No wonder. If something went wrong now it would be worse than if we had just left the damn things under the ground. Nobody outside would have known anything about them. But if we were exposed right now I can't bear to think of the shambles there'd be.'

'Don't worry. Another two or three days and we'll be done.'

Chapter 19

THEY SET off for Hamburg just on midnight and drove for five hours with only two short breaks. They were just over half way but it was obvious that the pace was beginning to tell even on Levy's tough men, and they decided to rest until they could drive in daylight. It was late the next morning when they pulled up outside the warehouse at Lohbrügge.

Malik went with David Levy to look over the ship in the afternoon. She was moored down-river at Schulau, a drab-looking vessel with her name painted in white on her heavy bows – *Maresha*. The birthplace of the prophet Micah.

She was riding high in the water, tugging sporadically at her warps around the bollards on the quayside. A ladder with several missing rungs was the only access, and it shifted uncertainly as the ship rose and fell from the wash of passing boats.

Levy stood looking up, his hands on his hips, but there was nobody in sight. He cupped his hands and shouted.

'*Shalom!*'

A few minutes later a figure appeared. A heavily bearded man who rested his elbows on the ship's side and looked down at them.

Levy shouted again. '*Shalom, Maresha!*'

The man smiled and waved, then pointed to the ladder, and they made their way cautiously and awkwardly up the precarious structure. The man was the captain, a Jewish Arab from Joppa and he took them to the small saloon behind the wheelhouse.

They sat around the small mahogany table and Levy

talked to the sailor. He could speak only a bastard mixture of Hebrew and Arabic so Malik had to sit in silence as they talked. There was much nodding of heads, and once or twice the Arab pointed through the saloon window towards the city. Finally he got three glasses and poured them each a large measure of *arak*. The captain grinned as he held up his glass, saying, '*l'chayeem*'.

After they had clambered down the rickety ladder to the quayside, Levy turned and waved to the captain before they walked to the car.

'What was all that, David?'

'We were just going over the loading procedures. When we give him the word he'll move up-river and tie up so that we can use the big quayside hoists, and he says we can have everything loaded inside a couple of hours.'

'What about when we're dumping them?'

'It'll have to be one at a time – his deck cranes aren't built to take more than twelve tons, and by now he reckons that even a crate of ten tons might be pushing them hard.'

'What's he getting out of it?'

'We'll find him his next half-dozen cargoes and he'll get paid the normal rate.'

'Is that enough?'

Levy smiled. 'More than enough, Jake. He's an Israeli. He was skipper of one of the small boats that ran the British blockade to get immigrants into Palestine before the mandate ended. When he's asked by Mossad to help he's proud to be asked.'

'It would save time if we loaded the crates in the warehouse onto the boat now, and then we could bring the transporters with the last two crates direct to the docks.'

Levy stopped walking. 'Why not? Let me go back and tell him. He can move up-river right now. Wait for me in the car.'

Malik watched as Levy hurried back to the boat, breaking into a trot in his eagerness to get things moving. Typical Israeli. Totally involved and totally committed. No fears, no doubts.

*

With two weapons to remove, the visit to von Busch was inevitably going to take longer, and Meyer had hinted that von Busch might be more resistant than the others.

Malik had gone with Levy to see the first three crates loaded onto the *Maresha*. The ease and speed of the loading had been almost incredible. The chain slings were hooked up and five minutes later the crate had disappeared into the hold. The whole operation took just under twenty minutes. It made their previous laborious efforts seem crude and amateurish. And the big wooden crates swinging in the air no longer held any menace, they were just crates, part of a ship's cargo. Malik, watching them being lowered into the hold, felt for the first time that the disjointed operation was beginning to come under control. He and Levy had taken time off on the way back to the hotel to have a coffee together in a restaurant by the Alster. Levy looked once more like the smiling, amiable man that he had met at Morris's house.

'Have you contacted your family, David?'

'No. I never do when I'm away. It's best that nobody knows where I am. They understand. Well my wife does, and the kids are used to me appearing and disappearing like the Cheshire Cat. What about your girlfriend?'

'I saw her when we were in Cologne.'

'Do you miss her?'

'Yes. Too much.'

Levy smiled. 'Like Kipling said: "Down to Gehenna or up to the Throne, he travels the fastest who travels alone."'

Malik laughed softly. 'It depends where you're going.'

'When's the big day?'

'As soon as this lot's over and finished.' For a moment Malik hesitated. 'We're definitely going to live in Israel when we're married.'

'My God. Why are we drinking coffee? Let's have a real drink to celebrate.'

'Let's wait until it happens.' But Malik was smiling.

'Have your people agreed to a posting to Tel Aviv?'

'No. There's no point in asking.'

'Why not?'

Malik smiled. 'I'm a Jew, David. They wouldn't trust me.'

For a moment Levy glanced away, his fingers screwing up the paper from his sugar cube, then he looked back at Malik.

'My people would take you and be delighted at the chance.'

'I'm grateful for the thought, but I think I've had enough of this game.'

'Rubbish, you're just exhausted by this bloody shambles. I've seen your record on our files. You're just what we need. Experienced and capable. You're ideal for Mossad.'

Malik shook his head slowly. 'No. I've genuinely had enough. If I'd not met Lisa I'd have just gone on. There was nothing better to do. In an odd kind of way it was a natural progression from Auschwitz.' Malik smiled wryly. 'It sounds odd, but it's true. In Israel, with Lisa, I knew I'd escaped. From Auschwitz and all the seamy side of my life. I felt totally different. Like an animal let out of a cage. I can't wait to get there, and Lisa is the one who made it possible.'

'She must be quite a gal.'

Malik smiled. 'She's much younger than me. She's almost more Jewish than me, despite the fact that she's one hundred per cent *shiksa*. She's beautiful and gentle, and she loves me. Without her I might as well have died in that bloody camp.'

'When you come over, Jake, contact me in the first hour. I know lots of people who can help you both. Nothing to do with Mossad. Just ordinary people, but influential people. They'll see you get the breaks.'

'Thanks, David. We'd better go.'

An agitated Heinz Fischer was waiting for them in the foyer of the hotel. He sprang up from his chair as soon as he saw them.

'We've got a problem, Jake. I thought you'd better know before you saw Meyer.'

'Go on. What is it?'

Fischer sighed. 'It's probably my fault. I thought it might save time if Meyer phoned von Busch to check that he would be at his place tonight and tomorrow. When Meyer phoned, von Busch told him that he wouldn't cooperate. He wouldn't agree to the removal.'

'When was this?'

'About ten minutes ago.'

'Why did Meyer tell him on the phone what it was about?'

'He didn't, Jake. Rechmann had already phoned von Busch and talked to him. Warning him what was happening.'

'The bastard,' Levy said softly.

Malik stood there thinking for a moment. Then he looked at Fischer.

'Get Meyer down here. I'll bring the car round.'

Malik stopped the car after twenty-five kilometres and turned to look at Meyer in the back.

'You'd better give us some background on von Busch.'

Meyer shrugged his shoulders. 'He's Baron Theodore von Busch. Sixty-two years old. Widower. No children. Very rich and very influential.'

'Where does the money come from?'

'It was always a very wealthy family. He has substantial shares in many companies. Not just in Germany, but in the United States, France and England. And South America too.'

'What sort of place has he got?'

'It's about five hundred hectares. More than half is forest. A big timber mill and a small furniture-making concern. Too near the East German border to spend much on development.'

'What's he done apart from making money?'

'He rides well. Was in the pre-war Olympics team. Skis. Was an officer in the Wehrmacht. Good record. Served in North Africa, Italy and on the Russian front. Was a colonel when the surrender came.'

'What sort of character?'

'Who knows? I would have said completely loyal before today. He is used to giving orders, of course, not taking them. Nobody's fool, I would say.'

'What sort of security has he got?'

'I don't know. Nothing more than a couple of servants apart from the estate workers of course. That's all, so far as I know. Security precautions draw attention.'

'And the site?'

'In a clearing in the forest.'

207

Malik started the car. 'When we get there, Meyer, I'll do the talking, but if he tries to appeal to you, you lay it on the line. He does what he's told or he's in real trouble. Understand?'

'Yes, Herr Malik.'

Lauenburg on the Elbe had once been the seat of an independent duchy but now it was little more than a pretty tourist centre on the river.

Malik followed Meyer's directions and turned off the main road where a signpost said *Haus Vierlande*. For a few kilometres the narrow road was flanked by orchards and fields of beans and peas, and then as the ground rose and levelled out, there on the right was a pair of high stone pillars, their large wrought-iron gates wide open. As they drove in Malik saw fleetingly the big armorial shield on one of the gates. He noticed a coronet and an eagle, and a pair of crossed swords.

The road wound slowly uphill until they saw the house. It was built on a spur of the hill, a background of firs and cypress washing down from the steep hill behind. The house was built in stone, and its proportions were timelessly perfect. The main door stood open, a black and gold German Shepherd lay beside the steps, unmoving, but its brown eyes watching them as they got out of the car. It stood up slowly, its head thrust out, as they approached the door, but it neither growled nor made any move towards them.

Malik pressed the bell-button beside one of the Palladian pillars alongside the door. They could see inside the large hall. Glistening wood floor, oil paintings on the wall and small display cabinets holding pieces of porcelain.

The man who walked towards them was obviously von Busch. Thick white hair brushed back from his forehead. Hard grey eyes and a thin wide mouth. Tall and elegant, he looked a typical Prussian aristocrat. As he reached the door he raised his eyebrows as he looked at Meyer.

'So, Herr Meyer. You've brought your entourage with you. I expected you despite our telephone conversation. You'd better all come in, gentlemen.'

He turned, and they followed him across the hall, down a small corridor where he opened a door and stood aside for them to go in. He moved towards half-a-dozen *bergère* arm-chairs set round a long, low, glass table.

'Sit down, gentlemen.'

And when they were seated he sat down himself, pulling at his trousers to avoid stretching the cloth at his knees. He leaned back comfortably in his high-backed chair.

'Let me tell you, Herr Meyer, that your visit is in vain. I told you so on the telephone, but maybe you are entitled to hear it to your face. I have no idea who your companions are but I gather from Rechmann that one of them is called Jacob.' He turned to look at Malik. 'I think from his description that that must be you, sir.'

Malik nodded. 'Herr Baron. None of us wishes to be dis-courteous but I have to make clear that asking your agreement was solely a courtesy.'

'On whose part may I ask?'

'Mine.'

'And who might you be, my friend?'

'That's not important, von Busch. It's for your benefit that you shouldn't know.'

'Von Busch, eh? We shall be on Christian name terms before long.'

Malik sighed with impatience. 'I'm afraid I haven't got time for the niceties, von Busch. You're in great danger of going to jail, or even losing your life.'

'It would not be the first time that I've been threatened, my friend. So let us put aside your threats.'

Malik leaned back in his chair his hands in his jacket pockets.

'Have you got a man who can pack a bag for you, von Busch?'

'Is that a gun in your right-hand pocket, Herr Jacob?'

'Yes.'

Von Busch smiled. 'D'you intend shooting me?'

Malik stood up and looked from Fischer to Meyer.

'Go outside, both of you.'

When they had left Malik was still standing. Levy was sprawled casually in his chair. Watching and alert, but not moving.

Malik walked slowly round the table and stood looking down at von Busch.

'Baron von Busch. I know that what you did was done with good intentions. I accept all that. But it's over now. It was anarchy and treason, not patriotism. Nobody official will ever know what was done or planned. I give you my word. All I ask is your cooperation.

The pale, hollow-cheeked death's-head face looked up at Malik's face.

'Go to hell.'

Malik turned to look at David Levy, who nodded almost imperceptibly. Malik's hand grabbed the bush of white hair and forced von Busch's head back over the edge of the chair. He could see the tracery of red veins in the German's protruding eyes.

'Are you going to cooperate, von Busch?'

The German nodded as best he could and Malik withdrew his hand from the bush of hair. Slowly von Busch arranged himself back to a sitting position. His chest heaving to get back his breath, his hand trembling as he wiped the saliva from his thin lips.

Very softly he said, 'You would have made a splendid Nazi, my friend.'

Levy stood up slowly. 'You're a fool, von Busch. A dangerous fool.' He turned to Malik. 'I'll take the car and get my people, OK?'

'OK?'

'You hang on here with the other two.'

As Levy walked into the hall he beckoned to Fischer who hurried over.

'I'm going to get my team. You and Meyer stay here. Don't let von Busch out of your sight and don't let him near a phone.'

It was two hours later when Levy came back with his convoy and he picked up Meyer and von Busch, taking them up to the site in the woods. Malik followed in the car.

The clearing in the woods was strangely quiet despite

210

the presence of the men. The late sun touched the tops of the pine trees and left long shafts of light angled down between the trees. Woodpigeons cooed, and he heard the broken call of a late cuckoo. Even when the generator started up it sounded muffled in the cathedral-like enclosure in the woods.

The raised top of the emplacement had been turfed over, and already it supported small clusters of knapweed and ragwort with a sprinkling of daisies and purple saxifrage. Its surface sloped from back to front and a long swath had been cut in the woods facing the centre of the emplacement.

Malik stood on his own, watching Levy's team at work. There were two men he hadn't seen before, sitting in Levy's car. One was reading a newspaper, the other was asleep with his head back on the seat.

Half an hour later Levy came up out of the emplacement and walked over to his own car, tapped on the window and the two men got out. The three of them were talking as they walked over to Malik.

'Jake, meet a couple of friends of mine.' He pointed first to the taller man. 'Niko Bergman and Ben Goldberg. Meet Jake Malik. He's in charge here. My people are just doing the washing-up.'

Malik shook hands with both men but they didn't say anything. Levy turned to them. 'I'll join you later. Just keep watching.'

The two nodded briefly and walked back to Levy's car. Levy turned to look at Malik.

'What do you feel about von Busch?'

'He's a problem. And he'll be more of a problem when we leave.'

'And Rechmann?'

'I'm going to deal with Rechmann myself as soon as we've finished here?'

'How?'

Levy's eyes were intent on Malik's face.

'Don't ask, David, then it stays my problem alone and not yours as well.'

211

'Are you going to tell Fischer?'

'No. Rechmann's a friend of his family. It wouldn't be fair to saddle him with that.'

'He'll guess, of course.'

'Sure he will. But guessing ain't knowing. And guessing doesn't make you an accessory.'

'This is why I called up Bergman and his friend.'

'Tell me.'

'Let *them* deal with Rechmann and von Busch.'

'Why?'

'They've got resources and experience you haven't got. They've got time which you haven't got. They're not connected with the operation. Nobody's seen them, nobody knows them. It's safer, Jake.'

'What about the other two? The judge and the brick-field man?'

'I reckon they're safe enough. Especially when they hear what's happened to the other two. I'll send Bergman to let them know they're safe provided they don't talk.'

'I think I'd better do that.'

'Forget it, Jake. Twelve hours from now we'll have these two crates on the boat. My people will be on the first available plane to anywhere in Europe and you and I will be on that boat. After we've dumped the crates she'll take us back to Rotterdam or Copenhagen and that's it.'

'What about the missiles in Israel?'

'They'll be somewhere in the Med three days from now.'

'Why did you jump the gun? Why not leave it to me to decide?'

'If you're going to live in Israel I didn't want there to be any chance of you being connected with it. Israel's not Germany. It's a small country and you could be noticed and remembered if anything went wrong. There was only the one site, Jake, and you can shift sand quicker than earth and concrete.'

'They've actually been removed?'

'They're at sea right now.' He smiled. 'They'll be dropped off Gaddafi's coast the day after tomorrow. A present from Jerusalem to the gallant colonel.'

Malik half-smiled. 'What reasons did you give your people for all this?'

Levy shrugged and smiled. 'Mossad spends most of its time not letting the right hand know what the left hand doeth. We get crossed lines now and again. My job is to prevent that happening too often. The team I'm using here are from Section Three . . . *Modi'in*. The team in Israel are *Shin Beth*. I don't have a problem.' Levy paused. 'What are you telling your people?'

Malik looked away. 'Nothing. They weren't all that interested in synagogue-daubers and the like. It's not really our kind of job. We only got stuck with it because there might be a KGB connection. I'm going to leave the impression that it wasn't worth pursuing.'

'What about your Kraut?'

'Fischer?'

'Yes.'

'What about him?'

'Can you trust him?'

Malik smiled. 'He's going to be my brother-in-law.'

'He's still a Kraut.'

'He'll be no problem. Forget him.'

'OK. I hope you're right. I'll go and start Bergman on his way to Cologne.'

As Malik watched the convoy moving out of the clearing in the woods he looked back for a moment at Levy's car. Ben Goldberg sat at the wheel with von Busch sitting beside him. Goldberg flashed his headlights and Malik waved and got into the BMW. Fischer was in the passenger seat and Levy was sprawled on the back seat already asleep.

They caught up with the convoy well before Hamburg and where the E4 ended at Horn the two hoists headed north, back to the hire company. The mobile homes forked away a few minutes later, heading for the airport. The BMW followed behind the two transporters towards the docks.

The *Maresha* had had to move up two berths but the captain and two of his men were already on deck and they

213

called out to the foreman of one of the gangs on the quayside as they saw the transporters manoeuvring alongside.

An hour later the crew were battening down the hatches. Fischer had handled clearance with Customs and the captain had gone to the harbour-master's office with the *zollpapier* and been issued with a *verkehrserlaubnis*. The pilot had complained about the state of the boarding ladder as he came on board. Six hours later they hove-to and the pilots' launch from Cuxhaven had pulled alongside to take off the pilot and Heinz Fischer.

All night and all the next morning they followed the Dutch coastline. Past the necklace of off-shore islands to Den Helder. Then they headed WSW until the sun went down. Levy and Malik slept all day on the floor of the saloon and it was the captain's high-pitched voice talking to Levy that woke Malik. As he sat up rubbing his eyes, Levy said, 'He says we're there. They've opened the hatches and hooked up the first crate. He wants us to go on deck and check that he does it OK.'

There was an almost full moon apart from the two lights on the top of the wheelhouse and Levy and Màlik stood watching as the gears on the hoists turned slowly and noisily. Slowly the crate came up, and when it was clear of the deck the hoists slowly turned and the crate swung out over the sea. There was a crew-man holding each of the long warps to the shackles and when the captain raised his hand they pulled in unison. For a moment nothing happened and then the shackles opened and the crate plunged nose-first into the sea. Cleanly and smoothly like an Olympic diver. For a moment the sea foamed and lifted and then there was nothing.

The crew-men were greasing the gears at the base of the hoists as the men in the hold slung the chains on the next crate. One after the other, at twenty-minute intervals, three more crates went into the sea. Then there was a long wait. The heavy loads were distorting some of the metal links on the sling chains and two men were trying to hammer them back into shape.

Eventually the last crate was in the slings. Twice one of the hoists had seized from the excessive loads it had taken, and the crate hung askew over the deck until they had poured oil over the hot gears that were clamped together from friction heat and physical distortion. Finally it was over the sea, the men on the release ropes awaiting the captain's signal. As his hand came down they heard the grunts of the men as they heaved against the ropes. And then the ship shuddered and listed as one sling came free and the huge crate hung, swinging in long pendulum arcs as the second sling held its grip on one end of the crate. Slowly the swings decreased until the crate hung vertically down, ten feet or so above the sea. The boat's list had slightly eased, but Malik was scared that they would be seen by some passing ship. They had chosen this spot because it was marked on the charts as an official dumping ground for ammunition.

Levy was talking to the captain who was shrugging and shaking his head.

'What does he say, David?'

'He says it's locked because the chain rings have been distorted, and he's scared that the dead weight could drag the hoist out of the deck.'

'What does he suggest?'

'He suggests he wishes he'd never heard of us.'

'Ask him if a man climbed up the hoist could he file through one of the links at the top. He'd lose the sling and half the chain but we could pay for a replacement.'

Levy talked to the captain. It sounded as though they were haggling and finally Levy turned to him.

'He says it would work but it's too dangerous. His men wouldn't do it.'

'Tell him to get a file and I'll do it.'

'You must be out of your mind, Jake.'

'Somebody's got to do it.'

Levy turned to the captain, anger on his face. Hands on hips, his head thrust forward aggressively, he shouted and raved, barely heeding the captain's replies. Five minutes later Levy was calm, nodding his head as the captain spoke slowly and deliberately. Then Levy turned to Malik.

'Forty Israeli lira, the bastard wants. But I've told him to go ahead. So much for Israeli loyalty, the shits.'

'It's cheap enough, David. I get dizzy standing on a chair.'

'Would you have done it?'

'Of course I would.'

'You're a better man than I am, my friend. There he goes.'

There was complete silence except for the wind across the deck and in the rigging as they watched the man slowly hauling his way up the steel lattice-work of the arm of the hoist. Several times he rested, his feet splayed out and one arm hooked over a strut. The crew-man perched on the wheel-house followed him with the light, and then, very faintly, they could hear the rasping of a file on metal. It came in snatches on the wind. Twenty minutes later there was the rattle of the freed chain and the crate plummeted down to the sea. A spume of water rose four or five feet in the air and then fell back into the seething foam that was the only remaining sign of the crate's existence.

Malik shook the captain's hand and waited until the crew-man came down. He was a Polish Jew from Cracow and they chatted for an hour before Malik went back to the saloon.

They anchored in the roads at Rotterdam midday the next day. And two hours later they were signalled permission to enter.

Malik pushed his plate aside and stirred his coffee.

'What are you going to do now, David?'

'Are you going back to Cologne?'

'Yes. I'll have to pick up my things and work out a phony joint report with Heinz Fischer.'

'I'll come back with you and check that there's no untidy ends from Bergman and Goldberg. Then I'll go back to Tel Aviv.'

Malik called to the waiter and paid for their meal and they took a taxi to the main station. They had booked on a flight from Schipol at six o'clock that evening and they spent a few hours in Amsterdam. Malik bought a record of the Finzi cello concerto for Lisa, and a small bottle of perfume for Heinz to give to Ruth. There was an hour's delay at the airport and they touched down at Wahn just after eight o'clock. They shared a taxi into town, dropping Malik near the flat and Levy carrying on to book himself a room at the Dom.

The flat seemed cold despite the warm day and it looked deserted. The recording and projection equipment had gone and Heinz had cleared his things from his bedroom. Malik sat on the bed and dialled Lisa's home number. It was Heinz's voice that answered and when he had asked for Lisa the phone had been hung up. He dialled again with the receiver to his ear. He heard the ringing tone at the other end and the phone was lifted and replaced straight away. He realised then that he must have annoyed Heinz Fischer more than he had thought.

He looked at his watch. It was nine-thirty, and he was too scruffy to go out to see her without bathing and shaving, and that would make it too late. He would have to wait until the next day. He was lying in the bath, his feet on the taps, steam condensing on his face, and his eyes closed, when he heard the key in the outer door. For a moment he hoped it might be Lisa. He called out.

'Is that you, Lisa?'

But there was no answer. And no sound of movement. He climbed out of the bath, put on his bathrobe and walked through to the sitting room. Heinz Fischer was sitting at the table but he didn't turn to look at Malik.

'I thought it must be you, or Lisa. I called out but I guess you can't hear from the bathroom.' He paused, towelling his wet hair. 'There was something wrong with your phone earlier on.'

Fischer turned to look at him and Malik was shocked by the look on his face.

'What on earth's the matter, Heinz?'

'You're what's the matter, Malik. You don't suppose I thought it was accidental, do you?'

Malik shrugged. 'I don't understand.'

'Rechmann was killed this morning. Shot by a marksman as he came out of the office at the factory to get in his car.'

Malik sat down at the table. 'What did you expect to happen, Heinz? That we leave him running around to spill

217

the beans? He was warned. I warned him myself. But he's an arrogant bastard. Self-important. He talked to von Busch and told him to ignore us. And that wouldn't have been the last one he would have talked to. Especially when he discovered that his chat with von Busch didn't work. He endangered the whole operation.'

'You know what happened to von Busch?'

'Tell me,' Malik said quietly.

'I phoned his place this morning when I heard what had happened to Rechmann. Von Busch was found drowned in the lake on his estate. There was a rowing-boat floating upside down. A stupid old man drowns himself. No suspicious circumstances.'

'What would you have done, Heinz? Let it all come out despite the consequences?'

'You knew that Levy was going to kill those two?'

'Yes.'

'But you didn't know they were already dead?'

'No.'

'It didn't matter to you. You weren't all that interested in when and how.' Fischer's voice broke with anger, bubbles of saliva on his lips.

'Calm down, Heinz. If Rechmann hadn't played the fool it wouldn't have been necessary.'

'You could have tried to convince him. Threaten him, even.'

Malik looked at Fischer, his anger beginning to override his wish to be friendly.

'Heinz, you're talking about two men who were so stupid, so arrogant, that they were ready to start a world war. What about the Russians in those cities? Innocent people who would die in a holocaust without any choice.'

'The Soviets could pull back. The choice would be theirs.'

'You surely don't think that the Politburo would back down under a threat like that? They would have answered that it was organised by the Americans or the Chinese and they would have struck back immediately. A pre-emptive strike. That would give the Americans no choice. The result doesn't bear thinking about.'

218

'So if the Soviets or their stooges invade West Germany or Israel you give them away? And don't think I didn't notice the subtle difference about the sites.'

'What difference was that?'

'The sites in Germany are all near big cities. Those in Israel are in the desert.'

'I hadn't noticed that. But Israel's a much smaller country, you couldn't have hidden them in a city.'

'And that justifies the Red Army invading West Germany, yes?'

'That's up to the governments of the countries concerned. It's not for you or me to play God. Nor Meyer and the others.'

'The Rechmann family would have been guests at your wedding.'

'What's the point you're making, Heinz?'

'He was a friend of my family. He was a good man.'

Malik shook his head. 'The men who ran Auschwitz and the other concentration camps had wives and children, and they all sang *Stille Nacht* with tears on their faces at Christmas. But they weren't good men, Heinz. They were animals.'

'Like you, Malik, they would claim that they didn't actually kill. They just turned a blind eye to what others did.'

'Don't kid yourself, Heinz. If it had been necessary I would have killed Rechmann and von Busch myself.'

'Lisa and my mother have gone over to the Rechmanns' to comfort the widow and the two girls. How do you think they would feel if they knew that you were responsible?'

'They won't know, Heinz. Lisa will never know.'

'She will, my friend. Because I shall tell her.'

Malik looked for long moments at the German's face. Then he said softly. 'You would destroy her if you did that. Give me one reason why you should.'

'So that she doesn't marry you, Malik. That would destroy her too. Your hatred of Germans will be used on her some day if you get the chance.'

'You'd better justify that, Fischer.'

'There are only two people dead from this. They're both Germans. The Jews just live happily ever after.'

219

Malik shook his head slowly. 'You're letting *your* prejudices show, Fischer. You know why those two had to go but you choose to ignore it. You'd better go before I get really angry.'

Fischer stood up. 'Just keep away from my family, Malik. You're not welcome any more. You're mad. You ought to be put away.'

'D'you mean that, Heinz?'

'I swear I mean it.'

Malik took a deep breath. 'We have to discuss our joint report about the operation.'

'There's no need to, Malik. It was your operation. You do the report. Just send a copy to police headquarters here in Cologne. I shan't expose it. I'll sign it, whatever it says.'

Fischer stood up clumsily, knocking his chair over. As he bent down to pick it up he was trembling and when he stood up he stared at Malik for long moments.

'I'm glad I'm not you, Malik. You said something in the first days we met that I never understood, but I understand it now.'

'What was that?'

'You said you envied people who had the chance to be innocent. I know now why you envy them.'

Fischer turned and slammed the outer door as he left the flat.

Malik sat there for almost an hour until the cold finally made him shiver and he wrapped the bathrobe closely round his body. It was just before midnight when the phone rang. It was Levy.

'Hi, Jake. Our friends dealt with both parties.'

Malik couldn't bring himself to reply. He sat there as if he were paralysed. Unable to speak.

'Jake. Are you there, Jake?'

He put the phone to his mouth. So close that it knocked against his teeth.

'What the hell's the matter, Jake? Stay put. I'm coming right over.' And the phone went dead.

Malik stood up slowly and shuffled towards the outer door. He opened it and left it ajar, leaning back against the wall, his

220

arms wrapped round himself, shaking as if he had an ague. It seemed hours before he heard Levy's steps hurrying up the stairs from the street. For a moment Levy just stood there looking at him.

'For Christ's sake, what's happened? Are you ill?'

But Malik's eyes were closed and his mouth hung open, his head back against the wall. For a few seconds Levy hesitated, not knowing what to do. Then he bent and took Malik's arm and lifted him on his shoulder, carrying him through to the sitting room, looking desperately for the bedroom. He laid Malik gently on the bed and hurried to the bathroom.

Slowly and gently he wiped Malik's face with the warm, wet cloth, and then he took his hand.

'Tell me what happened, Jake. Please.'

Malik turned his head on the pillow and opened his eyes. He said softly, 'Fischer came. He told me about Rechmann and von Busch.' He sighed and closed his eyes. 'He says that if I see Lisa again he'll tell her what has happened. That I'm a murderer and a German-hater.'

'So let the bastard tell her. She knows you better than that.'

Malik's eyes fluttered open. 'Her mother once asked me if I hated Germans enough to end up hating Lisa.'

'Then she's a stupid old bitch.'

'She's not, David. She's an ordinary woman. And remember what von Busch said. He said I would have made a good Nazi.'

'Who the hell are these bastards to say what you are? They all watched the Nazis shovelling our kids into the gas chambers and they didn't holler then, by God.' Levy paused. 'Anyway, you didn't kill those two.'

'No. But I would have done if your people hadn't done it for me.'

'D'you want me to fetch Lisa?'

Malik slowly shook his head. 'No.' Tears ran slowly down his cheeks as his eyes looked up at the ceiling. 'That's all over, David. It's all over.'

'We'll see. We'll see,' Levy said softly. But he knew it was true.

He sat with Malik all night, watching him as he slept, shifting and moving restlessly in his sleep, mouthing in whispers words Levy couldn't understand because they were in Polish.

Early next morning he called the hotel and spoke to Bergman. Then he asked the porter to send over his things and his bill. He booked Malik and himself on to a flight for London later that day.

Chapter 20

LEVY HIRED a car at Gatwick and drove them up to the house at Hampstead. He had phoned his wife asking her to come over. He found the house sad and soulless and not likely to help Malik recover.

There was an Israeli Embassy house in Wimbledon for transient diplomats and when Helen Levy arrived Levy arranged for them all to move in. The improvement in Malik's condition was rapid and obvious. Slowly Levy realised what sort of life Malik normally led. He was a loner. Asking and getting nothing from anybody, and Levy realised then what a difference the German girl must have made to him. What she supplied was ordinary enough. Other men might have been bored by it. It was no more than any normal couple would take for granted. And it was well inside what a man could expect from a girl. She didn't need to make him feel special to succeed. She just made him a normal man. With hopes and expectations, and someone to love and be loved by.

He talked it over for hours with Helen, as to whether he should contact the girl, tell her what had happened and suggest that she came over. But Helen Levy was a woman and a realist. She had no doubt that the girl would rush straight over, but she equally had no doubt that the shambles that followed would ruin them both. The fact that he was a Jew would suddenly have significance. The fact that she was a German would be a constant threat. She would not only have to abandon a protective and loving family but would have to cut herself off completely. She would be utterly dependent on Malik, who would be utterly dependent on her. They would make friends of their own as time went by but always in the background would be those accusing ghosts.

The ghosts who hated her husband. For being a Jew, for being himself, and for taking her away from them all. Two normal people could work hard at a marriage and keep it alive despite those disadvantages. But these two wouldn't stand a chance. Cut off from her family the guilt and estrangement would take away the girl's confidence. And the time in Auschwitz had ensured that Malik would never have any real self-confidence. In a strange way the camp might have given him the toughness and determination that made him good at his job. Ideal for MI6, but far from ideal for Lisa Gertrud Fischer. A natural loner and an enforced loner were not the basis for a happy marriage. And running like a thread through their discussions was David Levy's awareness that on his part, his argument, although valid and the facts true, was all a polemic. For David Levy knew another reason why it could never be. A reason that he was never going to be able to tell to his wife.

Levy helped Malik put together his phony report. It gave a long list of names that had been built up during the early stages of the investigation. Names that had eventually proved to have no relevance or significance. It attributed the swastika-daubing to being no more than the irrational actions of juvenile malcontents. Students, foreign workers, the less well-off and the usual spectrum of non-political hooligans with some complaint against society or authority in general. It concluded that they were not organised and not politically motivated, and could be dealt with, as and when required, by the normal action of local police. They were neither funded, influenced nor controlled by any political party or any foreign Intelligence service.

Malik eventually phoned Jenkins and made an appointment to see him the following day. He went to Heathrow with Helen and David Levy to see them off, and when their flight was called and they walked through the glass doors to Immigration and Customs, Helen Levy turned and waved, and her lips silently shaped the word '*Shalom*'. But Malik's face was impassive.

He walked slowly to the cigarette kiosk, bought three packets of cigarettes and then walked to the cafeteria.

224

As he sat at the metal table with its used crockery, greasy bottles of ketchup and pools of spilled tea he slowly stirred his cup of coffee. While the Levys were with him he had tried to think what he would do. But no thoughts would stay in his mind for more than a few seconds. Levy had looked after the sale of the house and the money was in the bank. He could do whatever he wanted. But he knew as he sat there that there was nothing he wanted to do.

For four months, or was it five, he had lived in a different world. For the first time in his life the perspective had been reversed. His work was the background, his personal life the foreground. But nothing had really changed. He was in exactly the same situation now as if he had never met her. He had come back from an assignment and would be given a new one, and life would go on the same as it had always gone on. He stood up slowly and carefully and walked to the front of the terminal and waved for a taxi.

He had known as he listened to the sour words of Heinz Fischer that it was over. By the time Fischer had told her and her parents, no matter how guardedly, she would be left with making a choice. Her family or him. He had little doubt that she would choose him, but he had too little to offer to let her pay the price. She would have no idea what the price really was. He wished that he could see her to explain, but he doubted if he could explain. There was nothing to say that could override her loyalty to him. Only time would teach her how much she would be throwing away.

He told the taxi-driver to take him to the Hilton.

Jenkins spent twenty minutes or so expounding to Malik the problems that SIS were facing in Washington now that Nixon had gone and the CIA was taking the blame for every misdeed that could legitimately or otherwise be laid at its door. Laidlaw as SIS liaison with the CIA had done an excellent job. As things had turned out, too good a job. He was too closely identified as a CIA sympathiser. Even our Embassy was giving him the cold shoulder.

Malik took it all as social chit-chat before his report was

discussed. When Jenkins ran out of steam on the problems of Washington, Malik took the plunge.

'You got my report on the operation in the Federal Republic?'

'What? Oh yes. The usual mountain out of a molehill, but we've done our bit of cooperation. Should keep us in Bonn's good books for a few months anyway.' Jenkins looked at Malik. 'How do you feel about an overseas posting, Jake?'

'Where?'

'There are several places where we need an experienced finger stuck in a hole in a local dyke. I haven't decided. Hong Kong is one of them but there's so much going on at the moment that there are other places that are more important. But in principle you've no objection?'

'No. None at all.'

'How soon could you be ready?'

'An hour.'

Jenkins looked at him sharply. Despite his faintly Dickensian air, he was a perceptive man.

'Nothing wrong, is there?'

'No.'

Jenkins sighed and stood up, walking with Malik to the door. As he stood with his hand on the brass door knob he said, 'A pity about the German.'

'What German?'

Jenkins looked embarrassed. 'I'm afraid I can't remember his name. The German who was working with you.'

'You mean Heinz Fischer?'

'Yes. I think that *was* his name.'

'What's the problem with him?'

'They notified us that he wasn't able to co-sign your report until he came out of hospital.'

'Why was he in hospital?'

'Knocked down by a hit-and-run driver. He hung on for a day or two but the injuries were too severe. But they're willing to accept the report on your signature only.'

'You mean he's dead?'

'I'm afraid so. I sent our routine condolences.'

226

Malik stood silent for a few moments, his eyes closed. And then he said in a flat voice, 'When shall I hear from you about my posting?'

'I'll phone you later today or early tomorrow.'

She stood looking at the front of the house, her heart beating wildly, and she tried to think of a prayer as she opened the gate and walked up to the door. She could hardly breathe as she pressed the china doorbell.

A woman in her late thirties answered the door. She was wearing a dressing gown and green leather slippers.

'Can I help you?'

'I came to see Jake.'

The woman smiled. 'And who's Jake?'

'Jacob Malik.'

'I don't know him, I'm afraid. Try next door.'

'This is Jake's house.'

'It's . . . I see. I'm afraid the house has been sold. We moved in two weeks ago. Maybe he was the previous owner.'

'Is there any forwarding address for him?'

'I expect he made arrangements with the GPO and his mail is re-directed.'

'You didn't meet him?'

'No. We dealt with the estate agents.

'Can you give me their address?'

'Yes. It was Billings in the High Street.' She paused. 'You go across the green. It's about ten minutes' walk.'

'Thank you.'

She turned and walked down the garden path and across the triangle of grass to where the road forked up to Hampstead village.

The estate agents were obliging enough but they had no forwarding address. They hadn't met Mr Malik. A Mr David Levy had had power of attorney for the sale of the house.

She went to the Post Office but they couldn't help her. They were not allowed to divulge forwarding addresses even when they existed. She could write to the old address and then it would be automatically re-directed. The woman behind the counter was a kindly person and she noticed the tears brimming in the girl's eyes as Lisa said softly, 'Can I ask if the new address is in Israel?'

For a moment the woman hesitated, and then she hurriedly jerked open the deep wooden drawer and looked through twenty or thirty dog-eared cards. She stopped at one of them and read it carefully. She looked back at Lisa's face, shaking her head.

'I'm afraid not, love. I can't say more than that.'

She stood outside the Post Office, trying to think what else she could do. She could see the small restaurant where they had eaten, and the shop where he had bought the electric light bulbs. It had been a sunny day and the world had seemed so wonderful. It was a sunny day today but everything was so terribly wrong. She couldn't think of any reason why he hadn't contacted her. And the last two weeks had been like a nightmare. The night of Heinz's accident. He had said that morning that he wanted to talk to her. Something serious, he said. And Malik gone. No letter, no explanation. It was a terrible nightmare. The two days while Heinz was dying. Watching her parents hope against hope until their spirits disintegrated. The funeral and Ruth, and her guilt that her thoughts were still about Jake. The two days of terrible arguments with her parents when she had said she was going to London to see him, despite his silence.

The overwhelming silence of her parents' disapproval. A disapproval that finally became a tirade against Jake Malik rather than against herself or fate. And overlying it all, her own pain that he had just left, knowing what grief it would bring her. She could think of no possible reason why it should have happened. Jake Malik wasn't that kind of man. She remembered that he had once asked her what he could do that would cause her to stop loving him. And she remembered her answer, that nothing could do that, because if he did something she would know that it had to be done. Nothing would change her mind about Jake Malik. She knew by instinct that she would never be happy again. But there was nothing she could do. Except write the letter and see

228

what happened. But she knew in her heart that nothing would happen. If he had wanted her he would have contacted her. She wished that he had slept with her and that she was carrying their child. She could have . . . She sighed and turned on her heel, asking the first woman she met where she could find a taxi.

There were two vacant seats next to Malik and when the film started he tried to read, but his mind wouldn't absorb the words.

He took the envelope out of his pocket and slid out the single buff page and read it again.

Memo to Malik J.
From Dpy. H of D III

Your posting to Washington as liaison officer SIS-CIA is now operational.

You are required to effect takeover as quickly as possible, as your predecessor is required for urgent duties elsewhere.

It has been laid down that in future SIS LO is not accommodated at the Embassy and you should rent suitable accommodation on Washington Grade 3 scale. Authorisation 19074 applies.

You will report directly to London using the diplomatic bag but in future no copies of your report will be provided for Embassy archives.

Funds are available on existing imprest account but with no increase in scale, until the present Review Board has reported.

We expect you to improve on the existing SIS/CIA relationship as quickly as possible. There is much ground to be made up, as you know.

C. Jenkins

Malik stretched out on the vacant seats and pulled the airline blanket over his body, covering his head. As he closed his eyes, the noise of the aircraft as it strained through the night sky was almost welcome. For five more hours he wasn't even on Planet Earth. He wished that he had learned at least one Jewish prayer. Just one. He had been going to when they got to Israel, but . . .

The plane to Cologne was half-empty and she sat looking out at the moonlight on the thick cumulus clouds. Far away there was a flicker of summer lightning and she turned back to the open pages of the book on her lap. She read the line of the Shakespeare sonnet again and again – 'Love is not love that alters when it alteration finds . . .'

She put back her head and closed her eyes, the paperback copy of Palgrave's *Golden Treasury* held tightly in both hands. It was all she had left of Jacob Malik.

Jenkins shook the rain of the sudden storm from his umbrella on the steps of the Reform Club. Closing it carefully and giving it two last decisive swishes he saw Howarth step out of the taxi and hurry towards the steps.

'Let's go in the bar before it starts filling up, Jenkins. Leave your brolly with the porter . . . That's right, Mason, put it on my hanger, there's a good chap. Number thirty-two.'

Howarth chose two leather armchairs in the far corner of the room. Shoving away the third chair to join several others around an empty table.

'Wettest September for forty years, they say. The buggers have always got some story. Three weeks' time they'll be telling us not to use hoses in the garden. You see if they don't.' He turned to look at the waiter. 'Right. Put them down there. Leave the soda water . . . that's fine. Thank you, Fletcher.'

Howarth raised his glass. 'Cheers.' He took a sip, considered the taste and then put down the glass, satisfied that it really was Bell's. He looked at Jenkins. 'I got your message. What's the news?'

Jenkins looked around but the room was quite empty. Despite that he leaned forward as he spoke. 'It's finished. All wrapped up and no problems.'

'Are you sure about that, Jenkins? Quite sure?'

'Yes, sir.'

'What about your chap, Marples, or whatever his name is?'

'Malik. He's been posted to Washington. He's already on his way there.'

'You mentioned that he'd put in a very low-key report. What do you feel about that?'

'I don't understand, sir.'

Howarth shrugged. 'It shows he's unreliable.'

'But we intended that. We hedged him round so that he'd react that way. I chose him right at the beginning because I knew how he would react.'

'Fair enough, Jenkins. First-class thinking on your part. But the fact remains . . . he went his own way . . . not only made unorthodox decisions but kept us out of the picture.'

'But that was my intention, sir. Like I said, we had a problem and I chose him as the man who would solve it the way we wanted. We can hardly criticise him for doing what we intended him to do.'

'We can, my friend. I can, anyway.' Howarth leaned back in his chair. 'We can expect a lot of cooperation from Bonn and Tel Aviv from now on. Bloody amateurs despite their reputations. You'd better give me a note on what you'd like from them.'

'I'll do that, sir. There's two or three items I'd like to have the files on.'

'You're happy to leave your chap and the Israeli running around loose?'

'Tel Aviv are happy about their man, and I'm perfectly happy about Malik, my chap.'

'Well don't be. Keep a monthly check on him. In my book he's not to be trusted.' Howarth shrugged. 'However, it's your head, my boy, your head.' He raised his eyebrows. 'I'm having lunch with His Nibs. Another drink before you get back to the grindstone?'

Jenkins took the hint. 'No thank you, sir. I've had my ration.'

Howarth nodded as he took out a cigar from a leather case. 'Remember what I've said. It's not a cricitism, mind you, just a sensible precaution.' He nodded slowly to mark his words. 'I shouldn't be surprised to see your name in *The Times* on New Year's Day. Have a good weekend.'

'And you, sir.'